FROZEN FIRE

FROZEN FIRE

METAL LEGION™ BOOK TWO

CH GIDEON   CALEB WACHTER   CRAIG MARTELLE

LMBPN

DISRUPTIVE IMAGINATION®

LMBPN Publishing
PMB 196, 2540 South Maryland Pkwy
Las Vegas, NV 89109

Print ISBN: 978-1-64202-437-1

First US edition, December 2018

We can't write without those who support us
On the home front, we thank you for being there for us

We wouldn't be able to do this for a living if it weren't for our
readers
We thank you for reading our books

FROZEN FIRE TEAM

Thanks to our Beta Readers

Micky Cocker, James Caplan, Kelly O'Donnell, and John Ashmore

Thanks to the JIT Readers

James Caplan
Terry Easom
Misty Roa
Keith Verret
Micky Cocker
John Ashmore
Crystal Wren
Kelly O'Donnell
Jeff Eaton
Peter Manis

If I've missed anyone, please let me know!

Editing services provided by LKJ Bookmakers www.lkjbooks.com

PROLOGUE: THE NEXUS

"Event horizon in three minutes," the warship's helmsman reported as the faintly wobbling, ring-shaped gate loomed before the kilometer-long *Bonhoeffer*. The gate was wide, a thousand meters across the inner margin of the metal structure. Terran scientists had concluded that the League's gates pre-dated human civilization and, possibly, humanity itself.

The *Dietrich Bonhoeffer* followed a ballistic trajectory toward Jump Gate New America 2. Tension flowed like waves from a star gone supernova. The venerable assault carrier drew steadily nearer the gate that connected the Terran colonies through what the Illumination League called the Nexus.

"Gate handshake protocols established," called the comm officer, and to Lieutenant Colonel Lee Jenkins' eye, the gate seemed to briefly shimmer as ink-black ripples fluttered across its otherwise blank surface. The gate was large enough to fit a Terran dreadnought, which was nearly fifty times the volume of the *Bonhoeffer*. The dreadnoughts had been specifically designed to be as large as possible and still fit through the gates.

"Steady on," acknowledged Colonel Li Yu, the ship's hundred-year-old commanding officer.

The *Bonhoeffer* was the only ship commanded by a colonel. Non-Fleet personnel were only permitted to crew select warships deemed essential to a given branch's ongoing operations. Terran Armor Corps once had its own fleet, but funding had been cut incrementally, and over time, only a single mighty warship remained under direct command of the armor branch.

Jenkins, standing at the back of the *Bonhoeffer*'s bridge, shuffled his feet nervously as the vessel crossed the one-minute-to-go mark.

This was not his first time passing through the Nexus, but only once before had he been present on the bridge at the moment of transit. He intended to savor the experience. The ship was at condition two, per standard gate-transit protocols, and that condition would persist at least until they reached their destination: the Naga System. The men and women of the *Bonhoeffer*'s crew were trained professionals, and operations proceeded fluidly despite the indisputable anxiety of the situation.

"Thirty seconds," the helmsman reported mechanically.

"All hands, this is Colonel Li," the ship's CO announced over the intercom. "Prepare for gate transit in twenty seconds."

Jenkins would have been lying if he tried to say he wasn't nervous about passing through the gate. Approach velocity, angle, rotation, EM profile, and a dozen different measurements of the ship's mass and displacement needed to be precisely balanced in order to successfully pass through an artificial wormhole. Failure to properly calibrate a gate-approach-vector had resulted in nine warships being destroyed during transit in Terran Republic history.

"Event horizon in three...two...one...mark," the helmsman announced, and as he spoke, the murky black disc of the wormhole gate was replaced by the image of a particularly massive, multi-colored gas giant.

"Transit successful," the ship's navigator reported. "We have arrived in the Nexus system."

"Receiving League Peacekeeper Fleet ID challenge," the comm officer reported.

"Transmit our credentials and itinerary," Colonel Li replied staidly as a dozen warship icons flickered into being on the tactical plotter positioned prominently in the command center. That dozen quickly grew to over a hundred, and Jenkins forced himself to relax as he knew that at least half of them were a match for the *Bonhoeffer*.

And at that moment, they *all* had their guns trained on the Armor Corps warship.

"Credentials and itinerary acknowledged," Comm reported. "I'm receiving a P2P link request."

Jenkins cocked his head, making brief eye contact with General Akinouye, who seemed as surprised as he was.

"Accept the link," Li commanded, and a moment later, the image of a Jemmin appeared on the screen.

The Jemmin were remarkably similar to humans. They were bipedal, featured external paired organs such as eyes and ears, and largely interacted with their environments the same way humans did. They relied upon the same basic senses, had fingered hands with opposable thumbs, and organized themselves along similar social lines to those used by humans.

But in spite of those similarities, the differences were striking.

They had grey, porous skin with the barest hints of blue near their facial features. Their mouths were lined not with teeth, but rows of flexible bone plates that were more than capable of tearing through meat and bone alike. Their ears were long slits which ran from midway up their necks to the tops of their heads, and their noses were recessed rather than prominent like human noses. And none of their external organs were quite symmetrical, though a consistent left-right bias seemed indiscernible to Jenkins.

Still, it was their eyes—gray, featureless, and unblinking—that stood out the most.

"Human warship *Dietrich Bonhoeffer*," the Jemmin's auto-translated voice greeted, "this is Illumination League Peace-keeping Cruiser, *Azure Spire*. Your destination star system is under quarantine. We advise, for your safety, that you return to your home star system and wait until we declare it to once again be transit-safe. Acknowledge."

"*Azure Spire*, this is *Dietrich Bonhoeffer* actual, acknowledging your transmission," Colonel Li replied neutrally while tapping out commands which, when received by the helmsman, saw the carrier's engines fire and drive the venerable warship toward the Naga gate. "Our mission to the Naga System is considered top priority. My orders are to proceed there without delay, secure Terran interests in accordance with our lawful rights, and await further instructions from my government. Acknowledge," he finished, his lips pursed in a thin line as he returned the *Azure Spire* CO's command.

"Transmission acknowledged, *Dietrich Bonhoeffer*," the Jemmin replied in the flat, emotionless tone of the auto-translator. "Acknowledge receipt of this duly-issued warning regarding the Naga System's current status."

Colonel Li quickly examined a data packet, which he brought to General Akinouye for review. The ebony-skinned general nodded after reviewing the document and affixed his signature to it.

"*Azure Spire*," Colonel Li declared, forwarding the document to the comm officer, "we are transmitting our acknowledged copy of your warning." His lips twisted into a smirk. "We appreciate your concern for our well-being."

"Transmission received. Proceed to the Naga gate and do

not deviate from the indicated route," the Jemmin said before cutting the link.

"Frosty," Akinouye muttered just loud enough for Jenkins to hear. He leaned toward Jenkins and added, "Prepare for a hot drop."

"Yes, General," Jenkins agreed, having already issued orders to that effect. Better to be unnecessarily over-prepared. The alternative would get people killed.

The *Bonhoeffer* adjusted course and speed, as directed by the IL Peacekeepers, and soon the main viewer was filled with the image of their destination wormhole gate. Clustered around the most massive gas giant in the Nexus System, the gates assigned to humanity's sub-set of the FTL—faster than light—network were relatively close to one another. The other League species, and even those species like the Vorr and Arh'Kel who were no longer parties to the Illumination League but retained access to their wormholes, were similarly clustered at roughly equidistant points from the rest of the non-League worlds.

Dozens of Arh'Kel warships soon appeared on the farthest edge of the *Bonhoeffer*'s tactical plotter, and Jenkins could feel the atmosphere in command and control, the CAC go taut as the contacts were called out in the sensor pit. There was little real risk of a confrontation in the Nexus, but the bad blood the rock-biters had earned in recent decades made every human present take note at seeing their longtime enemy's warships maneuvering well within weapons range.

"Steady as she goes, Helm," Colonel Li said firmly, and the stiff shoulders around the CAC relaxed, if just a bit as people resumed focus on their duties. "Triple-check our approach vector to the Naga gate," he added for good measure.

"Aye, sir," came a short burst of acknowledgments as the *Bonhoeffer* moved toward its destination. At their present speed, they would arrive in just under an hour. During that time,

Jenkins observed no fewer than one thousand distinct sensor contacts appear on the tactical plotter, with eighty percent of those icons belonging to the Illumination League Peacekeeper Force.

Every single League member species was represented in the ILPF's ship roster, but Solar humanity's representation was pathetic by comparison to most. Just thirty warships bearing Solarian heraldry were present, and none of them made any effort to contact their Terran brethren as the Armor Corps drove toward the Naga gate.

"One Minders," grunted General Akinouye in muted disgust. "A hundred billion people call Sol home, sixty times as many as live in the Terran Republic, and they can't even be bothered to present a credible presence here at the beating heart of the Illumination League? Pathetic."

Jenkins quirked a brow in mild surprise. "The Terran Republic's official stance on Terran-Sol relations is one promoting reunification."

"Nobody on this deck is stupid, Colonel," Akinouye said pointedly. "When our wormholes were locked out by the League for seventy years—which only happened because of those One Minders' inflexible, collectivist mindset—the humans of Sol and those of us in the Terran Republic took radically different paths. We had to survive without interstellar commerce, and developed our own technology as a result, which is why we're able to stave off the Arh'Kel even though they outnumber us fifty-to-one." The veteran general sneered contemptuously. "When the gates re-opened, Sol was a little too eager to run into the League's open arms while we learned how to stand on our own. Nothing that's happened since Sol joined the League has suggested reunification is anything but a pipe dream. So 'official stances' are nice in theory, but reality on the ground is another thing entirely." He inclined his chin toward the tactical plotter. "Sol and the League deserve each other. We Terrans deserve *better*, which is exactly what we're going to build. One brick at a time if necessary."

"Yes, sir." Jenkins nodded, a slow smile spreading across his face as the *Bonhoeffer* made its final approach to the Naga gate.

"Thirty seconds to event horizon," the helmsman called out.

"Angle and velocity aligned," the navigator reported tensely.

"Gate handshake protocols established," reported Comms.

"All hands," Colonel Li raised the crew over the intercom, "prepare for gate transit in twenty seconds."

The transit timer counted down on displays throughout the ship. As the *Bonhoeffer* reached the event horizon, Jenkins felt his breath catch for those last few seconds.

Then, just as had happened an hour before, the dark, impenetrable wormhole was replaced by the image of a planet. But unlike the gas giant in the Nexus System, this one was monochrome teal and featured a dazzling, silvery ring system, not unlike those of Saturn.

"Transit complete," the helmsman reported as the *Bonhoeffer*'s engines fired and the ship's course was adjusted.

"Contacts," Sensors called out, "multiple contacts in orbit of EO-5293."

New icons winked onto the tactical plotter, one after another, until thirty-eight warships appeared in orbit of EO-5293, a planetoid known colloquially as "Shiva's Wrath."

"Break it down," Li commanded.

"Twenty-three Jemmin warships squawking ILPF idents, Colonel," Sensors reported. "Fifteen warships squawking Vorr codes."

Li's brow lowered as he turned to General Akinouye. "The briefing indicated no more than six Vorr warships would be present."

"That was our intel," General Akinouye agreed grimly.

"Apparently the Jemmin disapprove of their presence in this star system."

Li nodded, satisfied that the Armor Corps' ranking member was being straight with him. "All hands," he raised his voice, "this is Colonel Li. Set condition one throughout the ship. I say again: set condition one throughout the ship."

The XO confirmed the order, and Jenkins knew that meant his time on the bridge was at an end. He turned to leave, but the general motioned for him to stop. "Stay, Colonel. I want you as up-to-speed as possible before we drop you on that ball of ice."

Jenkins nodded before giving Li a deferential look, to which Li nodded approvingly before resuming his duties. "Helm, increase acceleration to make least-time orbit of Shiva's Wrath."

"Least-time orbit, aye," the helmsman acknowledged before adding, "estimate low-orbit in twenty-three hours, eighteen minutes, Colonel."

Li turned to Jenkins. "I hope you people trained for a hot drop. I can't risk hanging between two battle fleets poised to tear each other apart."

Jenkins flashed a confident smirk. "You give us a survivable approach trajectory and we'll be fine."

"Good." Li nodded, though he seemed unconvinced.

As was so often the case, Jenkins felt significantly less confident than he let on. But he had done his level best to prep his people for a hot drop. He just hoped he'd done enough.

"Come on, you monkeys!" Captain Xi Bao snarled at the scrambling rookies as last-minute preparations were made to the drop-cans, which the mechs would ride to the surface of Shiva's Wrath. "Podsy's dates move faster than you, and they're all *dead!*" she shouted as a nearby worker tripped over her own boots and fell, sending a loose-packed crate of ration bars skittering across the deck. "Trying to get a purple tag, is that it, Quinn?" Xi barked as the woman hurriedly picked up the scattered bars and refilled the crate. "Bucking for a doctor's note so you don't have to go to work like the rest of us?"

"No, ma'am!" Quinn replied. She was the green Monkey assigned to Lieutenant Ford's *Forktail*.

"Then why in God's name are you trying to make out with my deck?" Xi barked. "Get those bars loaded into your mech. Move! Move! Move!" she yelled as the harried Quinn did precisely that, entering *Forktail's* drop-can and disappearing from sight.

It wasn't until the rookie was out of sight that Xi shared a grin with her former Wrench, Andy "Podsy" Podsednik, who rolled his wheelchair over to her side and muttered, "You could be nicer to them."

Were *they* nice to *me* when *I* was in her shoes?" Xi retorted.

"No," Podsy allowed, "but you get to make the world you live in. You don't need to keep it the mess that you were raised in."

"This isn't a slumber party or a sorority hazing," Xi scoffed. "Military life isn't for the soft of ass. If she can't handle me getting in her face over some ration bars, what good will she be when we're knee deep in the shit and taking fire?"

"I know." Podsy sighed. "I just think there's more than one way to skin the proverbial cat. Bear that in mind when you're having all the fun down there, will ya?"

"I still wish you were coming, Podsy," Xi said seriously. "Koch's repair unit was absolutely gutted when we transferred over from Fleet to Armor. We need every qualified Wrench we can find—legs or no," she added with a pointed look at his amputated lower limbs.

Podsy grimaced. "You know I'd rather be down there with

you, too." He shook his head in bitter resignation. "But I'll do more good scrounging up care packages and delivering them to you on schedule. Unlike Durgan's Folly, it would be nice to have a steady supply line." He lowered his voice conspiratorially as he cast a look around the *Bonhoeffer*'s "veteran" crew. "And between you and me, I don't trust these geezers to be on time for anything but the Tuesday all-you-can-eat buffet line."

Xi laughed before turning serious again. "I'm going to miss you down there, Podsy."

"Well, at least you're in good hands," he said with a bemused smile as Xi's new crewmates appeared.

Xi grumbled at the sight of them. "Don't rub it in."

"*Elvira*'s can is loaded and secured, Captain," Private Miles "Blinky" Staubach, her new Monkey, reported.

The man beside him, Chief Warrant Officer Fourth Class Lu Kai, nodded in agreement. "I double-checked the reactor and ammo stores, Captain. We're five-by-five."

"Good," Xi said flatly before gesturing to the nearest drop-cans. "Now how about you help the rest of the headless chickens straighten themselves out so that ours isn't the only can that makes the drop?"

"Yes ma'am," Staubach replied.

Lu, on the other hand, made a distasteful look before acknowledging, "Aye, Captain."

"Hop to it," she said with an urgent look, and her mech's new crewmates did precisely that.

"You've gotten them into shape," Podsy said approvingly. "It's almost like you know what you're doing...almost."

"I know, right?" she deadpanned.

"Excuse me?" came the feminine voice of the one person Xi did not want to hear from. She schooled her features into a neutral mask while Podsy made little effort to hide his delight in

Xi's discomfort. "Captain Xi," the woman said as she approached, proudly displaying her press credentials between her obnoxiously-perfect breasts. "I was just wondering if there's a better place where I could store my backup data storage equipment?"

Xi bit back a dozen angry retorts she would have loved to deliver, but with great effort, she calmly replied, "The small arms locker is the only compartment in my mech where you haven't already stowed at least *one* piece of your gear, Ms. Samuels. And as I already made clear, that particular compartment is off-limits to civilians."

The blue-eyed, blonde-haired reporter wasn't deterred. "This equipment is more valuable than half of the mechs in the battalion. I was assured by General Akinouye himself that I would receive full cooperation, Miss Xi..."

"*Captain* Xi," she interrupted tersely. "When I'm on-duty, that is the proper form of address. Or was that not also made clear during your meeting with my superiors, *Ms.* Samuels?"

Sarah Samuels' eyes flashed with something between amusement and satisfaction. "Perfectly, Captain."

Xi did, however, eventually relent by gesturing to *Elvira*'s drop-can. "See those two, green, impact-rated munitions crates just inside our can's ramp?"

Samuels flipped her hair as she turned to look at the indicated crates before nodding. "Yes, I do."

"If you can neatly stack the ration bars I've got stowed in there under the port hot-bunk," Xi said in a slightly patronizing tone, "you can use one of those for the last of your gear. But that's the best we've got to offer. Take it or leave it."

"I'll take it," Samuels agreed, turning toward *Elvira*'s drop-can. Her hips swayed exaggeratedly as she walked, and more than a few heads turned to watch her as the reporter bent down to do as Xi had instructed.

"Now I *really* wish I was going with you." Podsy sighed wistfully.

"She's not your type," Xi quipped. "Still has a pulse, remember?"

Podsy snapped his fingers in mock disappointment. "You're right, you're right...but still..." He cocked his head while admiring the view as the reporter bent over yet again. "Without exceptions, what good are rules?"

"You're sick, Podsy," Xi said, summoning as much scorn as she could before breaking out into a grin.

"I'm going to miss you, Captain," he said seriously. "Good hunting down there."

"I'm going to miss you too," she said with feeling. He blinked quickly before turning his wheelchair around and rolling toward the drop-deck's main entry.

Stumbling out of a nearby drop-can, Private Quinn once again spilled an armload of supplies, this time, chemical heat packs.

Xi groaned before stomping over toward the harried woman. "Making out with my deck on company time again, Quinn?"

"No, ma'am," Quinn replied, her voice tremulous as she gathered up the scattered heat packs.

"The next time I see you hurl yourself at this deck," Xi snapped, "there had better be a ring on your finger demonstrating your undying affection. Is that clear?"

"As a Solarian's conscien..." Quinn began before halting mid-word and giving Xi a wide-eyed look.

Xi smirked. "The first smart thing you've said all day, and you couldn't even do *that* right. Move your ass!" she barked, spurring the woman into action as she collected the last of the scattered supplies. After Quinn had once again disappeared within one of the thirty-nine prepped drop-cans, Xi muttered, "What the hell have you gotten yourself into, Bao?"

1

INSERTION

Xi verified her neural linkage to *Elvira* with a brief diagnostic cycle. It caused her body to flush with alternating waves of tingling and emptiness, as the implants buried in her brain prepared to re-route her motor cortex and tactile senses. Everything was green, which meant all that remained was to wait for the drop timer.

Hurry up and wait. I live for that shit.

She drew a cleansing breath, nervously checking her mech's various data streams and triple-checking the manual controls. What had once been a mere pre-deployment ritual, learned after hundreds of hours of practice in simulators, was now seared into her brain after the deployment on Durgan's Folly when she didn't have a functioning neural link to her mech.

She looked down at her fingertips, seeing the traces of scars from the abuse she had put them through on that hellhole of a world. Doc Fellows had assured her that another couple rounds of nerve regeneration therapy would restore the last of her fingers' sensation, except that therapy would have to wait.

Her comm board lit up with the launch countdown timer,

showing three minutes to drop. The corners of her mouth twitched upward. The wait was over.

It was time to link up with her mech.

Activating the link required less thought than it took to blink an eye, and once active, the link washed her body with a familiar string of sensations. Just one in eighty humans had brain structures which permitted long-term linkage of the type used for directly controlling an external vehicle. Xi happened to be exceptionally suited to neural linkage, which combined with her extraordinary reflexes and focus made her a one-in-ten-million candidate. That was the reason they pulled her from prison and put her in a mech.

She went through the ritual of checking her direct neural inputs, seeing the correct indicators light up across her board as she completed a hundred and thirty-two distinct inputs in less than three seconds. Once satisfied her link was up, she raised the rest of the company on their dedicated channel.

"2nd Company," Xi called, "link up and relay drop status."

Her command board flared to life as each of the Jocks under her command verified their links and drop-readiness.

"All right." She nodded approvingly. "2nd Company, sound off."

Lieutenant Eugene Ford, her Company XO and 5th Platoon's CO, was first to reply, "*Forktail* here, drippin' venom."

Next came Lieutenant Nakamura, 6th Platoon's CO and Xi's third-in-command. "*Wolverine*, snikt snikt."

"*Masamune*, razor sharp."

"*Sam Kolt*, makin' us equal."

"*Eclipse* here. The blacker, the better."

"*Cave Troll*. Big and filthy."

"*Widowmaker*, breaking hearts."

"*Gym-Cricket*, wishing on a star."

"*White Zombie*, more human than human."

"*Heavy Metal Jesus*, thunder-strikin.'"

"*Holy Diver*, riding midnight seas."

Xi nodded in satisfaction before finishing, "*Elvira*, clicking my heels." She switched to *Elvira*'s closed-circuit intercom, "All crew report ready for drop."

"Ready, Captain," Chief Lu, her new Wrench, acknowledged. His voice was tight and anxious. Perfect.

"Ready, ma'am," Private Staubach replied more confidently.

"Don't 'ma'am' me, Blinky," she quipped. "My twentieth birthday's coming up in three months, which makes me the youngest person aboard this bug. Captain, Cap, or Elvira will do just fine on the closed-circuit."

"Yes, m...I mean, yes, Captain," Blinky replied nervously, causing Xi to grin with satisfaction. They were *all* on their toes, which was precisely where they needed to be.

The drop timer reached thirty-seconds-to-go, and the *Bonhoeffer*'s deployment clamps clanged loudly against *Elvira*'s drop-can.

"This is it, kids," Xi called over the company-wide. "Watch your altimeters, velocity, and initial approach angle to adjust trajectory as needed to avoid burnup, but no maneuvering thrusters after drop-plus-twenty-seconds. Pop your chutes at the deck but don't burn the brakes until you hit the red-zone. Let's get wheels-down ASAP."

A rapid sequence of acknowledging flickers appeared on the display before her. She could just as easily have piped the company reports directly into her neural linkage, but unlike most, she had little difficulty switching back and forth between her real eyes and *Elvira*'s myriad of cameras. In her mind, the less clutter she put in her combat-feeds, the better.

As the counter reached the last few seconds, she felt her own nerves begin to fray and she called out, "Drop in five... four...three...two...one... Drop!"

The drop-can released from the *Bonhoeffer*'s clamps, and the external video feeds sprang to life to show the white orb of Shiva's Wrath below. Looming beyond the relatively tiny planetoid was the blue-green gas giant that served as its parent. Xi focused on her initial approach trajectory and, after a few seconds' calculation, she fired her drop-can's thrusters to re-orient the flat, rectangular container that held her mech.

The thrusters roared to life, pitching her bow up and rolling the can to an upside-down orientation per drop protocols. The pure-white horizon of Shiva's Wrath loomed below as Xi worked to fine-tune her approach vector.

Suddenly, one of the can's four thrusters died, causing it to briefly pitch as the other three continued burning for a quarter-second before she could cut their fuel supply.

"Get my thruster back, Lu," she snapped before isolating control for that thruster and carefully re-igniting the other three. If she didn't trim more off their angle, she would risk a fatal approach velocity that her parachutes and braking jets might not be able to overcome.

"On it, Captain," Lu replied tersely, but the seconds ticked by and nothing happened. Her thruster-fire window was closing. Fast. She needed that last thruster angle.

"I need that thruster, Chief," she growled, performing a quick calculation and finding there was nothing else she could do until he gave her back the fourth thruster. They were *barely* on the survivable end of the approach angle spectrum and had only another five seconds she could fire her thrusters before they would be unable to adequately compensate.

The thruster sprang back to life. "Three Thruster back online, Captain."

He hadn't spoken the second word before she was already burning all four at maximum. The can's approach vector slowly climbed until it was just over one percent above the minimum-survivable angle for her drop can's profile.

Going against her own pre-drop instructions, she let the thrusters burn for another two seconds before their fuel supplies were fully exhausted. "Yeah, yeah," she muttered, imagining the razzing her company would give her when they found out about the breach of protocol, "sue me."

The topside of the drop-can began to glow yellow-orange as it kissed the thin atmosphere of the frigid world below. The planetoid's embrace intensified with each passing second, but thankfully, the icy worldlet's atmosphere was thin enough that the display was rather less spectacular than drops into dense-atmospheres like those on nearly all of the Terran colonies.

The unfortunate side of the thin atmosphere was that it would provide significantly less braking effect as the drop-cans skipped through and accelerated toward the surface, which made drop-chutes and braking thrusters even more important.

To compensate, the cans had been put into extremely narrow and precise approach vectors, which kept them in the atmosphere for as long as possible.

But even Shiva's Wrath had enough gas in its atmosphere to make the drop-can, and everything in it, begin to vibrate with worrisome intensity.

She performed a quick damage check of the can's topside and found nothing remarkable. But the simulations had suggested this level of vibration would not take place for several more minutes.

"Diagnostics," she barked over the intercom.

"It looks like Three Engine's housing took some damage," Private Staubach promptly replied, and Xi re-oriented one of the drop-can's external cameras onto Three Engine to find that there was damage to its external housing.

"Manually isolate all feeds to Three Engine," she

commanded while doing so remotely. She didn't like the idea of making her people get out of their drop-couches during approach, but they simply couldn't afford to have Three Engine's pending destruction impact the rest of their systems.

Lu hesitated for a trio of seconds before acknowledging, "Yes, Captain."

She gritted her teeth, knowing that Podsy would have jumped out of his drop-couch before she had ordered him to. Thankfully, Lu was technically competent and completed the task in twelve seconds, evidenced by a thrill of sensory feedback sent through her neural link showing that a handful of fuel and coolant lines had been manually closed off.

"Three Engine isolated," Lu reported as he clicked back into his "crash-couch," as they had come to be known.

"Good work," she replied, and a few minutes later, the glowing, damaged engine was torn completely off its mount. With it gone, the vibrations temporarily abated, and the drop-can continued its parabolic trajectory toward the surface of Shiva's Wrath. Xi hoped no one was coming in behind them to get clocked by the engine. Most of the times, the drop-cans maintained separation, but sometimes, atmospherics funneled them together.

The drop-can's approach vector arced gently toward the surface of the planet, and eventually resumed its vibration, but this time, it did so in accordance with what the simulations predicted. Xi had no way of checking on the rest of her company until they touched down and freed their mechs, which would happen in another eight minutes if all went according to plan.

Consciously, she knew it was all a matter of physics that gave the vehicles no choice in how they manifested. Mass, velocity, gravity, air drag—these variables had been pre-calculated and were now playing out like some kind of unholy Rube Goldberg machine, which held her people's fate in its convoluted machinations. She rationally knew that nothing could be done to change their date with the surface, but that didn't banish her mounting anxiety during what was only her second combat drop.

The minutes thankfully ticked by as the company's drop proceeded according to plan, and soon the surface of the world below dominated her fields of view. The "deck," which was slightly different for each drop-can due to their physical profiles and drop characteristics, was less than thirty seconds away. It was time to flip the can topside-up.

"Flipping the coin," she declared, using the same terminology she had employed during the myriad simulations.

She test-ignited the orienting rockets, found them all in working order, and waited for the ideal moment to flip the can with a controlled, asymmetrical burn of chemical drivers.

The drop-can slowly rotated, just like in the simulations. Once it had achieved landing orientation, it remained there by the force of a hundred micro-rockets automatically regulating the can's orientation.

"Prepare for chute deployment," she intoned over the intercom.

The "deck" approached, and when *Elvira*'s can hit that precise altitude, Xi deployed the drop-chute. Her deployment input was logged so precisely that she only missed the bulls-eye by one two-hundredth of a second, a personal best after three hundred simulated runs.

A swarm of parachutes, each connected to the drop-can via carbon-fiber lines, blasted up from the still-glowing topside and deployed in perfectly-coordinated succession. Twenty-one distinct chutes blossomed, filling the sky and causing everyone inside *Elvira*'s cabin to snap down into their crash-couches. If they hadn't correctly braced for the lurch, someone might have lost a tooth. Or worse.

But the chutes' deceleration was nothing compared to what they were about to experience.

The chutes slowed their descent, but their impact was far less than would have been on a world with a thicker atmosphere. They flashed through the green-zone deck in a matter of seconds and fell through the yellow-zone only marginally slower.

"Brace for braking thrusters," she called, wincing in anticipation as the red-zone approached at a frantic pace.

This time when the drop-can fell past the red-zone marker, she missed by just under a tenth of a second. She would have snarled in frustration at such poor reactions, but the sudden jerk of the thrusters firing in unison was punishment enough. This was what made the couches crucial to so-called "hot-drop" deployments that required crews to ride their mech cans down instead of taking personnel shuttles.

She clenched her jaw to keep her teeth from shattering, and it felt as though her heart was being run over by a bulldozer. When the braking thrusters burned so loudly that even with several layers of armor between them and her ears, they were nearly-deafening. Then the drop-can struck solid ground. Hard.

"Touchdown," she declared unnecessarily. "All systems check."

Her board slowly began to flicker with confirmations as her Wrench and Monkey performed their post-drop checks. It took them twenty-two seconds, fully four seconds longer than their best run in the simulator to complete the checks.

"All systems green, Captain," reported Chief Lu.

"Confirmed," Staubach agreed. "All systems green."

While they worked through their system checks, she

swiveled the external cameras atop the tilted drop-can and saw that her best exit was to the left.

"Popping the left hatch," she intoned, reaching out with her mind to blow that panel's explosive charges. They blew in unison, and the panels fell away, allowing the frigid air of the snow-covered world to rush across *Elvira*'s external thermometers. Xi "felt" the sensation of cold air washing over the mech's hull much as she would feel it on her own skin, though it was considerably less intense. "Crab-walking," she declared, activating *Elvira*'s ambulation systems and causing the mech to rise a meter from the deck of the drop-can as the six legs engaged.

Her mech's first step into the ice-field was one she knew she would never forget, just as she would never forget the first steps she had taken on Durgan's Folly.

She slowly crawled her eighty-ton vehicle out of the drop-can, and once outside, she assumed a combat-ready posture. Her paired missile-launcher banks swiveled up and forward, locking into a fire-ready position. Her twin fifteen-kilo artillery guns ratcheted up off their cradles atop her Scorpion-class mech's hull and assumed a ten-degree angle before locking in place. Xi cycled her anti-personnel chain guns, filling the cabin with a faint whirring sound as they spun through a hundred phantom cycles apiece.

She activated the company-wide net after seeing a handful of her mechs' icons appear on the short-range tactical plotter. Soon she had accounted for each and every mech in her unit, which made her breathe a sigh of relief before she keyed her mic. "This is *Elvira* requesting encrypted status reports."

The reports flowed in, and it seemed that hers had been the most eventful drop of the entire company.

"Good work, people," she said approvingly. "You know the drill: *Eclipse*, put our birds in the air and establish P2P with Battalion Command. First, we hook up with 3rd Company and then rendezvous with 1st Company and the support vehicles. Roll out."

"Birds in the air," *Eclipse*'s Jock, Second Lieutenant Carl "Sargon" Benjamin replied promptly. "Estimate P2P in eight minutes."

"All right, people," Xi said with a grunt as she felt an insuppressible shiver when the cold air swept across her fast-walking mech, which crunched half-meter-deep footholes in the kilometers-thick ice covering Shiva's Wrath. "I hope you remembered your winter clothes."

———

"All pods touched down," Deck Chief Arnold "Jay" Rimmer declared over the drop bay's speakers. "Good work, people. Our crews have arrived on the surface and will rendezvous in two hours. First Shift, hit your racks. Second Shift, secure the vaults and visually confirm inventory before taking four hours" downtime. Third Shift, continue prepping a standard loadout of support cans; they need to be ready in six hours. Let's move."

A short-lived cheer erupted across the deck, and Andrew "Podsy" Podsednik shared the moment as he drove a forklift across the drop-deck. The lift was operable with manual inputs alone, and after much debate with Chief Rimmer, he had won the right not only to serve as Third Shift's supervisor but to help with the actual work of running the deck.

The drop-decks were typically served by teams of seven grease-monkeys and haulers, to go with three Wrenches who assisted with the tedious work or did actual machining when the need arose. Customizing replacement components before sending them to the surface via drop-cans similar to those which the mechs rode down was a crucial part of providing orbital support to armor on the ground. Without replacement parts, a relatively minor bit of battle damage could turn a mech into an oversized, useless "brick," hence the term's frequent use on the drop-deck.

For nearly an hour, Podsy helped his subordinates load a can of ordnance. It was mostly standard fare: high explosive and armor piercing (HE, AP) and incendiary shells, short-range missiles (SRMs), mid-range missiles (MRMs) and even a few long-range missiles (LRMs), heating pads, and relatively stable furnace fuels to keep the PDF—Planetary Defense Force— troopers from freezing to death, and of course, foodstuffs and water purification equipment. All in all, everything about this batch of cans was by the book, and thanks to Podsy's direction and subtle modifications of established Armor Corps protocol, they were nearly an hour ahead of schedule.

"Attention all hands," came Colonel Li's iron-hard voice over the ship-wide. He was usually the epitome of a command officer: calm and stoic, but ready on a moment's notice to rip something's throat out.

But right now, Podsy heard unmistakable anxiety in his voice.

"Two minutes ago," the colonel continued, "the Vorr and Jemmin forces in orbit of Shiva's Wrath exchanged fire. Three ships are already down, but the Vorr and Jemmin appear to be disengaging, moving to a stand-off."

As Li spoke, Podsy accessed the *Bonhoeffer*'s external feeds. At first, he saw nothing untoward, but then he noticed the faint trails of surface-bound vehicles headed for the same mountainous outcrop where the battalion was deployed.

And those vehicles had come from the Jemmin fleet.

"Maintain focus, people," Colonel Li said with firm resolve threaded through every syllable. "It's time we earned our pay."

The speakers went quiet, and the small red light beneath them darkened to indicate the address was complete.

"All right, people," Podsy called over the shift-wide channel while moving his forklift to a more central spot, "gather 'round."

Second and Third Shifts did as bidden, but Podsy couldn't immediately locate Second Shift's deck boss.

"Where's Chief Batista?" Podsy asked.

A pair of Second Shifters shrugged. "Haven't seen him in forever, Chief."

Podsy shook his head. "Define 'forever,' please."

"Eight minutes?" The Second Shifter didn't sound confident.

Podsy set his jaw. The standard break-time allowed was ten minutes, which meant that every smartass liked to use some variant of the "eight-minute rule" when covering for their fellows' absences.

"Fine," Podsy allowed before gesturing to the line of partially-prepped drop-cans behind him, "you can tell him when he comes back that we're re-packing half of these cans. One and Two need to have all of their LRMs removed, and we need to pull the Hawkeye MRMs too..."

"You can't override a load order," interrupted one of Second Shift's Wrenches. "Those have to be confirmed by the colonel and Chief Rimmer."

"I'm not telling anyone to stop working or to remove anything just yet," Podsy said firmly. "I'm saying to stop loading the LRMs and Hawkeyes since Jemmin countermeasures will make them useless, and prep all eight pallets of jammer drones. We can pull the unwanted ordnance back out of the cans as soon as we get confirmation from command. Third Shift, go," he commanded, and his people did while the Second Shifters looked on with mixed approval and reluctance. "Second Shift," he continued, "you can keep working on cans Five and Seven because their inventories won't need any modifications...go. That's an order," he snapped when they failed to jump, "and until Chief Batista comes back, I'm boss of the deck. Move!"

Most of the Second Shifters did as bidden, but a pair of stalwarts looked ready for a confrontation. They were older crew, ossified in their tendencies and disliking of anything that upset their formerly-established routines—routines which apparently included covering for naps taken by the shift boss.

Just as Podsy opened his mouth to argue with the rebellious crew, the main door swished open and Chief Rimmer moved onto the deck.

"Where's Batista?" he demanded after sighting Podsy and making a bee-line for his forklift.

"I'll go find him, sir," one of the Second Shifters said hurriedly.

"I didn't tell you to find him," Rimmer snarled as he rounded on the crewman, "I asked where he was, and now I want to know what he's doing."

The Second Shifter hesitated. "Napping in the Hawkeye bunks, sir."

"Wake his sorry ass up," Rimmer scowled before resuming his trek to Podsy's forklift. "Chief Podsednik, a word."

The disobedient Second Shifters smirked triumphantly as Rimmer approached, and Podsy was legitimately concerned that the boss of the deck might have some sort of problem with his orders to re-pack the cans.

"Yes, sir?" Podsy wheeled the forklift over to cut down on Rimmer's trek.

"We need to re-pack these cans," Rimmer explained. "If Jemmin forces are down there, the Hawkeyes and longer-range missiles are de-prioritized. We need to send down all of our jammer drones and a couple extra packs of exo-suits since detached infantry patrols are in the book for potential Jemmin encounters."

The flabbergasted looks on the rebellious Second Shifters' faces was priceless, but Podsy kept his expression neutral as he nodded. "Yes, sir, I was just coordinating that effort."

Rimmer's brow rose in surprise before he looked over at the stationary Second Shifters. "Is that true?"

"Yes, sir," replied one of the Second Shifters promptly, while the others nodded in agreement.

"Then why in the name of our Lord and savior, Mister Murphy, are you still standing here?" Rimmer barked.

Podsy quickly interjected, "They were reminding me that Cans Five and Seven didn't need modification."

Rimmer glared at the trio of Second Shifters. "Then get back to it. Now."

The trio scattered, and Rimmer gave Podsy a brief look of approval. "You're quick on your feet. I'll have the official orders revised in three minutes. Do you need First Shift's help to get this done on schedule?"

Podsy shook his head confidently. "We'll make the window, sir."

"Good." Rimmer nodded before his eyes locked onto the person of Chief Jose Batista, Second Shift's deck boss. "I'll have Chief Batista and his people stick around afterward to clean up, while you and Third Shift take their bunk schedule."

Podsy wanted to object, but he knew the extra duty shift that Batista's people were about to serve was less a reward for Third Shift than a punishment for Second. So he gave the only sane response, "Thank you, sir."

Rimmer set off for what was likely to be a lengthy upbraiding for his napping shift boss, but Podsednik's mind was already back on the task at hand.

He needed to get those cans ready. Captain Xi Bao and everyone with her would need them.

2

FROZEN HELL

"Good of you to join us, *Elvira*," Colonel Lee Jenkins greeted after all four companies were assembled at the rendezvous point. "I heard you had a little excitement on the way down?"

"Just keeping my people on their toes, sir," Xi replied with faint irritation.

"It's where we need to be," Jenkins acknowledged. "2nd Company will take point, 1st Company will take center with the infantry, and 3rd Company will break out at nine o'clock to the line of march two clicks. We'll arrive at Alpha Site in two hours. Roll out."

"2nd Company, on point," Xi acknowledged before leading her mechs to the front of the column. 2nd Company was consolidated from the remains of both 2nd and 4th Companies, with Xi in charge. Elvira was also one of the mechs in 4th Platoon of 2nd Company. She never knew from one battle to the next who would survive the engagement to become the next company. The entire battalion was a mish-mash of equipment and people forced into a formal structure that wasn't a perfect fit.

Round peg, meet square hole.

"3rd Company, nine o'clock, two clicks," replied Lieutenant

Winters, a newcomer to the battalion who had transferred over from Terra Han's PDF after eight years in their mechanized infantry.

Only Jenkins, Styles, Xi, Winters, and Koch were aware that this mission was more than simple protection duty. Only Styles and Xi shared Jenkins' knowledge that this was, in fact, a highly-secretive diplomatic meeting between the Terran Republic and an unknown species. Only a few people up the Fleet ladder even knew about the diplomatic nature of this mission. It seemed that Director Durgan had been much more circumspect in presenting this mission to the Terran government than Jenkins had initially suspected.

So when Jenkins said his next statement, he knew that only his hand-picked group would understand its full meaning.

"I just received confirmation that the Vorr are pulling out," he said as his column assumed formation. "Jemmin forces are inbound and will assume the Vorr position within the hour."

The brief delay before Xi replied told him she understood loud and clear. "Looks like sushi's off the menu. Damn."

Jenkins chuckled at her dark humor. The Vorr were an aquatic species which, as part of their customary greeting ritual, offered bits of their bodies for consumption as a gesture of good-will and openness. He would have been required to partake in this ritual had formal introductions taken place, and Jenkins wasn't ashamed to admit he was glad he would no longer have to.

"Jemmin or Vorr, who cares?" Lieutenant Winters asked enthusiastically. "We're here to prove Armor can do the job that others can't."

"Love the spirit, *Generally*," Jenkins approved, both of Winters' expressed sentiment and his ability to react in real-time. This was it. Jenkins had spent months prepping the crews for a situation like this, and now they needed to prove their worth. "Roll out."

Shiva's Wrath was cold. Incredibly cold. With a mean surface temperature of seventy degrees below zero Celsius, and an icy mantle ten kilometers thick with an ocean six times that deep beneath, it was a literal ball of ice. Its ultra-thin atmosphere was, surprisingly, breathable with only minimal concentration and humidification, so every vehicle had been equipped with the necessary gear to make it usable. Even the infantrymen were equipped with respirator units that did the job of protecting their lungs from the bitter cold and eventual desiccation that would come from breathing the worldlet's dry, unmodified air.

But to Xi, it wasn't the bitter cold, the mantle of ice, or even the breathable atmosphere which boggled her mind. Even the blue-green gas giant looming above the horizon wasn't enough to unnerve her.

What unnerved her, far more than she had expected, was the near-complete lack of *weather* on the planet.

During the early mission briefings, she had built the image of a blizzard-bound world in her mind's eye. Thick cloud banks, swirling snowstorms, drifts of white powder so deep she could lose her mech down one. All of these images had filled her apparently over-active imagination until, mid-way through the briefing, she had learned none of them would be featured on Shiva's Wrath. She had consciously accepted that updated information immediately without a single doubt.

But now, walking her mech across the smooth, icy landscape, she was thoroughly stunned by the lack of weather on the bleak, frozen planetoid.

Polymer hitting metal clattered behind her, and Xi turned to see Sarah Samuels bend down to retrieve one of her many video drones. Not much larger than a human hand, she seemed to have hundreds of the tiny things stowed throughout *Elvira*. As she moved into Xi's cockpit, the blond woman apologized, "I'm sorry about that, Captain."

"As long as this neural linkage is working," Xi replied tersely, "you're free to roam this mech just like the colonel said."

"You don't like me very much, do you?" the reporter asked with a bemused smirk.

"And why ever *would* I like you?"

"Because even the greatest deeds are meaningless without their proper recognition," Samuels replied all too easily. She had played this game. A lot. She was a predator who hunted information, and judging by the other woman's casual demeanor, Xi knew she needed to stay on her toes. "I heard you might know more than most about that," the reporter mused as she fidgeted with the camera now situated across her enviro-suited lap. "Recognition for one's deeds, that is?"

Xi was wrong-footed by that particular turn in the conversation. *Is she talking about Durgan's Folly?* she wondered in alarm. *Is this bitch* that *good?*

Xi shook her head. "We aren't in this for the glory, lady. The only way society works is if people like you are protected while you do...whatever it is you do," she said with an intentional hint of derision. "Sometimes that means people like me have to come to hellholes like this and stare down Nietzsche's abyss just to ensure everyone's ability to sip their lattes, argue with each other on the data nets, and I guess occasionally do something productive to keep the wheels of civilization from grinding to a halt."

"That sounds like an awful lot of disdain," Samuels observed neutrally. "Why risk your life to protect people you dislike so much?"

"First off, I don't dislike people," Xi replied as *Elvira* navigated a five-meter-wide fissure in the ice, carefully extending her legs and rotating the mech across the divide. The planet's surface was covered with such crevasses, crisscrossing hither and thither at seemingly random angles as the gravitational interplay between Shiva's Wrath and its parent gas giant constantly compressed and stretched the world's surface. "I dislike stupid people sucking off others while simultaneously judging them and, even worse, I hate bad ideas."

"Is that why you came to call a prison cell 'home' by the tender age of fourteen?" Samuels asked. "Not many people, even on the relatively authoritarian world of Terra Han, find themselves in max-sec before they've finished puberty."

"Puberty? At Fourteen?" Xi snorted. "Have you *looked* at me, lady? I had more curves at *thirteen* than an extreme drift-racing track."

Samuels laughed. "Fair enough. But that doesn't explain how you ended up behind bars."

"I thought you were here to document the battalion," Xi said irritably.

"I am," Samuels agreed, "but this battalion isn't made of machines and weapons. It's made of men and women, many of whom, like you, willingly chose to join military service instead of serving out their criminal sentences. As something of a scion for your unit, I thought an individual character bio of Captain Xi Bao, data criminal and information-thief-turned-mech-Jock, would be a good place to start my documentary."

Xi gritted her teeth. "I'm a data criminal, sure, but I never *stole* anything."

"That's not the way Terra Han's judiciary saw it," Samuels challenged. "They gave you a thirty-year sentence, one which would probably take you beyond your natural childbearing years, for stealing and broadcasting sensitive information across the data nets."

"That information wasn't stolen," she growled, "but yes, I did broadcast it."

"How can you say it wasn't stolen?" Samuels asked, and only then did Xi recognize the combative tone in the woman's voice. She had been so gradual in her lead-up to it that Xi hadn't even noticed, but now it was clear: she was being grilled.

Xi took a steadying breath. "The information I broadcast was government-collected statistical data on behavior patterns and their associations with multiple individual traits. Some of those traits were genetic, some had to do with individual social experiences, and some had to do with hormonal interplay with certain neural structures in the brain. The reason I didn't steal it...no, the reason I *couldn't have stolen it*, is simple: it was government-funded research, conducted using tax money. It belonged to *us*, not *them*, and the simple fact that they threw me in jail for shedding light on that information was all the proof one needs to know that my world's government does indeed view itself apart from the citizenry. That was the main point of my broadcasting the data."

"You stoked a lot of hatred with that data release," Samuels said sympathetically, though the sentiment was not directed at Xi. "Racial and sexual discrimination, ethnic violence, even several suicides were directly linked to your data release."

Xi shrugged with forced indifference as the last of 2nd Company traversed the icy chasm, though some required the aid of *Gym Cricket*, a multi-purpose non-combat mech that could create thirty-meter-long bridges in seconds. "I didn't cause any of that violence or hatred, and no sense in retrying the case. The government found me guilty. I served my time there before serving here. My sentence has been commuted and record expunged. If you're looking for some kind of daytime drama to create, go find it somewhere else. If you want to keep talking to me, then let's talk about 2nd Company and what we're facing right here on Shiva." Xi turned back to her console.

"Maybe you didn't cause the violence," Samuels allowed, "but you certainly fueled it." The reporter completely ignored Xi's attempt to end the conversation. The two women waited in uncomfortable silence. The reporter knew that the tension would grow.

"I'm not responsible for their hatred," Xi replied matter-of-factly, "and I'm not responsible for a society that self-destructs by choosing to coddle and shield itself from some of the harsher truths of the human condition. Some truths are nice to hear, others not so much. But instead of suppressing the flow of information which makes us feel bad, why don't we push it out there as hard and as fast as possible so we can collectively figure out how to deal with it? You're a reporter." she snapped, making angry eye contact with the blonde woman. "You, of all people, should know the answer."

Samuels' expression remained impassive, and she stayed silent for a moment while her hand-sized hover-drone recorded every second of the conversation.

Xi shook her head in disappointment. "Do you know what Thomas Jefferson said about an informed populace?"

"Tell me what he said." Samuels' eyes flashed with a peculiar, intense look.

"He said 'a well-informed populace can be trusted with its own government,'" Xi replied, having long-since burned those words into her brain. "But those words weren't what he was *really* saying. They were a negative image of his true message, which was this: an *uninformed* populace absolutely *cannot* be trusted with its own government. I was informing the public with my data release, whether they were going to like what I showed them or not. *I'm* not the enemy here. The real enemies in my criminal case are the institutions which think they get to decide what information is or isn't fit for public consumption. I broke the law, and I knew I'd be punished for it, but I did it anyway in part because I thought that the information I was putting out there was important and needed to be understood. Not because I agreed with what it suggested or represented, or because I thought it would lead to a particular outcome, but because I always, *always*," she repeated emphatically, "think that more information is better than less. My government threw me in jail because they disagreed, and I can't really blame them for dropping the hammer on me since I disrupted their plans." She shrugged. "The real problem in my case, Ms. Samuels, is the media that failed—and *continues* to fail—the people who depend upon it to present all of the facts so that we, the people, can make up our minds. You and your ilk waited for me, some random, fourteen-year-old girl, to throw myself on the proverbial grenade before you swooped in and spun the facts to suit your preconceived narratives."

Samuels' expression was flat, like the icy landscape before them, and for a long moment, she sat in silence before deactivating the recording drone. "Thank you, Captain Xi," she said neutrally before exiting the cabin.

The next few hours passed by in relative silence as the column rolled toward a nearly-vertical mountain looming fifteen kilometers above the ice-field around it.

"Alpha Site secured, Colonel," Captain Xi reported precisely on schedule. "The facility is ready for the infantry."

"Copy that, *Elvira*," Jenkins acknowledged. "Sergeant Major Trapper, you're 'go' to secure the facility."

"Roger," replied the grizzled Tim Trapper Sr., whose no-

nonsense approach stood in stark contrast with his son's more relaxed style. "Moving in."

Roy's tactical plotter showed a stream of icons emerging from the APCs—advanced personnel carriers—which bore Trapper's PDF troopers, all of whom had come from Terra Han. The Terran Armor Corps had only a handful of active infantrymen, most of whom were near-retirement and too high-ranking to warrant deployment as Pounders. So Sergeant Major Tim Trapper, Sr. was one of the few long-serving Armor Corps infantrymen present on Shiva's Wrath, with the rest of the veterans working to train an entire regiment of fresh recruits back at Armor Corps HQ on Terra Americana. But most of the recruits, like these PDF troopers, would come from Terra Han for a variety of reasons.

Uniquely in the Terran Republic, Terra Han was an Earth-class world. Its gravity was only six percent above Earth norm; its atmospheric content was nearly identical save for CO_2 levels of 4,000ppm, which was four times Earth's pre-FTL levels in the mid-twenty-first century; and, most important of all, it featured an axial tilt and mean temperatures that supported icy polar caps and Earth-like seasonal changes on much of its surface. Combined with its population of one billion humans, five times that of the second-most-populous colony, Terra Americana, this made Terra Han prime recruiting ground for the rebuilding Armor Corps.

Sergeant Major Trapper directed his people into the mouth of the subterranean facility, which bored straight into the side of the towering mountain. Without the forces of tectonic instability, erosion from weather, or tides lapping against the base of the rocky prominence, the mountain had stood unmolested for hundreds of millions of years. The sea of ice stretching out in all directions was less uniform near the base of the mountain, but Durgan Industrial Enterprises (DIE) had cleared several approach paths using a combination of careful orbital strikes and heavy equipment several decades earlier.

Two minutes after deploying from the APCs, Trapper reported, "Main facility secure, Colonel Jenkins. All internal monitoring systems read five-by-five. I'm sending four platoons to investigate the mining tunnels."

"Good work, Tim," Jenkins acknowledged. "Arrange a detail to finish securing the rest of the facility and rejoin the column once you're satisfied. We need to secure the other three facilities."

"Roger, sir," Trapper acknowledged, and to Jenkins' surprise, the venerable warrior emerged from Alpha Site's massive, iron-walled cave mouth four minutes later at the head of half the troopers he had led inside. "My people will conduct visual inspections to confirm the site's integrity, after which they'll reinforce the entry point." Trapper's people filed into the APCs, with the sergeant major's boots the last off the ground. As soon as he regained his APC, he reported, "Ready to roll, Colonel."

"1st Battalion," Jenkins called over the command channel, "proceed to the Beta Site."

Three hours later, the Beta Site and Charlie Site had been secured, and the column had nearly reached the Delta Site.

But before they arrived, *Roy*'s tactical board lit up like a Christmas tree. "Multiple contacts, Colonel," Styles remarked, and Jenkins leaned over the technician's shoulder to get a better look at the confused stream of data. "I'm reading Jemmin forces surrounding the facility," Styles reported tightly.

Jenkins set his jaw. "1st Battalion, hold position."

The column came to a halt a few seconds later, during

which time Styles worked to parse the data feeds, "They must have been using some kind of stealth systems, Colonel. It looks like they intentionally deactivated them as we approached."

Jenkins saw no fewer than eight vehicles, each at least twice the size of *Roy*, arrayed in front of the Delta Site's cave-mouth entrance. Each of these four facilities was a fully-automated, deep-mining operation funded by DIE. They extracted ultra-rare minerals, which were remotely-transported twice-a-year off the surface and collected by DIE transports for return to the Terran Republic.

"What are the Jemmin doing down a DIE mine shaft?" Jenkins wondered aloud.

"Can't be for the minerals," Styles mused. "Word is they've already mastered deep-core mining of all but the largest gas giants. Running remote operations like this one are inefficient by comparison."

"And the other three sites' cargoes are just sitting there," Jenkins agreed, "waiting to be collected."

"There's either something other than minerals being extracted down there," Styles suggested, "or the Jemmin are here for something from the facility itself...but what would they need with our relatively primitive tech?"

Jenkins grimaced. "Things look like they're about to get interesting."

Styles' board lit up again. "I'm receiving an incoming trans-mission from the Jemmin, Colonel."

"Let's hear it."

3

KEEPING THE PEACE

"Greetings, human paramilitary forces," greeted the Jemmin's auto-translated voice, which somehow seemed even colder and less...well, *human*, than the *Azure Spire*'s commanding officer during their brief jaunt through the Nexus System. "This location is under quarantine by the authority of the Illumination League Peacekeeping Force. Do not encroach while we secure the area in accordance with ILPF protocol."

Jenkins turned to Styles. "Get General Akinouye on the line. I don't like the sound of this."

"The *Bonhoeffer*'s currently repositioning, sir," Styles replied promptly. "I haven't been able to establish a real-time secure P2P for about eleven minutes."

Jenkins bit his lip irritably before gesturing for Styles to put him on with the Jemmin. "This is Colonel Lee Jenkins, commanding officer of the Terran Armor Corps forces currently deployed on this world. We are here under lawful writ in accordance with both Terran Republic sovereignty and pursuant to Sol's colonial recognition of the Terran colonies. We are thereby permitted to transit within Solar space, to conduct exploratory operations while doing so, as well as to extract and utilize essential resources from any territory which the Illumination League recognizes as under human domain. Acknowledge."

"Your transmission is acknowledged, Colonel Jenkins," the Jemmin replied, and something about its tone and cadence set Jenkins on edge. He doubted that effect was unintentional on the Jemmin's part. "We are here under the authority of the Illumination League Peacekeeping Directive, which subordinates parochial concerns whenever conflict arises with the sub-directives of member nations. Do not encroach until we have secured this facility and returned to our mobile command center, at which time you may carry out whatever lawful operations you see fit. Acknowledge your compliance with this directive."

Jenkins gritted his teeth in anger. They were here to meet representatives of a hitherto-unknown alien species, and that meeting was supposed to be facilitated by the Vorr—who the Jemmin had just shown the door after a short-lived exchange of fire that had killed at least three warships.

For all he knew, the Jemmin had the alien representative cornered in Delta Site.

But he had no options. The only potential moves left to him required General Akinouye's support, and the general was currently unavailable due to the unstable situation unfolding in orbit.

"Transmission acknowledged," Jenkins replied bitterly.

"Acknowledge your compliance with the previously-transmitted directive," the Jemmin repeated forcefully.

Before Jenkins could reply, the P2P light flickered to life, signaling he had just re-established contact with the *Bonhoeffer*. "Stand by, Jemmin Peacekeepers," he said and quickly switched over to General Akinouye's direct line. "General?"

"I'm here, Colonel," Akinouye replied. "We don't have much time, though. The shooting has stopped, and the Vorr are withdrawing to the gate, but the Jemmin are trying to push us off overwatch. It's taking some fancy flying just to keep us from bumping into the bastards."

"Sir," Jenkins urged, "I need you to invoke Terran sovereign military authority in dealing with the peacekeepers here. We've secured three of the four DIE facilities, but Jemmin peace-keepers occupy the fourth and they've assumed a hostile posture."

"Shoot me the details," Akinouye commanded, and Styles did precisely that while listening in on the conversation. A minute passed as the general silently examined the data. "I'll do what I can, Colonel, but our efforts up here haven't been very successful. I wouldn't expect them to budge a centimeter until they've had their way with that facility...and we didn't come here to start a shooting war with the Jemmin. Is that clear?"

Jenkins was disappointed, but kept it from his voice as he replied, "Crystal, sir."

"Put me through to the Jemmin commander on the ground," Akinouye ordered, and soon he was piped directly through to the ILPF commander.

"Good work on those cans, Podsednik," congratulated Chief Rimmer. "I'm glad you fought to get assigned to my drop-deck. The Corps needs more people like you."

"Thank you, Chief," Podsy acknowledged, having never been good with compliments. Or formal military interactions, for that matter.

He had found a home with Jenkins' battalion, which was filled with misfits and ne'er-do-wells like himself who liked to stretch the bounds of military discipline to the breaking point. Up here on the *Bonhoeffer,* the culture was a lot colder and less fluid. He would have to do something about that since it would be his home for at least the next six months as he fought to get up-to-speed with his prosthetics in what little downtime was available to him.

"Chief," Podsy ventured, "my people are heading back to their racks, but I was hoping you'd help me out with something."

"You're not tired?" Rimmer quirked a brow in both amusement and challenge.

"Of course I am, sir," Podsy replied with a weary, lopsided grin, "but I want to make sure we stay as far ahead of the curve as possible. The Vorr didn't come down here for no reason, and the Jemmin didn't open fire on them because they thought it would be fun. They were fighting over something, and I'm guessing it's going to be well below the icy crust of Shiva's Wrath. I'd like your permission to use your sensor feed access so I can scour the surface for signs of whatever it was they're looking for down there."

"You can't use your own access?"

"I could, but your access includes streams unavailable to me," Podsy explained. "We know Vorr technology isn't all that dissimilar to our own, but Jemmin gear works on entirely different systems. I can track Vorr activity on my access codes, but not Jemmin, *and*," he added pointedly, "I can't redirect any active scanners on my authority. But you can with yours."

Rimmer nodded slowly before moving to a nearby virtual interface panel. "Get comfortable, because I'm only authorizing you to use this terminal. And no active scanning of the Jemmin vehicles, only broad sweeps of their locations like would be normal for routine overwatch protocols. Understood?"

"Perfectly," Podsy said enthusiastically. "Thank you, Chief."

"Keep it to two hours max," Rimmer added firmly. "Then hit your rack and get ready for your next shift."

"Yes, sir."

After Rimmer had gone, Podsy delved into the *Bonhoeffer*'s sensor feeds and quickly found several key points of interest he honed in on to further investigate. His attention lingered for a few moments on the tense standoff between Jemmin forces and 1st Battalion at the Delta Site, but he forced himself to move on.

"Stay focused, Podsy," he muttered as he pored over sensor feeds and prepared for his first active-scan sweep of the formerly-Vorr-controlled base camp.

A camp which was now filled with Jemmin "peacekeepers."

"Human paramilitary forces," the Jemmin Peacekeeper declared as the ILPF vehicles lifted several meters off the ground, using their peculiar hover technology—which Jenkins had been assured was not anti-gravity, though it certainly appeared to be—and flew back in the direction of the now-Jemmin-occupied Vorr base camp, "we have secured the facility and are withdrawing as previously indicated. In accordance with the Illumination League's directives, you are now legally permitted to enter the facility for whatever purpose you wish to pursue."

"Acknowledged, Peacekeepers," Jenkins said flatly. Even General Akinouye's work over the last hour had yielded zero tangible results, and with each passing minute, Jenkins grew increasingly convinced that the Jemmin had taken something important from Delta Site. He switched to Trapper's private channel. "Sergeant Major, the Jemmin have withdrawn, but something doesn't smell right. I'm moving 2nd Company up to secure Delta's mouth, and I want you to lead an APC as far down the tunnel as it goes before deploying your people. I'll take a team of technicians to inspect the facility's control center."

"Negative, Colonel," Trapper replied firmly. "You await my go-ahead before disembarking the command vehicle. Armor Corps protocol says I put boots into every room before you do."

Jenkins nodded irritably. "Understood, but I want you leading the team down whichever tunnel looks to have gotten the most use by the Jemmin in the last few hours. And, Sergeant Major, if you find anything of interest, I want you to treat it like a crime scene and await my arrival."

A meaningful pause. "Understood, Colonel."

"Deploy at your discretion, Tim."

A few minutes later, with 2nd Company's mechs arranged in a reinforcing formation outside Delta's cave-mouth, Trapper's troops streamed out of the APCs just like they had three times before. Except while sixty troopers streamed into the mouth, leap-frogging with long-practiced rhythm as they worked their way into the potentially dangerous opening, the APC bearing Trapper himself remained silent.

Four minutes later, Trapper's APC leapt forward and he reported, "The control center is secure, Colonel. We're moving down the tunnel."

"Copy that, Sergeant Major." Jenkins nodded. "Chaps, take *Roy* to the cave-mouth. Styles, you're with me."

"Yes, sir," they acknowledged in rapid succession.

With just six minutes left in the two-hour window Rimmer gave him, Podsy worked frantically to run down every last byte of data the *Bonhoeffer*'s sensors could gather. Thus far he had revealed no fewer than fifteen distinct, artificial holes in the icy crust of Shiva's Wrath. They were spread out over a rough circle with a radius of eight hundred kilometers, and the Jemmin had occupied three of those holes with vehicles.

Each of the five-meter-wide holes had a dedicated fusion reactor pumping out enough heat to keep the water in the shafts from freezing by circulating reactor coolant down several kilometers of pipe. Sort of an inverse geothermal power system, to Podsy's mind. The tops of the shafts were covered with heavy-duty, special-alloy water-locks that prevented the water below from spewing upward like hydro-volcanoes. Each lock was a few meters thick, which meant it would be difficult to send anything large down them.

It was obvious to Podsy that the Vorr had come here to conduct some kind of exploratory mission, probably with the goal of recovering something specific from the ocean beneath the icy shell of Shiva's Wrath.

But the problem was that he still didn't know what they were there for. Or, perhaps more importantly, which of the shafts represented the best hope of finding it.

"Time's up, Podsednik," Rimmer declared as he came to stand beside Podsy's wheelchair. "Head to your rack."

"Chief," Podsy pleaded, "I need a few more minutes. I'm running an EM scan of the subsurface ocean, which won't be finished for another eight minutes. If I'm right, the Vorr didn't have time to recover all of their equipment from down there, which is why the Jemmin forced the issue by exchanging fire. It's why they keep trying to push us off overwatch," he continued, mindful of the irritated look coming over Rimmer's face. "I think there's something down there they don't want anyone to know about, least of all the Vorr but not us either."

Rimmer looked like he wanted to argue, but somewhat surprisingly, he pulled up a chair and sat down. "Why not hand this off to sensors?"

"Frankly?"

"Frankly," Rimmer agreed.

"I don't know the *Bonhoeffer*'s crew yet," Podsy admitted.

"The people down there are like family to me. Well...some of 'em, anyways," he amended with a snort. "Could you lay your head on a pillow not knowing if your family was in good hands?"

"You think you're better than Armor Corps veterans?" Rimmer challenged, taking some measure of offense at Podsy's suggestion.

"No, sir," Podsy said seriously, "but when I see crew chiefs like Batista wandering off for mid-shift naps...it doesn't instill the highest degree of confidence in the rest of the system. No disrespect intended."

Rimmer eyed him for a few tense moments before sighing. "None taken. You work with what you've got, and right now, Batista's what I've got. But I've also got you," he continued pointedly, "and it's obvious you're going to go far in this branch. I need you to remember your duties though, Chief," he said seriously. "You wanted to be a crew chief on my deck, which means that your duty to my deck comes first. If you can't do that, you need to tell me right now so I can adjust my system."

Podsy understood his meaning and nodded. "Understood, sir."

"Good," Rimmer allowed just as the monitor chimed with a notification.

Podsy looked at the sensor feeds and clenched a fist victoriously. "There it is...fifteen kilometers below the surface, on the slope of that rock. See it?"

Rimmer leaned closer to get a better look. The man was seventy-eight years old but had taken such good care of himself that he looked mid-forties. Spending the last thirty-five years in the largely-defunct Armor Corps had not caused him undue stress.

"I do," Rimmer agreed. "EM signature is consistent with a high-gain Vorr transceiver."

"My guess is they've got an automated facility down there," Podsy concluded, "and that whatever they're studying is something the Jemmin want to cover up so badly that they're willing to risk a shooting war with the second-most powerful star-faring nation in known space."

"But why wouldn't the Vorr just destroy the facility?" Rimmer asked, his brow furrowed in confusion.

"I don't know." Podsy shook his head irritably. "Just like I don't know why the Jemmin haven't destroyed it. They've got the ability to strike from orbit, and their sensors are better than ours, so they know where to shoot."

"What if the Vorr transceiver is a decoy?" Rimmer suggested.

Podsy's eyes went wide. "It fits...and now the fifteen distinct shafts make sense, too. They could be trying to throw the Jemmin off the trail." He pondered the situation for a full minute before shaking his head to clear it. "I need to forward this to Styles. He'll know what to do with it."

"Agreed." Rimmer nodded. "But send it through the chain of command. If they don't forward this, I'll personally do it. But only after you've put your head down in your rack for a few hours' sleep. Understood?"

Podsednik hesitated. He didn't feel like he could trust anyone, not even his deck boss, but he knew he needed to get past that. He also knew he had no choice but to do it Rimmer's way. He needed to do everything in his power to help the battalion, and right now that meant playing nice with the *Bonhoeffer*'s crew.

"Understood, sir." Podsednik nodded, pushing off from the table. "I'd appreciate if you could be the one to forward these findings, along with our preliminary theory, to the CAC."

"I'll do just that," Rimmer said seriously. "Good work, Mr. Podsednik."

As Podsy rolled back to his berth, he knew he wouldn't get any sleep after flopping into his bunk. But he also knew that right now, he needed to show he was a team player and get on Rimmer's good side.

Because if Shiva's Wrath was anything like Durgan's Folly, things were going to go south.

And soon.

"They pulled every data recorder and information storage system in here," Styles reported in frustration, his voice heavily-distorted as he spoke through his rebreather's external speaker. "There isn't even a relay switch that could hold more than eight bytes of data left in this mine, Colonel. I've never seen such a thorough cleanup job."

"Thank you, Chief," Jenkins replied in muted disappointment, taking steady, slightly-labored breaths as his own respiratory muscles provided most of the rebreather's air-cleansing power. "Sergeant Major?" He turned to Tim Trapper Sr., whose familial resemblance with his son was uncanny. Aside from a few deeper wrinkles and, surprisingly, a full head of hair on the elder version, it would be difficult even for an acquaintance to tell them apart.

"All three shafts were empty, Colonel," Trapper replied, his uniform stark-white from head-to-toe just like his troopers', and in contrast to the mech crews' white-with-brown-stripes running down the sides. "We conducted bio-sweeps and found nothing but trace Jemmin and human markers down the shafts."

"Are you sure other traces weren't scrubbed?" Jenkins pressed.

"Hundred percent, Colonel." Trapper nodded firmly. "The

integrity of the scenes was secure. The only living creatures that have been down those holes are humans and Jemmin."

"Vorr have self-contained enviro-suits," Styles observed. "They don't leave bio-material behind as a result. Just traces of the suits' skins and minor magnetic disturbances which are almost impossible to detect."

"Almost?" Jenkins asked hopefully, causing Styles to grin triumphantly.

"I found trace evidence of Vorr activity in the control center from about three months ago," the technician explained.

"They came here looking for something, too?" Jenkins asked in mild confusion.

"It's possible—" Styles shrugged. "—but at this point, all I've got is conjecture. My best conclusion, based on the available evidence, is that a single Vorr came in here, stayed for about six hours, and left. It could've monkeyed with the data storage systems, redirected the automated mining equipment, or just been scoping the place out."

"Vorr aren't innately curious, Chief," Sergeant Major Trapper grunted.

"Agreed," Styles nodded, "which means they came here for a specific purpose. But at the moment, I'm unable to present anything approaching a credible hypothesis as to what that purpose was. The data packet I just received from Podsy up on the *Bonhoeffer* makes me think the Vorr were looking for something on this world, but I'm confident they didn't expect to find it in here."

"Why not?" Trapper asked.

"Because they went to extreme lengths to establish over a dozen access shafts to take them down to the ocean below this world's ice sheet," Styles explained. "And it's obvious they didn't think they could extract whatever they came here for quickly, otherwise why go to all the trouble of drilling more than just a couple shafts?"

Jenkins shook his head. "We need to stay on point." He turned to Trapper. "Have your people secure this facility as planned. We'll move the column and establish base camp where we can support all four sites."

"Understood, Colonel," Sergeant Major Trapper acknowledged. "You moving up the rock or out on the ice?"

It was a good question. If his force had primarily been comprised of infantry, he would have chosen a spot up the steep mountainous slope. But his battalion was centered on the armor, which meant that maximizing mobility was key, even if that meant being more exposed on flat ground with little potential cover.

"The ice field," he replied, suspecting Trapper disliked his choice. "We'll rotate your people through the four mines to keep them fresh and to diminish radiation exposure. No longer than twelve-hour shifts in the mines, followed by no less than twenty-four hours at base camp. Every hour in the mines is equivalent to eight hours on the ice."

"The rock's hotter than the water," Trapper agreed with a curt nod. "We'll lock these holes down, Colonel."

"I'll have the *Bonhoeffer* deliver our first support gear within the hour," Jenkins explained, "so your people should be armed with everything they need to fortify the mines no later than four hours from now."

"Good." Trapper nodded before leaving to coordinate with his subordinates.

As the venerable warrior left, Jenkins and Styles shared a knowing look before returning to *Roy* and preparing to lead the column to their new base camp.

4

BRINKSMANSHIP

"Get those cans emptied, people," Xi called out over *Elvira*'s external speakers, directing the PDF troops to unload the eight drop-cans the *Bonhoeffer* had delivered to the site of their new base camp twenty minutes earlier. "Prioritize crew-served weapons, mortars, auto-cannons, and anything else we'll need to fortify our position. The mess gear can wait," she added pointedly as a pair of troopers began unloading crates of foodstuffs—specifically water purifier-heater units and boxes of coffee.

It seemed like half of the PDF troops from her home world were no-nonsense, by-the-book hard-asses like Sergeant Major Trapper. But the other half were at best more like summer interns, or at worst playing at being soldiers.

An alarm sounded from her status board signaling a failure of one of *Elvira*'s external systems. An anti-personnel cannon had just gone offline due to extreme cold, causing her to raise Lu. "Chief, we've got a failure on L-1."

"I see it, Captain," Lu replied shortly. "I should have it back up in two minutes."

"Two minutes?" Xi repeated in disbelief. "It takes you two minutes to melt a little ice off the ammo-feed manifold?"

"Pop the hatch and I'll have it in thirty seconds," Private Staubach offered as he took a bottle torch from its mooring and made for the cabin door.

"I like the initiative, Blinky," Xi said approvingly, hesitating before unlocking the door. "I've got a thirty-second timer on my HUD; you'd better beat it. If you don't, we might need to thaw you out next."

"Yes ma..." he cut himself short while pushing the hatch open and clambering outside the vehicle. "I mean, yes, Captain."

She snickered as he climbed over the top of *Elvira*'s hull, and her external video feeds showed him nearly losing his footing before he came to the spot directly above the L-1 anti-personnel chain gun. The temperature plunged significantly once the hatch was open, but in spite of the outside thermometers reading negative sixty-eight Celsius, the cold filling the cabin seemed less brutal.

It wasn't until Blinky lowered himself down, bottle-torch in hand, that Xi noticed a pair of video drones whizzing about him as he worked.

She silently swore, realizing Ms. Samuels had failed to ask permission before deploying her video drones to gather some footage. She thought about calling her out on it but instead decided to pretend she hadn't noticed. "Ten seconds, Blinky," she called, "nine...eight...seven...six..."

At that, the alarm icon vanished, and L-1 went through a routine diagnostic cycle. Private Staubach slipped and scrambled across *Elvira*'s armored back, making for the door, and somehow maintained his footing while Xi continued the countdown.

"Five...four...three...two...one..."

Using acrobatic grace, Blinky gripped the upper lip of the

hatchway, pivoted his body, and smoothly slid himself inside before landing on his feet with cat-like agility.

"Zero," Xi finished, closing the door almost fast enough to prevent the last of Samuels' video drones from zipping back inside the compartment. "Thirty seconds and he even got back inside," she said approvingly. "Somebody ought to reward you for that, don't you think, Lu?"

"Definitely," Lu grunted, making no attempt to hide his animosity toward the mech's assigned Monkey.

"Glad to hear morale and team cohesion aboard *Elvira* is on the up-and-up," Xi continued blithely, reminded once again just how much she missed Podsy's steady, capable hand.

An incoming communique flashed across her neural interface, which meant it was directly from Colonel Jenkins. The first part was a general status update to be disseminated among the crew and read:

All but one of the Jemmin warships have withdrawn. Bonhoeffer *is maintaining active overwatch of our position.*

"Good news," Xi reported before opening the second, classified half of the message. "All but one of the Jemmin warships have withdrawn from orbit. The *Dietrich Bonhoeffer* is no longer being harassed by their aggressive maneuvers and is now in optimal overwatch position."

"Good to hear," Blinky said enthusiastically. "I was starting to get a little nervous with all those guns floating around over our heads."

"*You?* Nervous?" Lu deadpanned. "I would have never guessed it possible from a man whose nickname is 'Blinky.'"

"All right, all right," Xi said, hoping to forestall an escalation of what would normally be a healthy bit of posturing, "I want you two running full diagnostics on the rest of our systems. This cold is messing with everything, so let's increase the cabin's temperature by another three degrees and spill a little more heat off the reactor onto the sinks."

"Yes, Captain," acknowledged her crew as she opened the classified portion of the transmission.

Jemmin stealth systems are hiding half of their vehicles' locations from our sensors. Stay alert and keep anti-missile systems hot.

She acknowledged the missive via P2P connection relayed by her Owl-class drones, which were the only aerial drones the battalion had that could fly in the thin atmosphere. She then confirmed that *Holy Diver*, her company's most capable missile-interception mech, had relevant systems showing green.

Twenty-one hours later, *Elvira's* cockpit filled with alarms warning of inbound missiles. A pair of Jemmin vehicles appeared on scanners fifteen kilometers from her current position.

"Incoming!" she snapped over the company-wide. "*Holy Diver*, lock onto those missiles and prepare to intercept."

"Copy that, *Elvira*," replied the railgun mech's Jock. "Two LRMs inbound, Jemmin profile. Current trajectory...takes them thirty-one kilometers west of here," he finished in confusion. "Time-to-optimal-intercept, eight seconds."

She scowled as she raised *Roy* on the priority line. "Colonel, I have Jemmin missiles passing overhead with apparent target thirty-one kilometers west of this position. Permission to intercept?"

"Granted," Jenkins immediately replied. "Take 'em down."

"Engage LRMs, *Holy Diver*," Xi commanded, and a flash of light from *Holy Diver's* quad of railguns followed a half-second later.

"LRMs scrubbed," *Holy Diver*'s Jock reported confidently, silencing most of the alarms.

As Xi watched her tactical plotter, the two Jemmin vehicles vanished. She clenched her teeth in frustration before, a few seconds later, two more Jemmin icons appeared on the precise spot where those LRMs had been aimed.

Again, alarms flared to life, and *Holy Diver* reported, "LRMs detected. Apparent target...twenty-two kilometers east of base camp."

Xi raised Colonel Jenkins. "Colonel, I've got two more LRMs in the air, apparent target twenty-two kilometers east of HQ. Permission to intercept?"

"Confirmed, you are clear to intercept," the colonel acknowledged.

"*Holy Diver*, *Elvira*," Xi called as the missiles reached the apex of their flight paths, "intercept airborne LRMs."

"Roger. Engaging," *Holy Diver* replied, and another brilliant flash of light preceded the missiles' icons getting scrubbed from the tactical board. "Targets neutralized."

Just as before, the pair of Jemmin vehicle contacts disappeared. And again, they were replaced by a pair of fresh signatures, these sixteen kilometers to the south. Except this time, no LRM signatures appeared overhead. Tense seconds ticked by until, suddenly and without warning, a signal appeared nineteen kilometers to the east at an altitude of seven kilometers.

She had not yet reacted before a flash of light exploded from precisely that location. A thunderous crack followed eight seconds later, and early reports indicated the device had unleashed a terrifying ten megatons of energy.

And they hadn't even *seen* it in flight.

"What was that?" Sarah Samuels asked, appearing out of nowhere to stand at Xi's side.

"Ever played 'chicken'?" Xi grimaced.

Even the normally stone-faced reporter went pale at hearing that, but Xi was surprised to see her quickly regain her composure. "Have we done anything that could be construed as antagonizing?"

"You're a victim-blamer? Really?" Xi quipped, drawing a withering look from the other woman. "Buckle up, buttercup." She flashed a savage grin. "Because if I know my CO, things are about to get interesting."

"What the fuck are they doing?" Jenkins growled.

"The last of the departing Jemmin warships passed through the gate ten minutes ago," Styles observed.

"Which means they waited until they were gone to start playing games." Jenkins shook his head grimly. He didn't like where this was going. Not one bit. "Theories?" he asked the room.

"My guess," Chaps offered, "is they want to paint a picture of plausible deniability."

"Agreed." Styles nodded. "They'd be happy if we packed up and left like the Vorr, but if we don't, then I doubt it'll be long before warning shots become the real thing."

"Analyze every bit of sensor data the battalion collected prior to that nuke going off," Jenkins ordered. "If you can't find anything, we have to assume it was dropped from orbit rather than launched."

He carefully didn't add, "Because if it *was* launched, and we couldn't see it even with an active link to the *Bonhoeffer*'s sensors, they could wipe us out at any moment."

No point in worrying about things outside of your control, Lee, Jenkins silently reminded himself. *Focus on what you* can *control.*

Seconds ticked by, during which time he forwarded relevant sensor data to the *Bonhoeffer* via secure P2P. General Akinouye personally confirmed receipt of the information and replied that he was attempting to communicate with the Jemmin in orbit. The two sensor contacts to the south disappeared, and Jenkins suspected there would be no further demonstrations in the immediate future. They'd made their point: they had better tech and weren't afraid to use it.

With the towering mountain to the north and all of the mines located there fully-reinforced against attack, Jenkins knew things on Shiva's Wrath just got a whole lot more complicated than even *he* had expected.

"Establish roving patrols per aegis protocols," Jenkins decided. "Each platoon is to be assigned a mech capable of missile interception, and we rotate the patrol routes at five-kilometer offsets to provide overlapping anti-missile cover of both HQ and the mines. Distribute intercept drones to each company as they return to HQ, and supply each mine outpost with one launcher and ten drones apiece."

The orders went out, and the crews responded quickly. APCs bore the anti-missile systems and fresh troopers to the mines, and then returned to HQ bearing troopers whose mine shifts had ended.

Several hours passed, during which time he ran through a myriad of possible scenarios with Styles' help. Tension heightened throughout the battalion, and Jenkins did his best to project an aura of calm as *Roy* took part in its assigned leg of the aegis patrol scheme.

"Missiles inbound," Xi declared over the platoon-wide nearly six hours after the nuclear bomb had gone off. She spun *Elvira*'s missile launchers up, dropping the mech into firing position as she prepared to fire at the inbound projectiles. This batch of Jemmin missiles had an estimated impact less than six kilometers from her patrol's current position.

Holy Diver had been assigned to 5th Platoon, while *Elvira* was in 4th. Both mechs were technically capable of missile intercept, though *Holy Diver* was the superior anti-missile platform.

Colonel Jenkins' standing orders were to engage missiles that encroached on the Terran zone of control, or ZOC, which included a fifty-kilometer radius extending out from every Terran-controlled point of terrain. This latest pair of missiles originated from a point just inside that radius, near the Alpha Site mine, and were set to strike well within Terran-controlled territory.

She locked her rockets on the LRMs and fired, sending the quartet of interceptors streaking into the sky. Two rockets per target gave a greater than ninety-three percent chance of interception. While far from perfect, it was the best she could do with her current systems.

The rockets screamed through the thin atmosphere toward their targets, bracketing them and sending their wreckage in a fan-shaped cloud toward the ground.

"*Elvira* reporting two LRMs neutralized." Xi was surprised when she received nothing but static in reply. "I say again: *Elvira* reporting two LRMs neutralized."

Again, no reply.

As she ran a virtual diagnostic on the mech's comm systems, she keyed up the intercom. "Lu, check the comm system. I'm not getting a reply from HQ."

"Everything checks out, Captain," Lu reported promptly, confirming her virtual diagnostic's findings.

She ground her teeth as she checked the local RF—radio

frequency—bands, finding no apparent source of interference. The radio simply didn't work, and no one knew why.

"Establishing P2P with the platoon," she said, a rare note of anxiety creeping into her voice. "*Cave Troll*, do you copy?"

"*Cave Troll* here," came the Jock's deep, rich voice. "What's going on with the RF?"

"No clue, *Cave Troll*." She grimaced. "*Gym Cricket*, *Heavy Metal Jesus*, do you copy?"

"Copy, *Elvira*," came *Gym Cricket*'s reply.

"Loud and clear, Captain," replied *Heavy Metal Jesus*' Jock. "But *HMJ*'s seeing some funky background on the high-band RF."

"All right, stick to the P2P and maintain constant linkage," she confirmed. "They're broad-spectrum jamming us, but as long as P2P works, no one's alone. You have your mission orders. Protect Delta at all costs."

Suddenly, a pair of icons appeared on her tactical plotter just eight kilometers away.

"Contacts," she snapped. "Two Jemmin Specters bearing two-six-eight, distance six-point-one kilometers."

But just as soon as they appeared, they vanished only to be replaced by another pair of icons only three kilometers from her current position.

"Contacts," *Cave Troll* growled, "bearing one-one-five, distance three-point-two kilometers."

"Shit!" cried *Gym Cricket*. "My drive system just went offline!"

Xi felt her hackles rise. "Say again, *Gym Cricket*?"

"My drive system is in a self-protective restart cycle," *Gym Cricket* replied after a brief, but potentially lethal, delay. "I won't be mobile for another forty seconds."

" 4th Platoon, hold fast," Xi ordered, her mind racing before she latched on to one particular thought. "4th Platoon, shut down all RF transceivers and physically unplug them. Now!"

Her own systems began to behave strangely, just enough that she noticed hiccups in *Elvira*'s responsiveness, but she was able to deactivate the mech's RF transceivers while her Wrench and Monkey scrambled to manually disconnect the devices from her onboard systems.

"What's going on?" she heard Samuels call from the rear of the cockpit. Xi heard no fear in the woman's voice, which was a pleasant surprise, but the last thing she needed right then was a civilian reporter climbing up her ass with questions.

"Lock it down, Blondie," Xi snapped. "We're under attack."

"General, my people are experiencing targeted systems interference in tandem with enemy weapons fire and encroachment on our zone of control," Jenkins said, knowing that every word he now spoke would be recorded for later examination.

"Are you certain these are not merely malfunctions, Colonel Jenkins?" General Akinouye asked, his expression neutral as he leaned slightly toward the video pickup.

"One hundred percent, General," Jenkins replied with total conviction. "Three of my mechs have reported catastrophic system failures as a result of targeted takeover attempts. These failures have occurred within minutes or seconds of Jemmin weapons fire. Under the Illumination League's charter pertaining to the treatment of colonial organizations, even such colonies of questionable allegiance to their parent nations as some argue the case to be for our Terran Republic, the ILPF is prohibited from engaging in such acts of aggression."

Akinouye's visage darkened as he leaned closer. "You're the

commander on the ground, Colonel. What is your recommendation?"

"Recommend you contact the Jemmin in orbit and advise them to stand down," Jenkins said firmly. "Also recommend you authorize 1st Battalion to engage targets behaving in a hostile manner, deadly force authorized, sir."

General Akinouye's eyes narrowed. "Are you sure about this, Commander?"

Jenkins nodded. "I am, General. We came here to do a job, and my people are being harassed with potentially lethal consequences while we are in the performance of our legally-sanctioned duties. We're content to abide by League law in this matter if the Jemmin stand down, but if they refuse or fail to acknowledge our attempts at dialogue, then we're ready to engage them."

"Stand by, Colonel," Akinouye commanded before his visage vanished from the screen.

Jenkins sat in relative silence for nearly six minutes, while the *Roy*'s crew went about their respective tasks. He could hardly believe what he was saying: was he *ready* to engage the most powerful space-faring civilization in the known galaxy, or was it all just bluster? He sincerely thought he meant it, but the moment of truth had not yet arrived. He could still back out, find some reason to withdraw and save face in the process as any sane person would likely do.

But Lee Jenkins hadn't lived a life of making the safe decisions. The Jemmin were provoking him, probably in large part because they thought he would back down.

And nothing made Lee Jenkins madder than an enemy thinking they could intimidate him into submission.

"When have I *ever* given that impression..." he muttered under his breath.

General Akinouye's face returned to the screen, and the

longest-tenured member of the Terran Armed Forces seemed alight for the first time since Jenkins had met him.

"This is General Akinouye to all Terran forces on Shiva's Wrath..." he began, his grim cast and hard tone making clear he understood the gravity of the situation. Then he spoke the five magic words that every warrior longed to hear from his commander. "You are cleared to engage. The Jemmin warship is refusing our hails. We can only interpret this as an act of open hostility and are therefore prepared to defend ourselves. I say again: all Terran Armor Corps forces on Shiva's Wrath are cleared to engage Jemmin forces who take offensive actions against Terran Armor Corps assets. Good hunting, Colonel," General Akinouye said with a curt nod. "Make us proud, son."

The line went dead, and Colonel Lee Jenkins felt a thrill course down his spine. It wasn't exuberance or joy that filled him, but the knowledge that he was about to stand up not just for himself, but for all of Terran humanity.

He transmitted over P2P to every mech and declared, "This is Colonel Jenkins relaying our orders from General Akinouye: we are cleared to engage the enemy. I say again: we are cleared to engage the enemy. The next provocative maneuver by Jemmin forces is to be met with lethal force. Acknowledge."

The rapid stream of acknowledgments bolstered his resolve, and he swelled with pride at the lack of hesitation from his mostly-new mech crews. At that moment, they were united as only warriors under fire could be.

It was time to shoot back.

5

ILLUMINATION

"All right, people," Xi declared over 4th Platoon's P2P comm net, "weapons hot. The next non-Terran signature that appears within our ZOC gets cratered, and return fire is authorized on the point-of-origin for future missiles which encroach the ZOC."

A flurry of acknowledgments streamed across her screen, and then they were left to wait.

...and wait.

And wait.

Forty-nine minutes passed as Xi's people remained on high-alert. Without the neural linkage, Xi's body might have begun to tremble. But the cybernetic implants helped to regulate the physical manifestations of heightened anxiety, and as a result, she knew she could remain in a combat-ready defensive stance for at least nine continuous hours before requiring relief.

And that relief could come in the form of sleep or, in emergencies, chemical stimulants.

"Stay focused, Xi," she muttered, her senses awash with the neural link's sensor feeds. Interpreting those streams in real-time was far from intuitive, but after a few months' training and the combat experience, albeit limited, it felt like second nature. The outside cold assaulted the systems that she cycled in a sequence to keep them from freezing up. The inside temperature was steady.

The reporter poked her head out occasionally, but retreated under an enfilade of threats and cursing.

Xi could "smell" movement at the edge of *Elvira*'s optical sensor range, but to focus her attention on it, she needed to engage her visual cortex. She could "feel" seismic and atmospheric variations through the mech's myriad of specialized sensors, but to focus on them, she needed to engage her auditory system.

Switching back and forth to process the constant stream of data was routine to even a rookie Jock, and much as she hated to admit it, Xi Bao had only seen active combat duty once. On Durgan's Folly. And her neural link had been broken for the majority of her combat experience, so she was hardly a ten-year veteran mech Jock.

She "smelled" something behind her, and focused her visual cortex on the rocket trail of an inbound missile. "Mid-range missile inbound," she reported while spooling up her antimissile rockets and simultaneously re-orienting *Elvira* so her artillery could target the point-of-origin. "Engaging."

Two rockets flew from their mounts, streaking up at a near-vertical angle before arcing toward the inbound weapons. A muted flash confirmed the offending missile was down. Just as that confirmation came in, she locked onto the missile's estimated point-of-origin. Sixteen kilometers from *Elvira*, it was at the very edge of her ability to accurately engage.

"Target lock," she declared. "On the way!"

Elvira's dual artillery cannons thundered in rapid succession, driving the Scorpion-class mech's legs a full foot into the

ice from the recoil. She had laid her guns according to temperature, atmospherics, the worldlet's gravity—which was sixty
percent of the human standard, and every other variable she had
learned to account for.

The shells took parabolic arcs toward their target, whistling
through the thin air as they flew. The Owl drone assigned to 4th
Platoon put its eyes on the impact site two seconds before the
shells turned the pristine ice-field into a shower of icy shards
and snowy powder. The impact report registered several
seconds later as the faintest tickle on Xi's forearms, and when
the frozen cloud had settled, nothing but a misshapen crater
remained in the ice field.

"Missile point-of-origin destroyed," Xi declared, but she
knew that it was unlikely in the extreme she had actually struck
the vehicle responsible for launching the MRM. Humans had
mastered the art of firing vehicle-mounted missiles, and even
artillery, on the run several hundred years ago. The Jemmin
were superior in terms of technological advances, so it was
foolish to hope they would succumb to something as simplistic
as counter-battery fire.

"Copy that, Captain," acknowledged *Heavy Metal Jesus'*
Jock. "I'm moving the Owl in for a closer look."

"Jemmin use ceramics and noble metal composites," Xi
reminded him as the Owl swooped down toward the impact
site. "Some of their stealthier vehicles also employ special
polymer skins which redirect light and give them visual-spec-
trum cloaking capability."

"On it, Captain," *HMJ*'s Jock affirmed as he directed the
Owl-class drone down to a height of just two hundred meters
above the crater. "Scanning the site..." he reported as streams of
data came back from the Owl. "Negative, Captain," he finally
declared, "nothing but salty ice here."

Xi noted that there had, a few seconds earlier, been some

small quantity of liquid water at the bottom of the oblong crater. But as the Owl had conducted its inspection, the water had re-frozen into a flat, placid-looking pool.

"Bring the Owl home," Xi ordered. "They're still just fucking with us. Let's be ready when they come back for seconds."

Her platoon Jocks acknowledged her command, and she switched her P2P to link up with Colonel Jenkins.

"Jenkins, go," the colonel greeted.

"We need to use the *Bonhoeffer*'s sensors, Colonel," Xi urged. "There's no way for us to overcome their stealth capabilities from down here."

"The Jemmin in orbit aren't making it easy for them to support us," Jenkins replied. "They've deployed some kind of drone-cloud in the upper atmosphere which interferes with the *Bonhoeffer*'s systems. Our people are forwarding whatever telemetry they can, but it's been hit-and-miss for the last hour or so. And frankly, I can't trust we're receiving accurate data from them. If the Jemmin are able to interfere with our communications gear, we have to assume that even our P2P net is potentially compromised. We can't count on their sensor support, but Styles is working on cracking the Jemmin stealth systems."

"Good enough for me," Xi acknowledged, knowing there was nothing else to be said. If the Jemmin could break the high-security P2P network, which was nearly unthinkable, it would severely hamper the battalion's coordination. The colonel wouldn't have suggested such a thing was possible without good reason, and Xi had learned it was usually smart to follow her CO's lead.

"Contact," *Cave Troll* reported a few seconds before *Elvira*'s sensors registered a pair of icons nine kilometers from 4th Platoon. "Engaging."

Cave Troll launched four short-range missiles at the

encroaching targets, and those targets winked off the board less than a second before the SRMs struck the icy ground where they had been.

"Moving Owl into position," reported *Heavy Metal Jesus*. A few seconds later, the ice crater came into view. And just as before, nothing but ice and fast-freezing water. "Negative debris."

Xi's sense of "smell" was suddenly overpowered by thirty new missile signatures. Originating from three previously-unmarked locations, she locked onto one and barked, "On the way!"

Elvira's guns roared, sending high-explosive shells at the target twelve kilometers from her position. Xi locked onto eight of the inbound missiles, half of which were aimed directly at 4th Platoon, and launched sixteen anti-missile rockets.

The rockets sliced through the frigid air, fanning out in pairs to engage the inbound missiles. Bolts of light stabbed up from 5th Platoon at the opposite end of the teardrop-shaped patrol route, and four missiles were snuffed by *Holy Diver*'s precise railguns.

Elvira's anti-missile rockets tore into the approaching missiles, scrubbing eight-of-eight from the sky.

A warning indicator screamed at the edge of her hearing, and Xi was temporarily disoriented by it before realizing what it was. "I've got a reload failure on Two Launcher," she snapped.

"Forty seconds, Captain," Lu replied, and she would have upbraided him, but another wave of thirty missiles appeared at the edge of her vision.

Reloading the other launcher with fresh anti-missile rockets, Xi locked onto four of those missiles and fired, sending her interceptors into the sky.

"Engage missiles, *HMJ*," she called out as her mech's anti-missile rockets reloaded at a painfully slow rate.

"Engaging," *Heavy Metal Jesus* acknowledged, sending hyper-velocity tungsten bolts into the approaching missile swarm from the humanoid mech's dual railguns.

Another pair of icons appeared just three kilometers from 4th Platoon's position, and *Cave Troll* growled, "Plasma cannons engaging."

The squat, humanoid *Cave Troll*, which nearly displaced as much as *Elvira*, raised its thick weapon arms in preparation to fire. The thrum of *Cave Troll*'s charging capacitors vibrated the ice so powerfully that Xi could feel it through *Elvira*'s seismic sensors. Three seconds after *Cave Troll*'s charge cycle began, both guns belched roaring gouts of relatively sluggish plasma streams. The blue-white flames tore through the air, leaving a thick trail of smoke as they gently arced toward the three-kilometers-distant targets.

The plasma streams incinerated the impact site, sending a geyser of steam bursting hundreds of meters into the air.

Heavy Metal Jesus engaged two more missiles with its railguns, sniping them from the sky. The distant *Holy Diver* did likewise, scrubbing four missiles. Combined with unexpected support from HQ, the second wave of missiles was neutralized.

Xi barely had time to catch her breath before *Elvira*'s alarms once again screamed in warning: thirty missiles inbound.

With Two Launcher still down for at least another fifteen seconds, Xi had no choice but to launch just half of her mech's potential arsenal of rockets from the still-functioning tubes. "4th Platoon, intercept missiles," she barked, knowing that this time, it would be difficult to snipe them all before they arrived. "Fire! Fire! Fire!"

Eight rockets sprang forth from *Elvira*'s functioning launcher and were soon joined by twelve from *Cave Troll*. Even with twenty rockets in the air, only ten of the inbound missiles would be met by anti-missile rockets. The engagement book was clear on this point: no fewer than two rockets were to be sent against any given Jemmin missile. She had already seen a twenty percent miss rate on her own rockets, so Xi knew that the book was right.

Jemmin ordnance was so potent that it only took one missile strike to scrub a mech. Even one as robust as *Elvira*.

Railguns stabbed into the sky from every mech in range to lend fire support. 4th Platoon's anti-missile rockets tore all ten of their targets down, and the railguns brought another eight down. But the railguns were beginning to miss nearly half the time, and she had just three seconds before the missiles would impact.

Unleashing the interception drones that had arrived via drop-can mere hours earlier, Xi activated thirty of the already-flying devices, putting them on intercept courses with the inbound missiles.

Blinding flashes and deafening reports overpowered her senses, which were protected from the harsh inputs by *Elvira*'s neural link filters. But those filters rendered Xi blind for a full second before the streams resumed.

And when they did, she saw that *Gym Cricket* was nothing but a smoldering wreck with debris scattered across and around an icy crater.

Her mind instantly tried to grasp the hope that the crew might have survived, but she pushed the foolish wishful thinking from her mind. *Gym Cricket* and its crew were dead. She wanted to feel sorry for them, to mourn them as they deserved, but she knew that doing so would only endanger the rest of her platoon.

"*Elvira* to HQ," she said, projecting as much stoicism as she could muster, "*Gym Cricket* is down. Maintaining posture and moving drones to inspect impact sites."

Elvira's second missile launcher finally came back online, but it was too late. The damage had been done. The Jemmin had killed Terrans, but thus far, Xi was unable to confirm that a single Jemmin had been harmed in reply.

And that was unac-fucking-ceptable.

"Copy that, *Elvira*," came Colonel Jenkins' near-emotionless reply. "Perform search-and-rescue before resuming patrol. HQ out."

"Blinky," Xi called over her shoulder, "take a bio-scanner and search that wreck for survivors. And be quick about it."

"On it, Captain," Staubach acknowledged, and a few seconds later, he was out the hatch. Naturally, he was followed by Sarah Samuels' video drones.

"Ms. Samuels," Xi called, raising her voice, "up here."

The reporter arrived in the cockpit, her face no longer the perfectly-composed mask it had been during the earlier "interview." This woman understood the magnitude of what had just happened, and what it might mean for the Terran Republic. Had Xi not seen that realization on the other woman's face, she would have been even harsher than she decided to be.

"I know you're here to take pictures," Xi said, making firm eye contact, "but you need to remember that those men were sons of the Terran Republic who gave their lives to safeguard it. Be respectful with whatever images you gather. Do I need to spell that out for you?"

Surprisingly, Samuels shook her head and held Xi's gaze unflinchingly. "No, you don't. I met the *Gym Cricket*'s crew aboard the *Dietrich Bonhoeffer*..." she trailed off, and Xi found herself actively hoping the reporter was just putting on a show. But it seemed she was genuinely shaken by the deaths of the mech and its crew, so Xi decided to let it be.

Two minutes later, Private Staubach returned to *Elvira*'s cabin with a grim expression as he carefully replaced the bio-scanner to its locker. "All crew accounted for, Captain...no survivors."

"4th Platoon," Xi grunted, "resume patrol. Stay on your toes. We've got three hours to go before we return to the barn."

As Samuels and Staubach returned to their respective seats within the mech's cabin, Xi did her best to conceal the brief stream of tears she shed for the *Gym Cricket's* crew.

"Captain," came *Heavy Metal Jesus'* report, "I'm reading ceramic fragments and trace polymer residue in *Cave Troll's* target zone."

"The SRMs or the plasma cannons?" Xi asked, her spirits suddenly buoyed by the good news.

"Plasma cannons, ma'am," replied *HMJ*. "I don't think it was enough for a full Specter, but it was definitely from a vehicle of some kind. I'm logging the spot and would like to request an APC be deployed for immediate inspection and retrieval of the debris."

"Permission granted." Xi nodded. "Looks like we just got our first Jemmin trophy. Good shooting, *Cave Troll*. You just notched an entry in the history books: first human to scratch a Jemmin."

"Thank you, Captain," *Cave Troll* replied.

"It looks like the rest of us get to play catch-up," Xi continued. "You've got a target on your back, *Cave Troll*. Hope you can handle the pressure."

With that, the patrol resumed without incident as they eventually returned to HQ, where they restocked munitions and prepped for their next turn on the circuit.

"Report, Lieutenant," Jenkins greeted as he boarded Lieutenant Koch's mech, *Kochtopussy*.

Debris fragments, most of which were smaller than a human torso, were neatly arranged on the shop floor at the mech's center. Koch gestured to a few of the larger bits. "It definitely had some kind of light-bending skin on it before the plasma melted it away, and it's also pretty clearly Jemmin design. We don't know a lot about Jemmin technology, but their ships use ceramic composites similar to this stuff." He picked up a shard the length of his forearm and handed it to Jenkins.

Jenkins' eyebrows rose in surprise. "It's barely two centimeters thick."

"And it's ruined." Koch nodded bitterly. "But this kind of stuff has been theorized for centuries as being potentially stronger against impacts than thirty centimeters of conventional composite armor like what we use on most of the battalion's mechs."

"Good against kinetics," Jenkins mused, "but weak to sustained thermal attacks."

"Weak is a relative term," Koch snorted. "This stuff is still better than our best material at soaking up and dispersing heat, but anything over six thousand degrees will strip the camo skin right off it. Without camouflage, its only advantage would be speed and maneuverability."

"How big was this vehicle?"

"Hard to say for sure..." Koch cocked his head skeptically. "But I'd wager it was two and a half, maybe three meters long and a third as wide."

"Airborne?" Jenkins clarified.

"Almost certainly." Koch nodded, waving a shard of the vehicle's ceramic skin. "And given how lightweight this stuff is, it wouldn't take much thrust to get it off the ground. But we still don't know much about their drive tech, and it seems that whatever system propelled this vehicle was destroyed by the plasma strike."

"A fortunate coincidence for the Jemmin," Jenkins mused.

"Probably not a coincidence at all." Koch shook his head firmly. "And Fellows has gone over this debris with a fine-toothed comb. There is zero organic residue anywhere."

Jenkins' brow quirked in surprise. "That's strange."

"Indeed, it is," Koch agreed. "If this thing was handled by a Jemmin at any point in the past, there should be some kind of residue. Shed skin cells, secretions, saliva, something. But there's *nothing* here. Fellows even took a few of the best-preserved pieces and made a culture bath to try to find some kind of organic traces, but his preliminary results suggest he won't find anything."

"Questions upon questions," Jenkins mused.

"Oh, and with *Gym Cricket* down," Koch added, "we've only got one bridge-building mech left, the *Jamboree*. Frankly, with all the crevasses near this mountain, we'll need it operational if we want to perform time-sensitive retrieval operations. I think it would be prudent to reassign *Jamboree* to my command and keep it here at HQ."

"You're probably right," Jenkins agreed, having debated the inclusion of *Gym Cricket* and *Jamboree* on the patrols before ultimately deciding to include them. *Jamboree*'s pair of SRM launchers were probably less valuable on patrol than its bridge-building capability would be later on. Especially if they ended up investigating one of the Vorr underwater shafts.

"Were they specifically targeting the *Gym Cricket*?" Koch asked, breaking Jenkins from his brief reverie.

"We don't know," Jenkins replied. "Jemmin missiles corkscrew in flight, and make erratic flight path adjustments to throw off antimissile attacks. There's no way to know which mech they were targeting."

"But they did stop attacking once they scrubbed it," Koch observed.

"They did." Jenkins didn't want to indulge this particular line of dialogue just now, and thankfully Koch took the hint.

"I'm sending up the next batch of parts requests to the *Bonhoeffer*." Koch changed subjects. "Is there anything you'd like me to include?"

Jenkins snorted. "Other than a crystal ball?"

Koch laughed. "They hit us, we hit them back. It's what we came here to do. Shake it off, Colonel. We stood tall, and at the end of the day that might be the most important thing to come out of this: that the Terran Republic will stand up for what it thinks is right, no matter how steep the climb might be."

"I know." Jenkins ran a hand through his hair. "Keep looking over this debris and update me with any new findings."

"Will do, sir."

Jenkins disembarked the *Kochtopussy*, returning to the frigid, serene exterior of Shiva's Wrath. Before he had taken three steps, he was ambushed by Sarah Samuels.

"Colonel Jenkins, a moment please?" she asked in that annoying yet somehow commanding way that all journalists seemed to master.

"Walk with me, Ms. Samuels," he replied, knowing it was a full three minutes' walk to his next destination. He could give her that much time. God knew Xi had been forced to deal with her for more than ninety-eight percent of the woman's time in the battalion, which made her a more patient person than Jenkins would ever be.

"Do you believe the Jemmin attacked the *Gym Cricket* specifically?" she asked, surprising Jenkins with the acuity of her thought process.

"We don't have any reason to believe that at this time," he replied, hoping he could stall her by overloading the conversation with technical information. "Jemmin missiles release multiple micro-warheads before impact; there's no way to know precisely which vehicle was their target, given the altitude at which they were met by the interceptor drones."

"Why would the Jemmin openly antagonize Terran military forces on a human-controlled world?" she pressed, easily switching gears and not falling for his trap.

"That's unknown at this time," he said flatly. "We have conducted ourselves in accordance with every applicable ordinance, including Terran, Solar, Illumination League, and even Jemmin doctrines governing the peacetime deployment of military assets. The Jemmin violated two dozen interstellar treaties with their blatant hostility here on Shiva's Wrath, and I'm confident those who occupy the Terran Republic's highest offices will lodge a formal complaint with the Illumination League after we've reported this incident."

"Do you think the Jemmin will let us off this world?" she asked, causing Jenkins to stop mid-stride and round on her.

He removed his re-breather and fixed her with a stony look. "Re-phrase that," he said, his voice colder and harder than he expected it would be.

"Do you think the Jemmin will permit Terran forces to peacefully withdraw from Shiva's Wrath?" she reiterated, removing her own rebreather and steadily meeting his gaze.

"Let me make something perfectly clear," he started coolly. "Shiva's Wrath is a human-controlled world. We have the right under every known interstellar law to be here. The Jemmin are our guests, but they have chosen to abuse our hospitality rather than reciprocate it. Will *they* let *us* leave?" he asked, openly scoffing at the notion. "I think the question you should be asking is this: will *we* let *them* leave? And the answer, frankly, is that I don't think they've earned the right to a peaceful withdrawal. They've killed Terrans on this rock, Ms. Samuels, and have demonstrated nothing remotely resembling remorse for having done so. *You* might not be clear on how to reply to such wanton acts of aggression, but I can assure you that the Terran Armor Corps knows *exactly* how to speak this particular language."

She seemed genuinely surprised by his reply, but rallied and asked, "Why would the Terran Republic send Armor Corps out here, to safeguard a relatively minor mining operation funded by one of the wealthiest mega-corps in the Republic, Durgan Industrial Enterprises? Are a few crates of rare minerals worth a shooting war with the most powerful civilization in the galaxy?"

Jenkins set his jaw. "We're being tested, Ms. Samuels. The universe is asking if we're ready to stand out here on our own two feet and deal with whatever it can throw at us. Some might be tempted to retreat to the safety of their homes and hope that someone, somewhere, can keep them safe. But the Terran Armed Forces doesn't run *from* fights. We run *to* them. You don't point a gun at someone unless you're prepared to pull the trigger. And you don't deploy armor unless you're ready to use it. This isn't about minerals, Ms. Samuels. This is about standing up for what's right, and that's exactly what the Terran Armor Corps does every damn day."

"Even if it gets you all killed?" she challenged, her blue eyes seemingly searching his own as they flicked back and forth.

He smirked. "*Especially* if it gets us all killed."

"Thank you, Colonel," she said agreeably, and a trio of hovering video-recording drones flew to her where she plucked them one-by-one from the air and put them in her pocket. She replaced her rebreather mask and added, "That's all I need right now."

She turned and made her way to the hospital APC, while Jenkins re-donned his own rebreather and resumed his trek to *Elvira*.

He needed to make sure Xi was adequately coping with the *Gym Cricket*'s loss. She was the fastest-rising star in the entire Metal Legion and his battalion XO. Knowing where her head was at, especially after losing a team under fire, was important on several different fronts. Jenkins had crawled all the way down a bottle during his first brush with such a loss, and hadn't come out for a full decade.

He was betting Xi would pull through a hell of a lot better than he had.

6

CONTACT

"Lu, I need you to visually inspect Two Launcher," Xi commanded. The control systems weren't as responsive as they should be, which suggested there might be ice built up on the launcher's exterior. They had already fine-tuned the mech's temperature, resulting in a near-sweltering interior environment, and they had not suffered a mechanical malfunction in two days.

Xi intended to keep it that way. And she also intended to push her Wrench harder than he seemed to like.

"What's the problem, Captain?" Lu asked.

"It feels like ice buildup on the lateral servo housings," she replied. "Get eyes on it and tell me what you see."

Judging by his delayed reply, it was clear he didn't want to do it, but he thankfully complied. "Yes, Captain. Opening the hatch."

Xi fractionally slowed *Elvira*'s pace as Chief Lu clambered up the ladder beside the hatch. She wanted to see how he coped with the combined cold and unsteady footing, but to protect herself from the sudden chill, she closed the cockpit doors.

Blinky, *Elvira*'s dedicated Monkey, had already gone atop

the hull a dozen times during the last few days' patrols. His eager demeanor and surprisingly capable technical skills had been as much of a pleasant surprise as Lu's drag-ass, sandbagging tendencies had been an unpleasant one.

Despite his lack of internal fire, Lu made it all the way to Two Launcher, albeit in twice the time it would have taken Blinky. He soon reported, "There's a little ice on the laterals and maybe some on the recoil mech. It's hard to see from here."

"Torch it off," Xi ordered, "then take a quick look at One and tell me what you see."

"Acknowledged," he replied tersely before igniting a bottle torch and clearing the obstruction. The battalion had already gone through five full pallets of liquid-hydrocarbon fuel bottles, but fortunately, there were hundreds more on the *Bonhoeffer*.

Lu spent at least twice as much fuel as he needed before moving to One Launcher. He crouched there, examining its underside for at least a minute before standing.

"I don't see any buildup on One, Captain," he reported.

"All right," she acknowledged, "spray another layer of water-lock on Two before coming back inside. Keeping the topside gear above melting temperature means we have to maintain moisture barriers or we'll lock up again in the middle of combat. 2nd Company won't have another cold-related mechanical failure on my watch. Is that understood?"

"Yes, Captain," both Lu and Blinky replied.

Lu soon returned to the cabin, his work topside complete. He continued to shiver once inside, remaining still as he simply breathed.

Just as Xi was about to re-open the cockpit door, proximity alarms rang throughout *Elvira*'s cabin.

"Hostiles at three hundred meters!" Xi barked, halting *Elvira*'s forward motion and pivoting toward the new contacts. She set One Launcher to unload its anti-missile rockets and reload with armor-piercing SRMs. Meanwhile, she trained her dual fifteen-kilo guns on the newcomers.

She focused her high-resolution optics on the arrivals and was taken aback by what she saw. Crawling up and out of the ice was a quartet of seemingly identical vehicles...but aside from their sheer bulk, it seemed as though they were living organisms of some kind.

Each was eighteen meters long, with a dark yellow-and-green exoskeleton supported by twenty-two short, curved legs. Their main bodies, or chassis, were curved from front-to-back with the highest point approximately a third of the way back. They moved with impressive speed, clocking in at just over a hundred kilometers per hour before they opened fire on 4th Platoon.

Elvira's hull was bathed in plasma as two of the bizarre, insect-like vehicles concentrated fire on her. "AP up," Xi called, more from routine than by necessity since she controlled the ammo-loading systems via her neural link. "On the way!"

Elvira's fifteen-kilo guns were lowered as far as possible, so in order to aim them at the enemy, Xi crouched *Elvira*'s front and raised the stern to tilt them down even farther. At that moment, more than any other, the mighty battle mech resembled the Scorpion her class was named after. The fifteens thundered simultaneously, sending armor-piercing shells into the nearest of the four enemy vehicles.

Shockingly, the vehicle did not explode, but merely log-rolled from the kinetic energy of the impacts.

It quickly scrambled to its feet and re-oriented itself before returning fire with some kind of mortar near its "head" region. *Elvira*'s top-side was struck by the slow-moving shell, which did not explode and initially seemed to do nothing but go "splat."

"What the fuck?" Xi growled in alarm, swiveling her top-side cameras to look at the damage. She set her jaw when she saw smoke rising from the heavy, composite armor shell just a meter behind her pilot's chair. "Blinky!" she snapped. "Tap into the coolant line with the high-pressure hose. We've got some kind of acid burning a hole through the roof!"

"On it, Captain," Blinky replied, scrambling to do as instructed.

A quick check of 4th Platoon's status showed that *Cave Troll* had also been hit by acid, but its vertical posture seemed to have limited the damage. *Heavy Metal Jesus* had avoided an acid shell but was reeling from a plasma stream hit.

"All right," Xi snarled as One Launcher finished loading AP SRMs. "You want to play? Let's play."

Locking onto the vehicle she had inexplicably failed to do serious damage with her dual fifteens, Xi sent four SRMs straight at the bug-looking thing. Shockingly, two of the SRMs missed entirely, exploding fifty meters behind the insect-like vehicle.

But the two that struck were aimed low and tore nearly all of the legs off its left side. The thing toppled, desperately trying to remain upright with the few motive limbs remaining on that side, but ultimately failed and came crashing to the ground.

Xi spun up her left flank's anti-personnel chain guns and began pouring depleted uranium rounds into its exposed underside. Sweeping up and down its belly with her weapons, Xi whooped with satisfaction as it curled and contorted while fifteen hundred rounds found the mark and made a mess of its soft under-carriage.

She loaded HE shells into the fifteens and re-oriented *Elvira*'s artillery onto the helpless enemy. "HE up. On the way!"

Two high-explosive shells tore into the floundering vehicle, blowing it apart like a paint-filled balloon. The icy surface was covered in a forty-meter disc of greenish-blue gore, which confirmed that these things were at least as much meat as metal.

Elvira rocked from a plasma strike to her left flank, and both chain guns registered system failures before shutting down.

Another acid shell fell onto *Elvira*'s top-side just before Blinky popped the hatch open, hose in hand. "Over the cockpit first," Xi ordered, pivoting *Elvira* toward another one of the new enemies. She sent four more AP SRMs toward the overgrown bug-thing, but this time just one of them struck true while the others inexplicably missed.

At these ranges, a miss should have been impossible. But here she was, three-for-eight with her latest missile launches.

Blinky began to hose the acid off *Elvira*'s hull, standing tall in his duty as the nearby, humanoid *Heavy Metal Jesus* sent a hyper-velocity tungsten bolt into one of the bizarre vehicle-creatures. The railgun strike punched a deep, glowing hole in the thing's hunched back, but the damage did little to deter the beast as it spat plasma in reply and bathed *HMJ*'s left leg in fire. *Heavy Metal Jesus*, already down one railgun arm from a previous strike, fell when its left leg was critically damaged.

As soon as it hit the deck, a swarm of half-meter-wide crab-looking things sprang out of the damaged bug vehicle. They swarmed toward the fallen *HMJ*, and Xi growled, "This is a crabs-free outfit!"

Sweeping *Elvira*'s right flank toward the surging line of crab-things, she unleashed her still-working chain guns across the horde of skittering critters. Their bodies burst apart on impact, and half of them exploded so violently that their purpose was clear.

They were grenade-delivery systems.

She maintained focus, cutting the damned things down before they could swarm *HMJ* and kill its stranded crew. At her back, *Cave Troll* unleashed its super-powered plasma cannons on one of the less-damaged vehicle bugs. The thing was utterly annihilated, with a quarter-kilometer-long steaming rent in the ice behind it serving as the lone reminder of its existence.

The humanoid *Masamune*, recently re-assigned to 4th Platoon from 6th Platoon, fired its railgun and tore a second hole into the already-damaged vehicle. But the enemy seemed unfazed by the devastating attack, which tore six legs from its right side and burned a meter-wide hole in its lower carapace.

"Concentrate fire on the wounded," Xi barked as the two remaining platforms began to withdraw into the icy tunnel from which they had emerged less than a minute earlier.

Cave Troll launched SRMs, but only three struck true, and they did little but slow the enemy's retreat. *Elvira* and *Masamune* were unable to cycle their weapons fast enough to get another shot off before the bug-things disappeared beneath the ice.

Xi's jaw muscles bunched angrily for several seconds before she said, "Blinky, Lu, and Samuels: take extraction gear and first aid materials over to *Heavy Metal Jesus* and get our people out of there. Move!"

Impressively, the reporter made no objection as she joined the team. Fortunately, *HMJ*'s crew had no serious injuries and were brought aboard *Elvira*, which had the most spacious interior of any mech in the platoon.

"She'll walk again," Xi assured the trio of battered crewmen before switching to the P2P link with HQ. "HQ, this is *Elvira*. We have repelled an attack by unidentified hostiles and have one mech down. Requesting repair-and-retrieval team to our location ASAP. All personnel alive and accounted for, but *Heavy Metal Jesus* is going to need a miracle from Lieutenant Koch's team before it can walk again. Over."

"Miracle en route, *Elvira*. ETA: Thirty-nine minutes," Jenkins acknowledged, and by his tone, she knew he had taken her subtle meaning. By calling the enemies "unidenti-fied hostiles," she was suggesting it was possible they were the very alien species they had come to this barren ice ball to meet.

But why, if this strange new species wanted to initiate diplo-matic relations with the Terran Republic like the Vorr had clan-destinely suggested, would they ambush a Terran patrol rather than approaching them peacefully?

Xi shook her head. "Above my pay-grade," she muttered before switching to the platoon P2P network. "*Cave Troll*, secure this site. *Masamune*, send one of your hunter-killer drones down that hole. I want to see where those bastards came from."

"Roger," *Masamune* replied. "HK away."

A six-wheeled vehicle, just large enough for a human to sit atop but of similar design to the ATVs each of her mechs had been equipped with pre-deployment, dropped from *Masamune*'s left leg and sped toward the tunnel through which the alien vehicles had fled. HK drones were armed with high-explosives for largely the same purpose as the crab-things the bug had sent to finish off *Heavy Metal Jesus*. *Masamune* was a rare, anti-mech design that was purpose-built to kill other mechs rather than to engage a variety of targets. Armed with four HKs, it could use them as mobile landmines, recon drones, or even launch platforms for one of its mid-range missiles. And while the lack of RF linkage made real-time recon impossible, if the drone survived, it would return with all the telemetry it gath-ered during the trip.

Seconds turned into minutes, and eventually, the HK emerged from the ice passage. A few seconds later, *Masamune*'s Jock reported, "They collapsed the tunnel a kilometer down, Captain. I could try to blow it..."

"Negative, *Masamune*." She sighed irritably, "they're long

gone. Maintain position until the recovery and repair, R&R, team arrives, then we'll resume our patrol."

"Copy that," both *Cave Troll* and *Masamune* acknowledged, and forty-five minutes later, with *Heavy Metal Jesus* loaded onto *Kochtopussy* and en route to HQ, Xi's three-mech platoon resumed its patrol.

7

THE FIRST THREAD

Colonel Jenkins looked up to see Styles close the hatch to his cabin, sealing the compartment off from the rest of *Roy*'s interior.

"What have you got, Styles?" Jenkins asked after the hatch was shut.

"I've inventoried everything from all four mine sites," Styles replied, placing a data slate on the small table in front of Jenkins, "and compared it with the lists DIE provided. We already knew about the Delta Site's missing data storage systems, but what we didn't know about were the ice core samples."

Jenkins cocked his head in confusion. "Ice core samples?"

"Yes, sir." Styles nodded eagerly. "Fifteen of them in all."

Jenkins leaned back in his chair. "The same as the number of Vorr underwater shafts."

"Precisely!" Styles agreed.

Jenkins drummed his fingers in thought before venturing, "DIE found something on the surface of this planet...and that finding suggested to them that there might be something of even greater value on the bottom of the ocean."

"But human technology...or at least Terran tech," Styles

amended, "isn't up to the task of such a deep dive in near-freezing temperatures. The *Bonhoeffer*'s scans show a Vorr transceiver eight kilometers down, on the underwater slope of this mountain."

"So, the Vorr drilled each of the fifteen sites," Jenkins mused, "but ultimately settled on one. Why not shut down the other sites?"

"My guess is still that the fifteen separate shafts, their ice core samples, and even the transceiver are misdirection," Styles explained. "Vorr are an underwater species with technology rivaling that of the Jemmin. Of all the races in known space, they're the best bet to be able to retrieve whatever it is that DIE found down there. But the Jemmin probably aren't far behind them in terms of underwater tech. They'll likely work to modify a gas giant probe or some other ultra-high-pressure device with a return system, which they'll then use to retrieve whatever it is that DIE found."

"Any theories as to what that might be?" Jenkins urged, but Styles shook his head.

"I just don't have enough information to work with, Colonel. I would know more about what we're looking at if I could get my hands on those core samples," he said leadingly.

"We don't know where the Jemmin are storing them—" Jenkin shook his head firmly. "—or even if they kept them at all. They're clearly trying to stop us from following this thread, so why not destroy the evidence?"

"That's probable," Styles reluctantly agreed before leaning forward conspiratorially. "Do you think this might have something to do with those...*bug* things Xi encountered?"

Jenkins shrugged. "It's possible. The longer we're down here, the more it looks like the Vorr had ulterior motives for bringing us here beyond the simple facilitation of a secret diplomatic meeting."

"And they bugged out the minute we arrived." Styles nodded knowingly before hesitating and seeming to resist the urge to continue.

"Go on, Chief," Jenkins urged. "What are you thinking?"

"I've got Podsy running an analysis on the Vorr shafts," Styles reluctantly explained. "The thing is...I think they were made from orbit—originally, that is."

"I don't follow."

"If you precisely attenuate a high-powered laser," Styles explained, "and I'm talking *high-powered*, the likes of which humanity has yet to deploy, you could drill straight down through an ice crust like this and leave a hole no wider than a few meters."

"To what purpose?"

"That's the part I can't figure out," Styles replied in obvious frustration. "I mean, if you wanted to explore a subsurface ocean like the one here on Shiva's Wrath, there are better ways to do it than with a capital-grade laser fired from orbit. And if you were just sniping fifteen 'somethings' located on the surface, there would be no need to drill all the way through ten kilometers of ice. Someone wanted to access this world's relatively-inaccessible ocean, but I can't figure out why. And without those ice cores, I can't even tell you when they did it."

"Only two known species use lasers on the scale you're talking about," Jenkins mused.

"The Vorr and the Jemmin." Styles nodded knowingly. "Which narrows down the list of suspects, sure, but we don't know enough about their respective histories to have the first clue what they might have wanted with Shiva's Wrath. For that matter, we don't know why they would leave it essentially unmolested until DIE came along and started conducting private surveys. Whatever it is that's valuable enough to make the Vorr and Jemmin fight over it was here long before Terran interests arrived, but they're only now showing interest in it?"

"An honest-to-God mystery..." Jenkins boggled before chuckling. "Silly me, I thought the worst I'd face were treason charges for conducting unauthorized diplomacy with foreign nations."

"Instead we've exchanged fire with the founding nation of the Illumination League and encountered another seemingly hostile alien species with whom we've also exchanged fire," Styles snickered. "Makes treason look like a cake-walk."

"I'm not sure I'd go that far," Jenkins allowed. "Is there anything else?"

"Not from me." Styles shook his head. "I'll keep working with Podsy on those drill shafts. Once I know more, you'll know. I'm hoping to come up with an estimated position of the ship that made them. If I can, it might tell us a little more about who cut the holes in the first place."

"Keep after it." Jenkins nodded approvingly.

"Oh," Styles added as he went to open the hatch, "Doc Fellows was right behind me trying to get time with you."

"Send him in."

Styles left Jenkins' cabin, and a moment later, the battalion's doctor entered. "Colonel," the doctor greeted, bearing a data slate that he solemnly proffered.

"Why the long face, Doc?" Jenkins asked mildly, taking the slate and viewing its contents.

"The short version is this." Fellows sighed, sitting down in the chair opposite Jenkins. "There's about six times as much radiation on this patch of ice as we anticipated."

"What?" Jenkins demanded in surprise, and the doctor gestured to the slate. "This isn't some kind of mistake?"

"I've been taking and re-taking surface samples of the ice here." Fellows shook his head grimly. "Every area I've tested, which includes everything in our patrol circuits, has been covered with highly-charged dust that's already worked its way into everything. Decontamination is going to be impossible. I've already run the numbers and checked with the *Bonhoeffer*'s inventory. There is no way to effectively contain this radiation. The best we can hope for is to sterilize the mech cabins and limit exposure to the crews within them, but the troopers are getting hammered."

"Can we counteract the effects by upping the dosage of anti-radiation meds?" Jenkins asked in muted alarm.

"We can," Fellows agreed, "and I've already upped everyone's doses to the maximum allowed per person. But at that rate, we'll exhaust our supply of meds in fifteen days."

"Recommendation?"

"Transfer the troopers to the mine sites," Fellows replied. "We initially thought the mines would have double the radiation we're seeing out here on the ice, but now the ice is hotter than the rock by nearly that much again. Coupled with the quarantine measures of each mech and its crew, we can maybe double our stay on Shiva's Wrath before we all start to suffer permanent effects of radiation poisoning."

Jenkins set his jaw as he asked the obvious question, "Was the ice this hot when we got here?"

"No, sir." Fellows shook his head firmly. "While the stuff is no longer falling from the sky, it was coming down in such small amounts that it didn't trigger any of our alarms. My guess is a low-orbit dispersal pattern which blanketed, oh, a five-hundred-mile radius, probably centered somewhere between us and the Jemmin base."

"It wasn't the nuke they touched off over our heads..." Jenkins mused, wondering how the Jemmin could have delivered what was essentially a dirty bomb into low orbit without anyone aboard the *Bonhoeffer* noticing.

"No," the doctor agreed, "but it probably happened around the same time."

Jenkins sat back in his chair and considered the situation. If there had ever been doubts as to the Jemmin intentions toward the Terrans on Shiva's Wrath, those doubts were now eliminated. He had wondered why the Jemmin went silent after killing *Gym Cricket,* and now he had the answer: they had poisoned Jenkins' people and were merely waiting for them to retreat or die from radiation sickness.

"All right." Jenkins nodded decisively. "I'll contact Sergeant Major Trapper and transfer all non-essential personnel to the mines. We'll reverse the rest schedule, bringing whoever is needed out here to HQ while resting personnel inside the mines."

"Do you want me to inform the battalion?" the doctor asked.

Jenkins shook his head. "No, I'll do it. I want you to oversee the decontamination shed, and make sure to pack each and every mech with all the perishables they'll need for the next thirty days."

"That slate—" Fellows gestured to the one he had given Jenkins. "—contains my requisition list. I'll need those supplies before I can construct the decontamination shed."

"I'll call them down ASAP," Jenkins assured him. "Thank you, Doctor."

"Colonel." Doctor Fellows snapped a salute before exiting the cabin.

"May I have your attention..." Colonel Jenkins' voice crackled through *Elvira*'s interior speakers, rather than through her headset. Xi recoiled in surprise, realizing he was making a battalion-wide address.

"This can't be good," Xi muttered.

"Ten minutes ago, Doctor Fellows informed me that our HQ has been blanketed in a layer of radioactive material," Jenkins explained, causing Xi's throat to tighten in alarm. Visions of radiation-poisoned war victims flooded her mind, and for a moment, she thought her heart skipped a beat as she imagined herself with a patchy head of hair and an emaciated physique. "He has already increased our med dosages, and we will begin adjusting battalion-wide protocols to compensate. Within twelve hours, we will have a decontamination shed up and running, where all vehicles and personnel will be scrubbed as clean as possible. After each mech has undergone this procedure, quarantine protocols will be in effect throughout the battalion. I know you meatheads like to play in the snow, but fun time's over. The enemy has violated humanity's, and even the Illumination League's, most fundamental war-time conventions. I intend for us to stand our ground and deliver the only appropriate rebuke—right into their teeth."

Xi felt her neck-hairs stand on end as her CO gave voice to the anger she currently felt at hearing she had been poisoned by the enemy.

"Check with your unit commanders for revised deployment protocols," Jenkins concluded. "Jenkins out."

"Is this for real?" Blinky asked, stepping into the cockpit with a concerned expression.

"Seems like it." Xi nodded irritably, doing her best to project an air of calm and control.

Sarah Samuels pushed past Staubach. "Captain Xi, how can we confirm the Jemmin really used a dirty bomb of some kind?"

"Trust but verify?" Xi quirked a brow in mild approval of the reporter's suggestion.

"Something like that," Samuels said guardedly.

"Well…" Xi mused sarcastically. "We could gather up some

surface ice in cadmium-lined containers for later testing, or we could pop a section of the top-side hull off and stuff it in a box somewhere in the hope the *Bonhoeffer* can retrieve and analyze it, or..."

Samuels gave her a withering look. "Captain, if you don't intend to take my question seriously..."

Blinky's eyes lit up. "Or we could pull the Geiger-counter from the med-kit and test samples of surface ice against samples taken from a meter down?"

Xi rolled her eyes, but in truth, she was glad he had taken the initiative after she'd left the proverbial door wide open for him. "Well...I guess you *could*," Xi said grudgingly.

"But what about breaking quarantine?" Samuels asked with mild concern.

"It doesn't matter until after we scrub the mech," Xi shook her head. "This cabin is already full of irradiated dust. Once we've cleaned *Elvira* inside-and-out, we can't re-open the hatch without re-contaminating the interior." She twisted her mouth into a bemused smirk. "I guess that means you're going to have to choose where you'd like to ride out the rest of this mission, Ms. Samuels."

Samuels returned the smirk. "We'll just have to wait and see how things shake out. I've grown rather fond of *Elvira* and her crew, after all."

"Great..." Xi said with patently false enthusiasm, turning back to her HUD and sarcastically muttering, "Really, really great."

8

OFFENSE VS. DEFENSE

"Those are *way* too fragile to be packed like that," Podsy barked, driving his forklift over to the drop-can in bay four. "These are the last of our radiation meds, Gong," he explained, mustering as much patience as possible while dealing with the hard-headed grease-monkey. "They need to be packed in orange, drop-rated containers to make sure they survive the landing."

"The green boxes have more interior volume, Chief," Guo Gong argued. "We can put three times as many doses in the same space by using them."

"The green boxes are less protected, so three times nothing is still nothing," Podsy snapped. "I'd rather deliver half of the drugs safely than all of them like that—" He pointed derisively at the stacks of green-boxed meds. "Use the orange pipes, like I said fifteen minutes ago, and with any luck, we won't miss our drop." He checked the drop-timer above the can, which showed just seventeen minutes to delivery. "Let's move, people," he urged, clapping his hands as loudly as possible while the recalcitrant Guo grudgingly did as ordered.

His shift had been on-duty for fourteen hours, which was nothing as far as he was concerned, but they were beginning to fray at the edges. For most of Third Shift, this was their first deployment. They had responded well to the pressure of the situation, but a few rough edges still needed to be sanded down.

A Second Shifter drove a forklift past, carrying a positioning gyro for a Scorpion-class-compatible SRM mount.

"Hold up," Podsy called after the crewman, causing her to stop and make eye contact. "Is that for *Elvira?*"

"No, Chief." She shook her head. "This is for *Devil Crab* 2."

"Lift it up so I can see the plug mount," he urged.

She hesitated before doing as told, and once she had lifted the meter-square device high enough that he could see its underside, he shook his head irritably.

"*Devil Crab*'s control cable uses a thirty-one-pin connector, not a Scorpion's standard twenty-six like *Elvira*," he explained as he turned his forklift toward a nearby workbench. "We never got around to re-standardizing *Crab*'s connectors after Durgan's Folly. Take it over to the bench," he urged. "I'll re-do the connector, but you'll have to help me."

She complied, and he did his best to lean out of his forklift's seat to gather the needed supplies.

"Tell me what to get, Chief," she said when it became painfully clear he was moving far too slowly.

"A size fourteen stripper—" He gestured to the tools hanging above the bench. "—and a same-size set of crimps."

She retrieved the indicated tools while Podsy carefully opened the connector end and peeled back the wires, one by one, before clipping the whole thing off and tossing it into the re-usable parts bin. It took him less than two minutes to replace the twenty-six-pin connector with the proper thirty-one. Without needing to be told, the Second Shifter brought a test box and plugged it in to verify its status.

The diagnostic completed in a few seconds and all indicators flashed green.

"Good work." He nodded approvingly, high-fiving the crewman before urging, "Now get it over to the can."

The next ten minutes flew by as his team finished loading for the drop. Gong even managed to get the radiation meds correctly packed and secured with a minute to spare before the doors closed and the overhead lift mechanism began conveying the drop-cans to the launch tube.

Each can was loaded into the tube's airlock, which could hold eight such cans simultaneously, and soon Chief Rimmer broadcasted through the area.

"Initiating drop in five...four...three...two...one...can one away...can two away...can three away..." he intoned with the consistency of a metronome until, finally, all eight cans were out of the tube and en route to the surface of Shiva's Wrath.

During ejection, Podsy sat at the same workstation that Rimmer had previously used to grant him access to the *Bonhoeffer*'s sensors. He began poring over stored sensor data, specifically the information surrounding those fifteen Vorr shafts. He needed to access the *Bonhoeffer*'s main processor for a few minutes to crunch the numbers, and for that, he would again need Chief Rimmer's access codes.

"All cans down," Rimmer said grimly. "Can Four's braking thrusters failed and the impact exceeded green box tolerances. What was green-packed in Four?"

Podsy made brief eye contact with the wide-eyed Gong, but Podsednik had no desire to rub the crewman's nose in it. Everyone made mistakes; the trick was learning from them.

Podsy switched on his workstation's two-way intercom and replied, "Nothing perishable other than a few desalination filters, sir. All the radiation meds were orange-tubed by Mr. Gong."

"Good work, Gong," Rimmer congratulated while Gong

suddenly looked ashamed, but Podsy needed to focus on his sensor feeds.

"Chief Rimmer, a word?" Podsy asked over the intercom.

"On my way." The chief appeared at Podsy's side a few moments later. "What is it?"

"I need to run some simulations," Podsy explained. "These laser-drilled shafts were cut from orbit, but I don't know the laser's point-of-origin. I need access to the *Bonhoeffer*'s main processor for at least three minutes, maybe as much as five, to run the simulations and get a clear picture."

"So, what's the problem?" Rimmer asked bluntly.

"I need your access codes, sir," Podsy said warily.

"Not anymore you don't." Rimmer shook his head. "General Akinouye personally approved my request to have your privileges upgraded. In fact, you probably have greater access than I do at this point."

Podsy blinked in confusion. "Why would he do that, sir?"

"The general's been doing this a *long* time, Chief." Rimmer smirked. "If there's one thing a lifelong CO like the general can spot a click away, it's talent. And any CO's first job is to put the people under him where they can do the most good and then give them what they need to succeed." He clapped Podsy on the shoulder. "Carry on, Chief."

Too surprised to intelligently reply, Podsy said, "Thank you, sir."

He then refocused on the task at hand and began running simulations with the hope that they would paint a clearer picture of who burned those holes in the ice on Shiva's Wrath.

"My son was right," Xi heard a deep, gravelly voice call out from beyond the decontamination shed.

Xi turned to see what might have been a slightly-older clone of Tim Trapper Jr. emerge from the other side of *Elvira*, which was getting a thorough scrub-down by a team of PDF soldiers apparently serving out some kind of disciplinary sentence under Trapper's watchful eye.

"Excuse me, Sergeant Major?" Xi asked.

"He said you were a lot like my daughter," Trapper Sr. explained as he appraised *Elvira* with every purposeful, yet leisurely-looking step he took around Xi's mech. "He was right. Have to say, though... Between you and me, I prefer your taste in vehicles to hers."

Xi was intrigued. "You don't like TFMC dropships?"

"Not as far as I could throw them," he spat, meeting her eyes and sending a shiver down her spine at the uncanny resemblance between father and son. "Though I'd be the first to admit it's mostly because she rode one to her death. A person can learn to accept a profound loss, Captain Xi, but it's unreasonable to expect that person to forget it."

Xi nodded in agreement. "If it was forgettable, it wouldn't be very profound, would it?"

"Exactly," he replied approvingly.

A question sprang to her mind, and it passed her lips even before she realized it was on them. "What about forgiveness?"

"Forgiveness?" he chuckled. "Well...it probably takes a better man than me to pull that particular maneuver off. Dawkins," he barked at one of the troopers scrubbing *Elvira*'s acid-burnt top-side, "if I see one more half-assed thrust of that broom, I'll personally arrange an intimate encounter between the two of you. Is that clear?"

"As a Solarian's conscience, sir," Dawkins replied snappily before redoubling his efforts to wash down Xi's mech and avoid further aggravating the senior Trapper.

"What happened between you two?" Xi asked, this time fully conscious of the question and its potential hazards.

"Honestly?" The grizzled sergeant major sighed, and for a fraction of a second, he looked like a tired old man before his gruff exterior and stiff posture once again projected the air of a battle-hardened leader of men. "Loss happened. Some are better dealing with it than others, and it turns out I don't measure very high on that particular stick." He turned and critically eyed her from head to toe before chuckling. "When he's right, he's right." Trapper Sr. thrust his hand out. "I'm glad to have met you, Captain."

"Likewise," she acknowledged, accepting his hand before he climbed up *Elvira*'s leg with a demonstration of agility and spryness that should have been impossible for an eighty-two-year-old man.

He moved over to the acid-burnt patch of *Elvira*'s top-side and whistled. "Never seen a burn like that. Looks like it only missed the cabin by about a few centimeters."

"I've got a good Monkey," she said with conviction. "He hosed it off before it ate the rest of the way through."

Trapper nodded approvingly. "Hang onto him." His attention was taken by something, or someone, to *Elvira*'s stern, and he barked, "Who in the name of Hades taught you how to push a broom, Butte?"

He made his way out of Xi's sight and left her to marvel at just how uncannily Senior and Junior resembled each other.

"All right, Styles," Jenkins said after the door to his private cabin was shut. "Let's hear it."

"The angle of the strikes suggests they were made from a single position in low orbit," Styles explained. "Podsy used the

Bonhoeffer's main processor to run billions of simulations, and this is what they showed as most likely." He pulled up a visual display of the ship's probable location. "We can't be certain, but it looks like this one would favor a Jemmin, not Vorr, warship. The ability to remain stable while in low orbit takes a lot more technical capability than we have or the Vorr, most likely. By stable, I mean the ship can't move more than a millimeter from its geosynchronous orbit for the duration of the drill. Judging by the cleanliness of the holes, it didn't even move that far."

"How confident are you that it was the Jemmin and not the Vorr?" Jenkins asked.

"Eighty-five percent," Styles replied firmly. "With the ice core samples, I could tell you with absolute certainty, but we have to assume they're long gone."

"So, the Jemmin came here, punched a bunch of holes in the ice..." Jenkins wearily rubbed the bridge of his nose. "...and, what...left something behind?"

"That's our best guess." Styles nodded.

Jenkins shook his head dubiously. "But if that thing was important enough that reclaiming it justified the risk of a shooting war with the Vorr, why wouldn't they have come and picked it up before DIE ever came to this world?"

"There are a couple possible answers," Styles said as a gleam entered his eye. "One is that they didn't know that the humans were coming. The second, and I think more likely answer, is that the Jemmin didn't know about it until recently."

"But if they dropped it..." Jenkins trailed off as he slowly began to take Styles' meaning. "You're saying that whatever's down there was left by a rebel Jemmin faction?"

"Rebel? Based on what little we know, or think we know, about Jemmin society...probably not," Styles shook his head doubtfully. "But dissident? It looks that way to me, Colonel."

"So, the Vorr—" Jenkins steepled his fingers contemplatively. "—learned about this a few decades ago and...what?"

"Alerted DIE that there was something worth investigating down here," Styles suggested, "and asked them to establish a mining operation so they could clandestinely retrieve whatever's down there without violating interstellar law. The Jemmin found out, and..."

"Wait." Jenkins sat forward in alarm. "Are you suggesting that whatever's down there is related to the Vorr withdrawal from the Illumination League?"

Styles seemed genuinely uncertain, but more than that, he looked *uncomfortable* following what appeared to be the inevitable train of thought associated with his theory. "I'm saying," he began carefully, "that the timelines match up enough to suggest it."

Jenkins sat back in his chair, wondering just how deep this hole he'd lunged head-first into went. "Which means we might have been brought here..." He stopped, unable to finish the thought.

"...to form an anti-Jemmin alliance with the Vorr and whatever this third species is," Styles finished somberly. "If the Jemmin suspected as much, they would have driven the Vorr off as soon as possible."

"While leaving a contingent here to drive us off," Jenkins muttered in disbelief, "or, if necessary, to destroy us."

"The actions we've seen suggest this is the case. It's easier to deal with the fall-out from a 'rogue' warship's actions than to face an alliance which consists of Vorr, Terran, and whatever these insectoids are," Styles said with finality. "They left that one ship here so they could claim plausible deniability for its aggression."

"It's too transparent," Jenkins rejected. "There's no way it passes the sniff test...is there?"

"Stranger things have happened." Styles shrugged. "But this is all still conjecture. I have no hard evidence."

"It's the best we've got to work with," Jenkins mused, "and it explains why the Jemmin are willing to go to such lengths to drive us off Shiva's Wrath, including irradiating the planet in violation of most interstellar treaties." He gritted his teeth and flashed a wolfish grin. "Which means leaving is not an option."

"Do you think we should present any of this to the general?" Styles asked.

"The facts, yes." Jenkins nodded. "But we might be chasing a red herring. We don't know a whole lot about the Jemmin from which to base our guesstimates. I need something more concrete before we take it to the brass. For now, this theory remains between you and me. Understood?"

"Yes, sir," Styles agreed.

"All right." Jenkins nodded approvingly. "This could be a case of pattern recognition run amok," he said pointedly, causing Styles to chuckle.

"I've been guilty of that on a few occasions," the technician agreed.

"But it could also be that you're onto something here," Jenkins added heavily. "And if you are, we need to make sure that no one learns about it. If the Jemmin think we're onto them, they'll give us both barrels. Which only makes cracking their stealth suites that much more important," he said pointedly.

"Still no luck on that front, sir," Styles said sourly. "I'm going over every byte of data from the battalion's sensor logs, but I still can't see a way to punch through the fog."

"Negating their stealth advantage is now your top priority," Jenkins said severely. "Without the ability to reliably locate and target them, we're surrendering the initiative to the enemy. We can't surrender tempo against a technologically superior adversary, Chief."

"Understood, Colonel," Styles agreed, standing and offering a salute. "I'll get back to it."

"Good work, Chief." Jenkins nodded approvingly before the technician hurried out, closing the hatch behind him. After he had gone, the lieutenant colonel rubbed his jaw and muttered, "What the hell have you gotten yourself into, Leeroy?"

9

AMBUSH

Three days after *Elvira* had undergone decontamination, Xi was once again at the head of a patrol. This time, she led only *Cave Troll* and *Masamune*, deciding with Colonel Jenkins' approval that their combined anti-missile capability was more than enough.

"I can't believe I just heard you say that," *Masamune*'s Jock scoffed.

"Can't handle the truth, *Masamune*?" *Cave Troll* challenged.

"Anyone who argues that the early-twenty-first hip-hop scene was as impactful on human music as the late-twentieth metal peak is braindead," *Masamune* rebuked.

"A lot of this argument depends on how you define 'impact,'" Xi interjected with a smirk.

"Sure," *Masamune* agreed, "if by 'impact' you mean 'left a festering sore that took a century to lance and heal over,' then yeah, it was maybe as impactful as the metal uprising...*maybe*. It's like saying Billy Joel was as great a composer as Mozart just because they happened to both play piano. Man, I thought better of you, *Cave Troll*." *Masamune* registered his disappointment with a low and long sigh.

"Whoever said I liked hip-hop?" *Cave Troll* asked, unable to keep the bemused note from his voice.

"You've been arguing for the past twenty minutes for something you don't actually believe?" *Masamune* demanded in outrage.

For her part, Xi muted her mic to hide her laughter at seeing *Cave Troll*'s well-laid trap snap shut on his fellow Jock.

"It was either that," *Cave Troll* replied slowly, "or go through Styles' creepy porn collection...*again*. Between you, me, and this exceptionally limber-looking Arh'Kel, I had a lot more fun defending the indefensible against you."

"So, you *don't* actually like ear-virus music?" *Masamune* asked irritably.

"I'm hurt, *Masamune*. I may be big and stinky," *Cave Troll* retorted, "but that doesn't mean I'm stupid."

"You've got a sick sense of humor, *Cave Troll*," Xi quipped approvingly after unmuting her mic. "I knew we brought you along for more than just the BO."

The patrol resumed in relative quiet for a few minutes before *Elvira*'s tectonic sensors suddenly began to tickle Xi's left arm.

"Bugs," she snapped, pivoting *Elvira* and zeroing in on the point of the disturbance just as the ice erupted in a geyser of steam. One of the strange, bug-looking things emerged just as *Elvira* and her flanking mechs opened fired on the new hole in the ground.

The initial fire was focused and intense, combining anti-personnel chain guns and coilguns that tore the icy tunnel's mouth apart. Chunks of ice flew in all directions, with much of it pulverized or turned to steam by the ferocity of the barrage.

But less than two seconds into the onslaught, Xi got the

nagging suspicion that it was a decoy and spun *Elvira* to her six o'clock just in time to see another bug emerge from the ground three hundred and fifty meters from the first one.

"Multiple contacts," she barked, unleashing *Elvira*'s chain guns and locking on with her dual fifteens. She didn't want to kill these things since they were probably the species they had come to entreat, but they were ambushing her people, and that meant they needed to be treated as hostiles.

Her fifteens thundered simultaneously, lifting *Elvira*'s front legs fractionally off the ground, stabbing deeper into the ice following the recoil. The bug-looking vehicle was knocked over, but it managed to regain its footing before firing a stream of plasma fire at *Masamune*. Instantly, a second stream of fire erupted from the opposite side of the humanoid, anti-mech *Masamune*.

The coordination of those strikes was so precise that they struck *Masamune*'s left leg from both sides directly above the knee. For a moment Xi thought it would survive.

Then, like a tree felled in the woods, *Masamune* tilted further and further over its damaged limb. The deadly mech's Jock did everything he could to keep the vehicle upright and seemed to have halted the ponderous fall before a third plasma jet struck that same leg and blew the damaged joint apart.

The mighty *Masamune* crashed to the ice, sending a plume of snowy dust up around it. True to form, its pilot fought to train his damaged mech's guns on the enemy, and even managed to fire his railgun at one of the flankers.

The targeted bug vehicle's rear, tail-like section was shorn completely off by *Masamune*'s defiant fury. The loss of a full fifth of its body seemed irrelevant to the creature as it skittered across the ice while its fellows did likewise.

"Crab-cakes inbound," called out *Cave Troll* just as Xi noted the stream of meter-wide, crab-like grenade delivery drones that had tried to kill *Heavy Metal Jesus* during the first engagement.

Following Xi's pre-mission directives, *Cave Troll* re-focused his coilguns on the approaching lines of "crab-cakes." With four coilguns on his squat, roughly-humanoid mech, *Cave Troll* tore into the crab-cakes and annihilated at least a hundred of them in the first few seconds. Emerging from three separate holes in the ice, the suicide vehicles surged mindlessly forward without attempting to mask their intent.

They meant to destroy the downed *Masamune*, which was something Xi could not allow.

She unleashed *Elvira*'s chain guns on the stream of tiny enemies while locking onto the nearest of the larger vehicles with SRMs. She could not simultaneously control four chain guns and the SRM launcher, so she focused her attention on the SRM while letting *Elvira*'s auto-targeting systems deal with the crab-cakes.

She manually locked a pair of SRMs onto the circling target and growled, "Gotcha, bitch."

But less than a second before the SRMs left their racks, the other two bug vehicles fired their plasma cannons. *Elvira* was driven into the ice as a deafening explosion went off just above the mech's stern.

Xi's neural link temporarily cut out, and for a precious second-and-a-half, Xi was disoriented and unable to process what had just happened. But when the link's data-stream resumed, she knew precisely how bad they had been hit.

"Launchers One & Two are gone," she declared, quickly finding none of her top-side cameras functioning. "Lock off the ammo feeds and clamp down the ordnance," she snapped with bitter appreciation for her enemy's efficiency. Refocusing her attention on the battle, she loaded HE shells into her dual fifteens and growled, "HE up. Firing!"

Elvira's violent reply to having lost her SRMs was every bit as devastating as Xi had hoped. The dual high-explosive shells struck the same target she had previously bracketed, tearing two-meter-long gashes in its upper carapace. She focused her left chain guns on the vehicle's exposed innards, sending nearly two hundred rounds per second into the gory rents in the enemy's armor.

The unmistakable whine of *Cave Troll*'s plasma cannons cycling up filled her virtual ears. Capacitors thrummed and the ground beneath *Elvira* vibrated for a pair of seconds before *Cave Troll* delivered twin bolts of plasma fire at the last undamaged bug vehicle.

Just as before, nothing but steam and tiny armor fragments survived *Cave Troll*'s wrath.

But somehow, the encroaching crab-cakes had swarmed dangerously close to the mighty plasma-throwing mech. They had altered their target priority after *Cave Troll*'s devastating display of firepower, which suggested autonomous decision-making ability.

Xi turned *Elvira*'s chain guns onto the horde of grenade-carrying critters, but for some reason, her accuracy had fallen off completely. Instead of thoroughly devastating the enemy line as she had previously done, she only managed to pick off half as many per second.

"*Preacher*," she raised the HQ-stationed highly-specialized missile mech, "I need a Purgatory on *Cave Troll*'s position. Now."

"Purgatory on the way," *Preacher* replied two seconds later. "ETA: four seconds."

Xi continued to sweep her guns up and down the lines of oncoming grenade drones, while *Cave Troll* did likewise. But it seemed her vehicle was not the only one whose accuracy had nose-dived, and no matter how many rounds they put into the ice, some of the crab-cakes managed to slip through.

A pair of grenades went off on *Cave Troll*'s articulated feet, doing little damage but heralding worse to come as the crab-cakes clambered up the squat mech's massive legs. They were looking to damage sensitive points like the knee, but it seemed that *Cave Troll*'s armor was too tight for them to squeeze through. Dozens had already climbed halfway up its armored bulk, and it would only be a matter of time before they reached the relatively vulnerable cockpit.

Thankfully, before that happened, the Purgatory-class missile arrived.

The air was filled with a fiery roar as the air-burst missile exploded mere meters from the spot where *Cave Troll* stood. A Purgatory-class missile was a finely-tuned, broad-dispersal incendiary device. If correctly attenuated to the target environment, a Purgatory would instantly clear any unarmored target from a half-kilometer patch of ground, and they had been known to slag small arms and crew-served weapons alike near the blast point. They were unthinkably devastating and horrific but were also perfect for danger-close support of armored units like Xi's platoon. Only Arh'Kel were heat-resistant to such a degree that they could survive a Purgatory strike relatively unscathed without the benefit of armor, which was why the ordnance had not been used on Durgan's Folly.

Xi kept firing, half-blindly, in the hope of driving off whatever creatures somehow survived the hellish inferno. The smoke soon cleared, replaced with fast-dispersing steam, and when her visual systems were back online, Xi saw that *Cave Troll* was on the ground. There was no movement anywhere nearby, which suggested the Purgatory had wiped the critters clean.

But not before they had brought down *Cave Troll*.

Snarling in frustration, Xi locked onto the badly-damaged

bug vehicle she had hit with HE shells. "Come and get me, roaches!" she yelled as she loaded another pair of HE shells into her fifteens and sent them downrange.

One of the HE shells missed high, exploding nearly a kilometer behind the target. But the other struck one of the massive rents caused by its predecessors, and the resulting shower of gore was a thing of beauty as the bug vehicle exploded in all directions.

"One-on-one," she said triumphantly, turning *Elvira* toward the last remaining bug vehicle.

The enemy vehicle seemed confused, milling this way and that for a few seconds while Xi loaded fresh ordnance into her fifteens. She ran a quick diagnostic on her errant left gun's targeting system while staying the right gun for a moment. "Lu," she called over *Elvira*'s intercom, "check the gimble and the mount points for the left gun. Blinky, open up the targeting computer and tell me what you see."

Xi crab-walked *Elvira* to the right as her crew worked to diagnose the targeting problem. The bug vehicle, somewhat surprisingly, mirrored her movement and the two began to circle for several long, tense seconds while *Elvira*'s systems diagnosed the problem with the left fifteen. Just a hundred and twenty meters separated the vehicles, and Xi suddenly realized that unlike its previous, side-on posture, the hunch-backed, pillbug-looking vehicle was facing *Elvira* head-on.

"It's mirroring my posture..." she muttered in mixed alarm and curiosity. She stopped her right-ward progress, and the bug immediately did likewise. She slowly moved *Elvira* back five meters and, again, the enemy vehicle uncannily mirrored her movements.

Gritting her teeth, she knew there was something significant to the thing's maneuver. But what was it? The thing had ambushed them, torn two of her mechs down, and now it wanted to *dance?*

"Targeting computer looks good, Captain," Blinky reported.

"The gimbal's fine, Captain," Lu added, "but the mounts were tweaked when the SRMs blew. I'm inputting the new position into the computer," he said as those figures appeared on Xi's HUD.

"Good work." She nodded, confirming the HE shells up in her guns were ready to fire. She was less confident than she had been a minute earlier, but she knew that this bug needed to die. Now. "On the way," she declared, sending another pair of HE shells into the bug vehicle.

Both shells struck the mark, but shockingly, neither seemed to do significant damage. The thing's carapace was bent and now sported several length-wise cracks, but unlike previous strikes, there were no meter-wide holes in the thing's armored skin.

But even more surprising was the fact that, instead of returning fire with its plasma cannon, it skittered toward the nearest ice-hole from which one of its companions had emerged at the fight's outset.

"Oh, no, you don't." Xi grimaced, reloading HE shells. "HE up." She sneered as the thing's front-half moved into the tunnel. "On the way!"

Her guns thundered, sending their ordnance into the tunnel's mouth, but from the angle of impact, she doubted she'd hit the thing.

"Dammit!" she screamed in frustration.

And then a meter-wide beam of light stabbed into that tunnel from directly overhead, slicing through the ice-field like a scalpel as the ice boiled straight into steam. The constant laser gouged deeper and deeper into the ice, like a needle pursuing a splinter lodged beneath the skin, and it tore a three-hundred-meter long, fifty-meter-deep chasm in the ice before finally disappearing.

Steam boiled skyward and liquid water fell to the bottom of the chasm, most of which froze before it reached the floor of the icy gash.

The fallen *Masamune* was dangerously close to the newly-formed ravine and fell several meters down the gentler top-most section of its steep walls before coming to a stop. *Cave Troll*, on the other hand, had fallen far from the beam's path and was unaffected by the suddenly-unstable patch of ice surrounding the orbital strike's impact zone.

"*Masamune, Cave Troll*, respond," Xi called out over the P2P, but she knew that neither of the vehicles' point-to-point comm systems were likely to function after the Purgatory strike.

It would take relatively minor but critical repairs to their lateral P2P transceivers before they functioned properly. Still, the protocol was usually protocol for very good reasons, which meant she needed to try raising them at least three times before dispatching her crews in a search-and-rescue mission.

"*Masamune, Cave Troll*, respond," she repeated while walking over to the nearer *Cave Troll*, but again, she received no reply. "*Masamune, Cave Troll*, respond," she called for the third time before switching to *Elvira*'s intercom. "Lu, Blinky, Samuels: grab your gear and head over to *Cave Troll* in search of survivors. On the double," she snapped, unlocking *Elvira*'s hatch and knowing that she was poisoning them all with radioactive dust by doing so, "we've got two downed mechs whose crews need our help. Move!"

"Yes, Captain," came Blinky's immediate reply, while both Lu and Samuels were much more belated in their acknowledgment of her orders.

"HQ, this is *Elvira*." Xi raised the battalion on the priority channel. "I've got two downed mechs in need of retrieval. *Cave*

Troll and *Masamune* crew condition currently unknown. We're conducting emergency support at this time. Requesting immediate medevac, over."

"Copy that, *Elvira*," Styles acknowledged. "R&R team notified. ETA forty-five minutes."

"Be advised," she continued, careful not to make direct reference to the still-unrecognized alien species, "Jemmin warship opened fire on a fleeing vehicle."

"Repeat your last, *Elvira*," Styles said neutrally.

"Jemmin warship opened fire with capital-grade lasers on the last hostile as it fled beneath the ice, and the strike-zone was danger-close to *Masamune*," she reiterated, again careful not to refer to the bug vehicle. All official logs would be processed at a later date by Terran Armed Forces oversight agencies, and this mission was supposed to be as secretive as they could manage. "Suggest you notify Colonel Jenkins immediately."

"Copy that, *Elvira*," Styles acknowledged. "I'm sending Second Platoon out to replace 4th Platoon in the patrol. ETA: seventy-one minutes."

"Roger, Headquarters," she replied. "Holding position here."

Twenty minutes later, the final tally was in: all three of *Cave Troll*'s crew were dead, killed by crab-cakes that had somehow penetrated the cabin before the Purgatory struck. But the mech was largely intact, and with a new crew could probably be put back in service in a day or two.

Masamune's crew had all survived, but their mech would need more extensive repairs than *Cave Troll*. Still, given enough time, Lieutenant Koch assured Xi that it would be back on its feet within the week.

As Xi moved *Elvira* back to the barn, her crew prepared to tear apart every single system related to her targeting controls. Something was affecting them at the most inopportune moments, and she intended to find out what it was before it cost any more of her people their lives.

Cave Troll's death was a direct result of those targeting systems failing in the middle of combat. She was responsible for not taking more severe action after the SRM misses during the first bug engagement, and now three good warriors were dead due to her failure.

It wouldn't happen again.

10

JEMMIN ASSAULT

"Orbital strikes inbound!" Styles called out a few minutes after Jenkins had donned his uniform and entered *Roy*'s command center.

"All crews to their stations. Active sensors to maximum. Prepare to receive Jemmin missiles," Jenkins barked, perhaps unnecessarily as it seemed Styles had already coordinated as much. "Where are they hitting?"

"Four of our six APCs are down, sir," Styles reported tightly as he pored over the sensor logs. "Two were shuttling troopers back to the mines, and the others were on standby."

Jenkins quickly checked to find that the hospital APC was not among the targeted vehicles. Yet.

"Incoming missiles," Styles called out in a raised voice.

"All mechs, engage anti-missile countermeasures at will," Jenkins ordered, knowing that he would pour at least four times as much counterfire by giving the individual mechs their heads, but he also knew after talking with Xi and examining the evidence that the Jemmin had seemingly caused all manner of problems with various systems throughout the battalion.

Better to waste a little ammo than let missiles through.

"At will, aye," Styles acknowledged as *Roy*'s own anti-missile rockets tore from their mounts and soared into the sky to meet the enemy ordnance. "Missiles engaged...twenty-five scrubs...thirty-four...forty-two..."

Roy was rocked by an impact so powerful that it nearly launched Jenkins into the far bulkhead.

"*Preacher*," Jenkins snapped, "prepare to return fire on all priority Jemmin targets."

"Priority targets, aye," *Preacher* acknowledged.

"All crews," Jenkins continued, "this is the Colonel. Execute fire package Hades. I say again, fire package Hades is authorized."

Explosions erupted throughout HQ as fifteen out of two hundred Jemmin missiles slipped through the missile shield. Most of the missiles were near-misses, but a handful hit their targets with devastating effect.

Holy Diver was struck twice, knocking all four of its railguns off the board as its status changed to critically-damaged. The downed *Cave Troll* was struck once, but its robust armor protected it from being taken out of commission. *Hawkeye* and *White Snake* were destroyed outright by precise missiles strikes, and even *Kochtopussy* suffered a near-miss that blew two of the relatively unarmored legs clear off its chassis. Dozens of troopers were killed in five separate nests built around anti-missile rockets and micro-railguns.

Then, with a degree of precision and timing that would make any commander proud, Jenkins' people executed fire package Hades in four seconds from start to finish.

Five hundred SRMs and MRMs flew from their mounts, and artillery cannons spat fifty shells of depleted uranium fury. The missiles streaked outward in nearly all directions, and the artillery screamed through the thin air of Shiva's Wrath, as Jenkins' people showed the Jemmin how humanity replied to her enemies. There was enough conventional ordnance in fire package Hades to destroy a mid-sized warship or to completely devastate all but the biggest Terran metropolis. That combined firepower was the most destructive fire order of Lieutenant Colonel Jenkins' career.

But the beating heart of fire package Hades were *Preacher's* four tactical nuclear devices, which were aimed at the four most likely Jemmin stronghold locations. In addition to the nukes were four Purgatory-class air-bursters, which would illuminate secondary points of interest that might be hiding the stealthy Jemmin vehicles. The Purgatories would, at the very least, shred the camo-skins from any Jemmin vehicles and make them much easier to target with conventional weaponry.

The Terran anti-missile shield continued to pour fire into the sky, sniping ninety-five percent of the inbound Jemmin missiles as their human counterparts tore through the frigid air toward their targets. For a moment it seemed as though the Terran missiles would reach their targets unmolested, as enemy counterfire failed to intercept at the optimal point of those projectiles' flights.

But then, with chilling precision, laser beams erupted from two of the most-likely Jemmin base-camps, sniping nearly every single missile bound for them. Luckily, the Purgatory and nuclear missiles were more heavily-armored, and one of each pierced the Jemmin missile shields.

The Purgatory blossomed, its flames rolling outward with terrifying speed until the blast zone was briefly transformed into the gaping maw of Hell. Steam exploded outward, propagating the blast wave even faster than would normally be possible in such a thin atmosphere. The fireball managed to stay ahead of the steam cloud while seemingly gathering strength from it. Three distinct Jemmin vehicles were outlined by the blast-wave, their camo-skins stripped away by the raging inferno, and Jenkins' mech crews immediately bracketed and eliminated the exposed hostiles with combined artillery and railgun strikes.

The tactical nuke was, predictably, even more devastating. Flaring with the luminosity of a short-lived star, the light-wash forced every sensor system in the battalion to self-protectively deactivate for two seconds. When they resumed operation, it was clear that at least two more Jemmin vehicles had been scrubbed by the one-hundred-fifty-five kiloton device.

Another dozen confirmed Jemmin kills flashed across Jenkins' board, bringing the confirmed kill total to seventeen. Unfortunately, he had no way of knowing what class each of those vehicle kills had been, which meant he didn't know how much damage he had actually dealt to the enemy.

Roy lurched from left-to-right as impact alarms rang out through the cabin.

"Railgun strike," Styles reported urgently. "Point-of-origin... bearing two-one-niner, azimuth...forty-three degrees. Distance: eight kilometers."

"*Devil Crab* 2," Jenkins commanded the battalion's second Scorpion-class mech, "scrub that bird."

"Engaging," *Devil Crab*'s Jock declared, and surface-to-air rockets streaked up into the sky in pursuit of the flying vehicle. Another railgun strike hit a nearby mech, the *Fistandantalus*, and blew one of its four legs off at the mid-joint.

"*Widowmaker*," Jenkins called with forced calm, "return fire on second bogey with your railguns."

"Railguns hot," *Widowmaker* acknowledged before sending a pair of tungsten bolts into the sky in the opposite direction of the first airborne target. "Target neutralized," *Widowmaker* reported with satisfaction as an intense explosion marked the Jemmin flyer's end.

Devil Crab 2's rockets failed to hit the mark, causing its Jock to report, "Negative impact on target, *Roy*. Oh-for-eight."

"Seismics!" yelled Styles. "Emergence points throughout the camp!"

The tactical plotter filled with two dozen unique signatures as Jemmin vehicles emerged from the ice. They immediately opened fire with rockets and railguns, causing HQ to erupt into total chaos.

"All vehicles, maintain missile shield and engage local targets," Jenkins commanded as Chaps put *Roy*'s coilguns on target and smoked a Jemmin vehicle that looked identical to the one whose hull fragments had been examined by Koch. He was pleased with the tweaks to their sensors that allowed the system to gain lock on stealthed technology. It was small, less than four meters long and a quarter as wide, but bore both rockets and railguns that it used to destroy a nearby infantry nest before Chaps tore it apart with coilgun fire.

The roar of rotary chain guns filled the camp as guns cycled at maximum speed. Twenty Jemmin targets were whittled down to ten in a matter of seconds, but then more Jemmin vehicles emerged from the tunnels and soon more than fifty of the teardrop-shaped, hovering platforms filled the camp.

Roy's coilguns killed another, and another, but a trio of railgun strikes tore into the command vehicle's right flank. Myriad system failure alarms went off as Jenkins' mechs moved into mutually-reinforcing positions from which to fight off the invaders.

Roy tilted dangerously to the right and Chaps yelled, "I've got failures on Two and Four Legs. Fix them or we're sitting ducks!"

The Jemmin seemed to have correctly identified the command vehicle's importance, and soon four more railguns stabbed into *Roy*'s left flank and stern. Rockets tore into its already-exposed flanks, causing even more alarms to go off.

"All guns, this is the colonel," Jenkins declared over the

battalion-wide P2P net, "calling in strikes on *all* enemy targets inside HQ perimeter. Fire! Fire! Fire!"

Coilguns whirred and chain guns roared, but their accuracy began to plummet as the enemy circled their primary targets and ruthlessly set about the task of eliminating them.

Then Jenkins' people answered his call, and the Terran base camp's former chaos gave way to apocalypse.

Dozens of artillery shells slammed into the ice, tearing five-meter-deep craters out of the formerly-pristine surface. SRMs struck the ice near enemy vehicles, with even near-misses knocking Jemmin fighters to the ground. A dozen Jemmin vehicles, half of which had previously fired on *Roy*, were scrubbed from the board and another dozen fell in the ensuing seconds as they tried and failed to resume their jerky, evasive maneuvering before being bracketed by Terran guns.

Somewhat alarmingly, the few Terran infantrymen who survived the initial attack proved to be the most effective at countering the Jemmin vehicles. RPGs were more than eighty percent accurate, with each one destroying a Jemmin fighter as the Terran infantry turned their weapons on HQ's interior. Crew-served machine guns spat depleted uranium slugs at Jemmin fighters, and even those relatively light weapons were able to do enough damage to turn the tide of battle against the alien vehicles when they slowed their erratic, evasive movements enough for the mechs' larger guns to sweep through and finish them off.

Slowly, but surely, the Terran forces began to push the Jemmin incursion back. *Roy*'s damaged drive systems were temporarily repaired, and the command vehicle waded toward the heaviest concentration of enemy with coilguns spewing high-velocity pellets at anything that moved.

Enemy rockets and railguns returned fire, skewering the more lightly-armored mechs at *Roy*'s back and knocking several out of the fight. *Wolverine* collapsed with its hip badly damaged by railguns, and *White Zombie* fell to concentrated rocket fire on its left foot that rendered it immobile and sent it to the deck. But even with those recent casualties, the Jemmin push had been halted. Now it was only a matter of time before the Terran armor ground them to dust.

Which was why Jenkins was anything but surprised when the Jemmin turned and fled down their holes. He didn't need to give the order to intensify fire on the fleeing fighters, but he did feel it necessary to remind Styles, "Expect another wave of missiles, Chief."

"All units acknowledge ready to intercept," Styles replied promptly.

"Return fire on all missile points-of-origin as they appear," Jenkins commanded as the last Jemmin disappeared beneath the ice. "I'm authorizing use of our remaining Purgatories on high-confidence targets."

"*Preacher* acknowledges weapons hot on three remaining Purgatories," Styles reported.

Sure enough, two seconds after the last Jemmin vanished, the tactical board lit up with a hundred and fifty-six inbound missile signatures. Jenkins' people returned fire with deadly precision, targeting each of the seven points of origin with artillery and missile strikes while their anti-missile systems reached out to scrape the sky clear of inbound ordnance.

Preacher sent a Purgatory missile streaking off at a target as soon as it was visually-confirmed by one of the roving Owl drones. Another went off in the opposite direction even before *Roy*'s board confirmed the target's location. The second was soon followed by the third, and last, Purgatory missile in Jenkins' arsenal.

All three of the incendiary devices were intercepted by last-second laser fire, but only one of them was destroyed outright while the other two slammed home on their targets.

Raging domes of fire erupted, and each of those hellish fire-balls revealed what appeared to be a Jemmin Specter-class platform.

Elvira, out on patrol to the west, was the first to engage an exposed Specter with her fifteens. HE shells exploded, one a near-miss and the other a direct hit on the Jemmin vehicle. Exploding in a primally-satisfying shower of ceramic debris, the briefly-exposed Jemmin Specter was annihilated by *Elvira's* textbook-precise fire.

The second Specter was likewise taken down by artillery fire from *Generally* on patrol to the south, and soon the guns fell silent as the Jemmin disengaged completely.

For the moment.

"Get General Akinouye on the horn," Jenkins commanded.

Styles made to obey but soon reported with a look of unmasked concern. "Colonel...the *Bonhoeffer's* currently engaged with the Jemmin warship in low orbit."

Jenkins set his jaw before barking, "Have the *Sam Kolt* acquire target lock and order *Preacher* to prep her last two nukes for low-orbital fire solution. Now!"

"Get those racks back to the magazines," Podsy shouted as the *Bonhoeffer* lurched beneath his forklift. "If that ordnance goes, it'll blow half the deck!"

"It's too late for that!" Chief Rimmer shouted as grease-monkeys worked frantically to secure the pallets and racks of munitions which, just a few minutes earlier, had been staged for loading into the next wave of drop-cans. "Shove all this loose ordnance into Can Three and load it in the tube!"

Podsy nodded, knowing it was probably the right call even though it wasn't the one he would have made. He rolled over to a rack of eight mid-range missiles, picked it up, and drove toward Can Three while others worked to secure the already-loaded supplies. "Forget about the perishables." Podsy waved off a pair of crewmen working to secure pallets of foodstuffs. "Our people aren't getting this can!"

Looks of comprehension came over their faces, and they backed carefully away as Podsy drove the fully-loaded rack of missiles toward the open back.

The *Bonhoeffer* lurched again, nearly causing the rack of missiles to slip off the front of the lift's forks, but Podsy managed to keep it from falling by dropping it to the deck and letting it self-right. Breathing a sigh of relief at avoiding catastrophe, he was just about to call out for help when one of the grease-monkeys from Second Shift ran past the forklift and gestured hurriedly for Podsy to slide the rack into place.

Podsy did so, and the crewman locked the rack down with the quartet of manual clamps before hopping onto the forks and riding the lift back out.

"Good work," Podsy congratulated as another forklift ran past him bearing four of the extremely valuable Purgatory LRMs. He wanted to tell the lift's driver not to throw them in the can since Can Three was about to be sent into the void—hopefully to be retrieved at some later date—but he knew that securing the drop-deck was more important than salvaging half of their remaining Purgatory supply.

"Go! Go! Go!" he urged as the lift driver slowed, apparently sensing Podsy's reticence. The driver sped off for the can, into which he and his lift's attached grease-monkey moved to load the Purgatory missiles.

Soon the can was filled, and the rest of the deck had been likewise cleared of live ordnance.

"All right," Rimmer barked, clapping his hands emphatically, "everyone off the deck. Move! Move! Mov—"

His words were cut short when a deafening roar filled the deck. A bright-red beam of light stabbed through the outer hull, tearing into two nearly-empty cans. Four crewmen locking those down were incinerated, and the beam carved deep into the heavily-armored secondary hull that protected the *Dietrich Bonhoeffer's* keel: the innermost segment of the ship which contained fuel stores, reactors, drive systems, and main processors.

The powerful beam cut through two full meters of armor but failed to pierce the rest as the *Bonhoeffer* rolled its damaged flank away.

And when the beam disappeared, the air in the drop-deck began to roar out through the five-meter-long rent in the outer hull.

Podsy's earpiece was barely able to convey Rimmer's voice over the howling gases as they vented into space. "Everyone to the control room!" the deck chief yelled, but thankfully none of the crew needed to be told. Podsy drove his forklift over to the windowed control room's main door, reaching it before half of his crew. He unbelted himself as the roar of escaping air steadily began to die down in its intensity, which meant that the breathable gases were nearly gone from the compartment.

He tried to lunge for the door but fell after failing to achieve a firm grip on the forklift's doorjamb. His head struck the deck, and all he could see were stars until he dimly became aware that he could no longer hear the roaring gases. *This is it*, he thought sourly. *Dying of asphyxiation on a drop-deck...not the blaze of glory I hoped for...*

He reached out, hoping to find something to grip and use to haul himself toward the door. But instead of a workbench leg or even the forklift's tire, all his hands managed to grasp were soft, round bags of some kind.

Lubricant pouches? he wondered, not remembering seeing any of those on the *Bonhoeffer*'s drop-deck.

It took him several more seconds to realize he was already inside the control room, and that the "lubricant pouches" were, in fact, the mammary glands of the same grease-monkey who had locked down the missiles in Can Three.

She looked down at him with something between annoyance and amusement as she said, "I'm glad you're all right, but you won't be if you don't get your mitts off me."

He hastily withdrew his hands and cracked a weak grin. "Sorry...but if it's any consolation, you're not my type."

"So I've heard," she grunted, and Podsy felt a firm hand grip his shoulder.

He looked up to see Chief Rimmer looking down at him approvingly.

"How many did we lose?" Podsy asked.

"Eight," Rimmer replied grimly, and through the control room's main window, Podsy saw a flash of light from the void beyond the gash in the hull.

He blinked hard enough to clear the cobwebs and re-focused on the hole just in time to see the sleek, curved hull of the Jemmin warship erupt in a series of rapid explosions that swept it from stem to stern. The *Bonhoeffer* was laying into the damaged enemy with missile after missile, tearing massive wounds in the advanced warship's hull.

After at least forty distinct impacts, those relatively minor explosions were dwarfed by a blinding flash of light that caused everyone in the control room to reflexively shield their eyes. When they turned their attention back to the hole, the *Bonhoeffer* had rolled to an orientation that would not permit them to see the Jemmin warship.

But if Podsy knew anything about anything, the Jemmin warship had either gone reactor-critical or been struck by a nuke.

Either way, it was off the board. Permanently.

"Thanks for the assist, Colonel," General Akinouye greeted after the Jemmin warship had been destroyed, finished by the last of *Preacher*'s nukes. "We couldn't get any of our fusion torpedoes out of their launchers."

"How's the *Bonhoeffer*, General?" Jenkins asked intently.

"Our forward armor is down to twenty percent, and we took severe damage to our main propulsion, port drop-deck, and power systems," Akinouye replied. "We're maintaining support posture, but I'm going to be frank. If the Jemmin return with even one more warship like that one, we'll have no choice but to withdraw. I'm of a mind to scrub this mission right now, Colonel."

"I advise against that, General," Jenkins said firmly. "I think we're on to something big down here, and it's obvious that the Jemmin don't want us to find out what it is. And without that Jemmin warship up there, we should be able to coordinate between the *Bonhoeffer*'s sensors and our surface-based systems to locate and neutralize the Jemmin in future engagements. In my opinion, we've come too far to pull out now, General."

Akinouye leaned toward the pickup, causing his image to loom on the display, "Colonel Jenkins, we've already crossed several lines I hadn't thought we would come within sight of, let alone brush up against. I appreciate your enthusiasm, but this situation is nearly out of control. This might be our last opportunity to prevent it from devolving into outright chaos, and I don't think I need to remind you of the consequences for the entire

Terran Republic if the entirety of the Metal Legion is destroyed."

"I understand, General," Jenkins said with conviction, "but we've got a theory we're working on down here, and if we're right about it, then we absolutely cannot withdraw from Shiva's Wrath until we've seen this mission through."

"A theory?" Akinouye repeated with mild disapproval. "Why is this the first I'm hearing about it?"

"We didn't have enough supporting evidence to present it, General," Jenkins replied guardedly before adding, "and we couldn't jeopardize sensitive, mission-critical information security."

Akinouye nodded slowly as he seemed to take Jenkins' meaning. "All right, Colonel," he said, seeming to arrive at a conclusion, "I'll oversee repairs up here until we've got the other drop-deck up and running. When that's complete, I expect you to deliver a personal debriefing on this 'theory' of yours."

Jenkins cocked his head in concern. "General...are you ordering me to return to the *Bonhoeffer* in the midst of deployment in an active combat zone?"

Akinouye smirked, and even at his venerable age, the expression was every bit as savage and primally-disconcerting as it had likely been a century earlier in the general's life, "No, Colonel Jenkins, I'm not bringing *you* up *here*."

At that, the line went dead, and Jenkins leaned back in surprise.

"Did I hear that right?" Styles asked under his breath.

"I think you did." Jenkins nodded seriously, gesturing to the privacy of his cabin. "You'd better prepare a top-sheet."

"On it, sir." Styles nodded, standing from his station and making for Jenkins' private cabin at the rear of *Roy*'s compartment.

"Captain Xi," Sarah Samuels insisted, "the people have a right to know."

"Right now, you know as much as I do, Ms. Samuels," Xi replied irritably.

"You won't give me a straight answer," Samuels snapped, her usual veneer of total control melting away in the aftermath of the devastating attack. "I just lost my uplink with the *Bonhoeffer*. Is it still in orbit or did the Jemmin destroy it?"

"Wait." Xi rounded on the reporter. "*You* have a direct link with the *Bonhoeffer*? Do you have any idea how many regs you violated by not informing me about that?"

"My data-stream's integrity is protected by the most fundamental laws of the Terran Republic's Founding Articles," Samuels retorted. "Don't change the subject, Captain Xi. Is the *Bonhoeffer* still in orbit or did the Jemmin destroy it?"

"Honestly?" Xi did her best to control her temper, which she suspected would soon tear loose of its moorings no matter how hard she tried to lock it down. "I don't know the answer to that."

"My drones picked up multiple EMPs indicative of Terran nuclear warhead detonations," Samuels continued. "Under the Terran Military Doctrine, tactical nuclear devices are *only* authorized for deployment in wartime, Captain Xi..."

"I think you need to sit down, Ms. Samuels," Blinky said, taking the reporter by the arm and trying to gently drag her from Xi's cockpit.

"Get your hands off me!" Samuels snapped, rounding on *Elvira*'s Monkey before returning her focus to Xi. "Terran humanity has a right to know, Captain Xi. Is the Terran Republic now officially at war with the Jemmin—or with the entire Illumination League?"

"First off," Xi said steadily, clenching her fists so hard that her nails dug into her palms, "tactical nukes are only authorized for deployment on *inhabited* worlds during wartime. Those restrictions don't apply to uninhabited worlds like Shiva's Wrath."

"You're evading my question," Samuels retorted, her professional veneer reasserting itself with each passing second. "Is the Terran Republic at war with the Jemmin?"

Xi thought about playing word games or invoking operational security as was technically her right during combat conditions. But for reasons she could not immediately identify, she declined the chance to dance around the question and instead answered as honestly as she could.

"How in the holy fuck would a mech driver know something like that? You know more of what's going on outside this tub than I do, so why don't you ask one of them. Do you want to know all that I know, Ms. Samuels?" she asked.

"Yes," the blond woman snarled, her eyes lighting up in anticipation.

Xi shook her head darkly. "Then here's the truth: I don't know. All I know is they openly antagonized us without cause, and we didn't return the favor. Then when they shot at us, we defended ourselves like we've been trained and authorized to do, but we didn't chase them down to retaliate. Then they fired from orbit on a position danger-close to my unit, and again we declined to escalate the situation since no damage was done. And just now, they opened fire on our APCs from orbit, killing at least a hundred Terrans before launching a multi-pronged attack on our HQ," she growled, thumping her fist against the arm of her pilot's chair. "You're Goddamned right we fired back with everything we had! But are we at war? Officially?" She snorted in derision. "That's a question for the politicians, Ms. Samuels. My job is to locate and engage threats to Terran sovereignty...and that's *exactly* what I intend to do for as long as I live."

The reporter seemed genuinely conflicted. It was clear that Xi had not given her the sound-bite she wanted, but it was also clear that she was far from disappointed by what Xi had given her.

"Now..." Xi gestured to Blinky. "Private Staubach will escort you back to your station. I suggest you comply with his direction because I can assure you *mine* will be nowhere near as gentle if you make me unplug from this chair."

Samuels' mask of professional detachment once again covered her face, and she wordlessly exited the cockpit with Blinky at her back.

After she had gone, her question rang in Xi's ears like the aftermath of a fifteen-kilo gun's report:

Are we at war with the Jemmin?

11

AFTERMATH

"Here's what I've got, Colonel," Styles reported after Jenkins closed the door to his private cabin two hours after the Jemmin assault on Terran headquarters. "Using the *Bonhoeffer*'s sensor logs—" He handed Jenkins a data slate. "—the Jemmin completed their deep dive to the Vorr transceiver's location, and that three minutes after they reached the site, they opened fire on us from orbit."

"But those fighter platforms didn't tunnel under the ice instantaneously," Jenkins grunted.

"They'd been prepping this attack for days," Styles agreed.

"Why didn't any of our thermals or seismics detect them?"

"That, I can't tell you," Styles said with open frustration. "There is no way they should have been able to tunnel that many times, that close to us, without our seismic scanners going off. Xi and I have been working on a theory, and you're not going to like it."

"Let's hear it." Jenkins sat down in the chair opposite Styles.

"We think they've corrupted every single sensor and targeting system in the battalion," the technician explained. "We also think that we prevented them from a complete takeover of our information-processing systems by disconnecting every RF transceiver in the unit. Our guess is that their remote takeover has to occur in stages, either to prevent it from being detected or because it simply takes a certain amount of time for each takeover to complete."

Jenkins' hackles rose as he realized that, as usual, Styles was right: he did *not* like that theory.

"We've run diagnostics on every piece of gear *multiple* times since we've had targeting issues," Jenkins observed. "They've all come back green."

"We think the first stage of this takeover is to re-write the diagnostics, so they're blind to the effects of later stage modifications," Styles explained. "I've looked as hard as I can, using every trick I know, but I still can't see where they re-wrote our code. I've got the base firmware settings for every piece of hardware in the battalion stored on hard, unmodifiable systems up on the *Bonhoeffer*," he explained. "I've already compared *Roy*'s systems to those on the hard copy and can't find anything wrong, which means the problem is beyond my ability to see."

"Recommendation?" Jenkins asked grimly.

Styles sighed in frustration. "A total reboot of every sensor and targeting system in the battalion, which means each mech needs to have its main computer rebooted as well."

"That could take two hours per mech—" Jenkins shook his head adamantly. "—and would return all custom neural link settings to default. It would take our pilots *days* of constant practice and *tens of thousands* of rounds of ammo to dial-in combat-ready settings."

"It's what I've come up with, sir," Styles said heavily. "We could switch everyone over to manual inputs and rotate the reboots through a modified off-duty schedule?"

Jenkins shook his head. "Including Xi and Chaps, there are only five or six pilots in the battalion who could operate near-peak effectiveness on manual controls, and maybe that many more who would clear combat-readiness tests across the board. We simply haven't had enough time to train everyone on their rigs."

"It's what I've come up with, sir," Styles repeated, a rare helpless note entering his voice.

"All right." Jenkins decided to change subjects. "What about the deep dive? Have we got any idea what they found down there?"

"Not yet." Styles shook his head. "But using the *Bonhoeffer's* sensors, I've been able to locate several half-kilometer spheres of liquid water a kilometer or so below the surface. There are five of them, and they appear to have been Vorr staging areas of some kind, but the Jemmin have overtaken these sites. I can't get a clear look at what the Vorr were keeping there."

"The Vorr are aquatic," Jenkins mused. "They might have been storing perishables or something there."

"That would hold," Styles agreed. "I just can't confirm or refute that theory since I can't get a good picture of what's there. There are bits and pieces of Vorr machinery, but again, it's too deep to get accurate information of what, exactly, that machinery does."

"All right, forget about the pools," Jenkins decided. "Focus on the attack. Why assault us mere minutes after reaching the Vorr transceiver?"

"That's complicated." Styles sighed. "Either they found what they were looking for and decided to eliminate us, which doesn't seem logical..."

"Agreed." Jenkins nodded urgently.

"Or," Styles continued, "they didn't find what they were looking for and decided that the risk of us having it was too great to ignore—and that, if we did have it, erasing us and it while risking an interstellar conflict was preferable to letting whatever it was get out in the open."

"Your theory's looking better," Jenkins mused. "It seems like whatever the Vorr came here to retrieve is something the Jemmin can't risk letting us see, or heaven forbid, remove from this rock."

"I agree." Styles nodded. "But I still don't have any evidence. It's all speculation at this point."

"It's the best we've got to go on." Jenkins shrugged. "Never let perfect be the enemy of good."

Styles snickered. "I'm not *sure* that saying applies here."

"I think it does," Jenkins said matter-of-factly. "Information is just one variable in conflict resolution. It's an important one, but anyone who thinks the best way through a difficult situation is always to have the maximum possible amount of information doesn't understand the way this universe works. Indecision kills a group faster than any enemy could. In a choice between risking paralysis from lack of information, or risking failure because of ill-informed action, I'll take an unproven working theory that keeps things rolling every time."

"More is lost to indecision than wrong decision?" Styles cocked his head skeptically.

"Definitely."

Styles seemed comforted by that, which was Jenkins' primary objective. "All right, then I'll keep scouring for evidence," Styles declared with seemingly renewed energy.

"And see if you can come up with an alternative to mass-reboots of our mechs," Jenkins added after the other man had made for the hatch. "If you can't come up with anything in the next sixteen hours, I'll need to make a decision on that front."

"Yes, sir," Styles acknowledged.

A few minutes later, Jenkins' wrist-link chimed. "Jenkins, go."

"Colonel," came the voice of the comm stander temporarily taking over for Styles, "I just received a coded message on White Band."

"Put it through," Jenkins ordered, and the encrypted file appeared on his link. A quick series of inputs decoded the file's contents, which were comprised of just two words:

Havoc Inbound.

Jenkins immediately connected with Captain Xi. "*Elvira*, do you copy?"

"*Elvira* here," acknowledged Xi.

"We have a delivery en route bearing mission-critical supplies," he half-lied. "Proceed to the following rendezvous coordinates and await further instructions."

There was a brief but pointed delay. "Copy that, Colonel. Who should I take as escort?"

"No escort, Captain," Jenkins replied firmly, knowing that Xi had yet to formally re-structure her battered company following its repeated encounters with the bugs. Three other platoons had engaged with the bugs since their first appearance, with each suffering serious damage, but only Xi had encountered the bizarre aliens more than once. "Take *Elvira* out there, and I'll ensure you're covered in-transit."

"Yes, sir," she said, making clear she disliked the idea of running out on the ice field alone and exposed. But while Havoc was inbound, he knew that its LZ was the safest place to be on Shiva's Wrath.

Elvira was less than three kilometers from the rendezvous point, but nothing was showing up on the scanners. "No escort," Xi muttered irritably. "If this is some kind of game, Colonel..."

She temporarily stopped herself from finishing that particular thought, and a moment before she was about to finish it with gusto, a flicker appeared on the edge of her neural-linked "vision."

"Finally," she grunted, "a drop-can..."

She trailed off as she realized what she saw was not, in fact, a drop-can. It was coming in on an aggressive approach vector and was too small to be a can. Then another icon appeared, followed by another, and another, until ten of the things registered at an altitude of thirty thousand meters.

"What the..." She finally realized what she was seeing. "Aerospace fighters?"

The *Dietrich Bonhoeffer* was outfitted with sixty void fighters and twenty aerospace fighters. The void fighters were only capable of maneuvering in space, but the aerospacers were able to come all the way down to the surface if atmospheric pressure wasn't greater than three standard units.

The fighters, flying an offset diamond formation, were soon joined by an eleventh icon, which approached at an angle far more aggressive than any drop-pod could survive.

Her eyes went wide when she realized what was inbound.

"*Bahamut Zero*..." she whispered, feeling goosebumps rise all across her body.

Tearing through the atmosphere of Shiva's Wrath, flanked by ten decelerating aerospace fighters, was the most terrifying vehicle ever deployed by the Terran Armor Corps. Angry orange flames poured off its hull as *Bahamut Zero* plunged through the worldlet's frigid atmosphere.

The massive vehicle was so large it would have taken a specially-designed drop-can twelve times the size of the one that *Elvira* rode down. Deploying such an enormous can would have required a special launch tube to be installed on the *Dietrich Bonhoeffer*, so *Bahamut Zero* was specifically designed as one of the few active-duty Armor Corps vehicles that did not require such a system to safely make planetfall.

Designed as a would-be revolutionary armor platform, *Bahamut Zero* was a prototype that had eventually been abandoned due to the outrageously high costs of deploying it. Featuring both track-based locomotive systems as well as an eight-legged hybrid walker-roller system similar to *Roy*, the vehicle cut the distinctive image of a multi-legged beast conjured from the darkest nightmares humanity could endure.

The aerospace fighters broke their diamond formation as *Bahamut Zero* reached the forty-thousand-foot mark. Two of the fighters broke for the deck, diving like pelicans while two more pairs swept left and right.

Elvira's sensors lit up with Jemmin missile blooms just eighteen kilometers from her current position. Using her newly-installed SRMs, she locked onto the Jemmin weapons and engaged with anti-missile rockets. Her rockets tore upward, but the Jemmin missiles were moving nearly as fast as her anti-missile rockets.

"Dammit," she grunted, loading extended-range HE shells into her fifteens and targeting her guns on the missiles' point-of-origin. "ER-HEs up! On the way!"

Elvira's guns cleared with a deafening roar, sending the twin extended-range shells toward the enemy position. She didn't expect to hit the target directly, so she had spread her strike-points far enough that she might hit the stealthy vehicle with enough shrapnel to outline its position.

The shells whistled through the air, taking a ponderous arc before striking exactly where she had aimed them. She felt a thrill course through her as a glimmer of sensor contact flickered into position at the furthest edge of the HE shells' blast zone.

Before she could even think to coordinate with the incoming fighters, a pair of railgun bolts skewered the Jemmin vehicle. Its power core containment failed, and the vehicle exploded in a brilliant dome of light that left nothing but a steaming crater of ice.

Bahamut Zero hurtled toward the ground, passing the fifteen-thousand-foot mark where its braking thrusters engaged. Giant wings unfurled along its sides, and a maneuvering tail unfolded at the vehicle's rear as the mighty war machine took control over its descent to the surface of Shiva's Wrath.

Xi watched with unvarnished awe, giggling with excitement as *Bahamut Zero*'s deployment chassis came down to seven hundred meters, stabilized its speed for two seconds, and dropped the peerless vehicle. The unburdened deployment frame pulled up, its condor-like wings sweeping back as rocket engines engaged and drove the now-hollow aerospacecraft up toward the heavens from which it had come.

A combination of parachutes and braking thrusters delivered *Bahamut Zero* safely to the icy surface, where it landed with an authoritative crack less than a kilometer from *Elvira*'s present position.

The battlefield behemoth immediately began to tear across the open ice-field, accelerating to a speed fully twice *Elvira*'s maximum in just six seconds. As it reached peak speed, Xi saw an inbound P2P connection request appear on her HUD.

She accepted the request and fought to steady her voice amid the excitement of the moment. "*Elvira* here, over."

"This is *Bahamut Zero* with a message for all Armor Corps units on Shiva's Wrath," came the unmistakable, commanding voice of General Akinouye. "Havoc is on deck and operational."

Seeing *Bahamut Zero* arrive at the battalion's new HQ was nothing short of breathtaking, even for Lee Jenkins. Displacing nearly five hundred tons, it bristled with more weaponry than a full company of mechs and had enough armor to stave off at least as many enemy platforms while it eliminated them with murderous precision.

Sixteen railguns in quad-mounts, four LRM launchers with four tubes apiece, four MRM launchers with six tubes apiece, twelve SRM launchers with eight tubes apiece, twenty-two coil-guns scattered across its hull, and four plasma cannons of the same design as *Cave Troll*'s comprised the arsenal of the Armor Corps' pride and joy.

Fielding *Bahamut Zero* was normally impractical due to the extensive costs associated with deploying and retrieving it. It took two heavy lifters, working in tandem, to pick the thing off a standard-gravity world and return it to the *Dietrich Bonhoeffer*. In fact, it had been sixteen years since *Bahamut Zero* last moved under its own power.

And that had been for a Founding Day parade.

All of which meant that, as shows of support went, the general had just given the most meaningful one that Colonel Jenkins could have hoped for. Akinouye's message upon arrival was never once uttered, yet nonetheless remained loud and clear to every Terran on Shiva's Wrath:

We're staying until the job's done.

Bahamut Zero rolled to a stop fifty meters from *Roy*'s position. In deference to the general's arrival, Jenkins had removed *Roy* from the central point of the HQ and ceded that territory to his superior officer as both protocol and professional courtesy demanded.

Unexpectedly, *Bahamut Zero* failed to assume the central position, opting instead for one even more removed than that which *Roy* occupied.

Elvira, following close behind *Bahamut Zero*, assumed her assigned slot in the parking lot just as *Bahamut Zero*'s main boarding ramp lowered and a company of Black Berets disembarked. Black Berets were the special guard units of the Terran Armor Corps, and against the icy white backdrop of Shiva's Wrath, their all-black uniforms seemed somehow more intimidating than usual.

And as far as Lee Jenkins was concerned, that was saying quite a lot.

He made his way toward the Black Berets' formation with Styles at his side. They came to a stop just outside the quickly-assembled honor guard and waited at attention for the go-ahead signal.

One of the Black Berets made no show of discretion as he ran a scanner over Jenkins and Styles from a safe distance, while his fellows steadily trained their weapons on the duo.

"Clean!" declared the scanner-wielder.

"Good," General Akinouye's voice boomed from the massive vehicle's speakers.

"Permission to come aboard, General?" Jenkins asked, as protocol dictated.

"Permission granted," Akinouye acknowledged.

They moved up the steep ramp and came to the mech's interior, where a young officer silently greeted them and gestured to the rear of the vehicle. Jenkins and Styles silently followed, turning a dozen times along the cramped passageway before arriving at an open door.

Beyond the door was a conference table that looked like something from a trillionaire's boardroom, and at the head of that table sat General Akinouye.

"Come in, Colonel," the longest-tenured member of the Terran Joint Chiefs gestured to a pair of unoccupied seats adjacent to his own. "Let's hear this theory of yours."

12

ASYMMETRY

"I never thought I'd see the *Zero* make planetfall," whistled Lieutenant Ford as the newly-formed six-mech patrol, led by Captain Xi, drew nearer to its teardrop-shaped route's apex. "It must have been something seeing her come down with your own eyes, Captain."

"I'm not going to lie, *Forktail*," she said, "I think I got wetter than you did, which I'm sure is a surprise to us both."

"Ha-ha," Ford deadpanned.

"Good work on the target reveal, Cap," came the newly-assigned Jock riding *Cave Troll*, a 2nd Lieutenant named Yuan. "You painted that Specter like Bob Ross conjuring a cloud."

"Like Havoc even needed the help," Ford chuckled. "The *Zero*'s so heavily-armored, I doubt *six* of those Jemmin bottle-rockets would have scratched the paint."

"Confidence to the point of cockiness is one thing, *Forktail*," Xi chided, "but there's nothing smart about getting hit in a fight, no matter how tough you are."

"Yeah, yeah." Ford sighed. "You're right as usual, Captain. But in the three days since the *Zero* arrived, the Jemmin haven't done so much as pop a recon drone above the deck. And with

Bahamut Zero enhancing the missile shield back at HQ, we've been able to boost these patrols to six mechs apiece. I doubt *anyone* comes messing with us now. They're probably hunkered down in their hidey-holes, waiting for a cloaked ship or something to come pick them up."

"A worthy enemy strikes when you least expect it," Xi replied irritably.

"*Elvira*'s right," agreed the Jock riding *Widowmaker*, the hundred-ton spider-shaped mech. "Forgetting *Bahamut Zero*, this patrol is the heaviest unit in the battalion, and we're near max-distance from HQ. If the Jemmin attack, it will be when we're stretched as thin as possible, which will be in the next ten minutes."

"Agreed," *White Zombie* confirmed. "*Eclipse*, are you reading anything out there?"

"Not yet," *Eclipse* replied tersely, "but I'd have better luck if y'all weren't nonstop jabbering in my ear."

"Copy that, *Eclipse*," Xi said. "Pipe down and keep your eyes peeled."

Two minutes later, *Eclipse* declared, "Contact bearing zero-seven-niner, range: eight kilometers."

A swarm of missiles bloomed from the indicated target point just as Xi put *Elvira*'s sensors on the area. Sure enough, a Jemmin Specter and at least three other, smaller vehicles appeared on the screen. About half of the Jemmin missiles were headed Xi's way, with the other half headed to HQ.

"Railguns, target inbound missiles and fire," Xi barked as she zeroed in on the enemy missiles with *Elvira*'s rockets. Of the thirty-nine missiles sent up by the Jemmin at that location, three were instantly scraped off the board by railguns while rockets downed another four. That left twelve missiles inbound on her patrol's location, and six of those weapons found their targets.

Elvira's rear-left leg was blown completely off by a direct hit that made her mech lurch so badly, Xi bit her tongue. With blood briefly spewing out of her mouth, she snarled and re-positioned her Scorpion-class mech to compensate for the lost leg.

Cave Troll was struck by a pair of missiles, with one impact blowing its left plasma cannon completely off and the other tearing a hole in its left flank. Fortunately, the thickly-built mech maintained its footing and sent a burst of SRMs at the enemy in reply.

The exact center of *Forktail's* long chassis was struck by a missile, which by all rights should have destroyed the mid-sized vehicle outright. But the design of *Forktail's* spinal armor was such that it distributed much of the explosion's energy to the side and away from the central section, so instead of being killed outright, the nimble mech merely lost its front-left leg and was rendered all but immobile.

"*Eclipse*, send a flare-burst to that position," she commanded, deciding to test a theory her company had come up with in the last few days.

"Flares on the way," *Eclipse* acknowledged, and a quartet of specially-modified anti-missile rockets sped off on a low trajectory toward the Jemmin location.

"Artillery solution plotted," Xi declared after taking precious seconds to confirm her onboard computer's firing solution. "Transmitting now. Fire! Fire! Fire!"

Elvira and *Widowmaker*, sporting a pair of fifteen-kilo guns apiece, sent HE shells downrange using Xi's hand-calculated solution. The shells burst in a near-perfect diamond pattern, showering the area with shrapnel and exposing two Jemmin vehicles. Unfortunately, neither was the heavy Specter.

"APs up," she declared, zeroing in on the now-visible targets. "On the way!"

She cleared her guns a quarter-second before *Widowmaker*, and both targets were destroyed in radiant displays that briefly illuminated the other two Jemmin vehicles. But just as quickly as they appeared, the enemy craft faded off-screen and out of view.

Eclipse's flare rockets, moving low and slow by design, reached the target and exploded directly over the briefly-illuminated vehicles' location shortly after the Jemmin disappeared. The entire area was showered in superheated metal fragments, which scattered like Founding Day fireworks over the town square. An oblong dome of ice was covered by the flare residue, and sure enough, *Eclipse*'s theory proved out as both Jemmin vehicles were revealed by the relatively crude devices.

"Good shot, *Eclipse*!" Xi congratulated as she loaded a pair of HE shells into her fifteens.

Elvira bucked as her guns cleared, sending explosive shells to the slow-moving Specter's location. *Widowmaker*'s guns cleared beside her just as the Specter flew apart in an eminently satisfying shower of glowing ceramic shards. The smaller vehicle was also scrubbed before it could repair its camouflage systems, and for a moment, Xi thought they had wiped out every enemy in the area.

Then the railguns struck from above.

Widowmaker, the only vehicle in the patrol larger than *Elvira*, was struck by four precisely-aimed tungsten bolts, which skewered it center-mass. One of those slivers of hyper-velocity tungsten pierced *Widowmaker*'s power core, which exploded with a force equivalent to three kilotons. The heaviest vehicle in the patrol had been destroyed before its crew even realized they'd been hit.

Only *Forktail* was close enough to be struck by destructive shrapnel from *Widowmaker*'s death throes, but its low profile kept it from anything but fist-sized shards of the dead mech's hull.

"Target lock," *Eclipse* declared, and Xi saw a fire solution appear on her HUD.

"Firing," she snarled in rage at having her patrol so badly hit by the enemy, with one mech destroyed outright. SRMs leapt out of their tubes with murderous intent, and the quartet of offending Jemmin aircraft were destroyed before they could evade the fast-moving missiles.

"All bogeys down, Captain," reported *Eclipse*. "Scanning local area."

"This is *Forktail*," Lieutenant Ford said anxiously. "Our fusion reactor containment is critical. Shutting it down and requesting pickup."

"Moving to your position, *Forktail*," Xi said urgently as she turned her mech and used its remaining five legs to walk as fast as possible to Ford's mech. As she did so, she checked on HQ's status and saw that they were still taking fire from enemy positions on the far side of the ice-field. Her weaponry would barely let her engage at those ranges against relatively stationary targets, so there was little point in worrying about lending fire support from here.

It looked like *Bahamut Zero* was making its presence known to both friend and foe alike. Icon after icon of enemy positions winked out while the platform delivered devastation to the Jemmin attackers.

But before she could pore over the combat logs, her board erupted in another burst of signals.

"Contacts," she instinctively called out as six distinct signatures erupted from the ice-field around her battered patrol. Where a few minutes earlier she'd had six mechs, now she was down to four, and just two of those were undamaged.

But instead of Jemmin signatures, it was bug vehicles crawling up from their ice tunnels.

"*Cave Troll.*" She smirked while pivoting *Elvira* to face the nearest insect vehicle. "Clear one of those."

"With pleasure," *Cave Troll* acknowledged, and soon the ice beneath *Elvira* began to vibrate. *Cave Troll*'s ultra-powerful, limited-range plasma cannon belched a gout of blue-white fire that annihilated the bug. But unlike previous kills from the dual cannons, this single shot left behind enough wreckage to positively identify what it had been.

White Zombie squared off on two of the insect-like vehicles. The metal plates over that humanoid mech's shoulder sections folded back to reveal a variety of SRM and MRM launchers, which fired four SRMs and two MRMs on each of the bugs. Xi approved of the enthusiasm, though the MRMs were probably a bit more than she would have touched off given the choice.

The left bug was hit by one MRM and two SRMs, which sent it skittering across the smooth ice-field. It came to a stop nearly eighty meters from its previous position. It reoriented itself head-on to *White Zombie*, and its "mouth" began to glow as its fellows' had done prior to firing plasma streams.

The right bug was missed by both MRMs, but the SRMs struck and blew the thing apart in a shower of gooey, metallic chitin. It was the first time Terran missiles had killed one of the things outright, and Xi felt no small measure of satisfaction watching the thing die.

But as she squared off against another bug, she noticed something curious: two of the six bugs were hanging back, relatively motionless, while the other two survivors pressed the attack with their plasma cannons.

"What are you waiting for?" she sneered, loading HE shells and locking onto the bug that *White Zombie* had sent skittering across the field. Raising *Elvira*'s stern to get a close-quarters firing angle, Xi's dual-fifteens thundered and delivered their shells into the already-wounded thing a quarter-second after it sent a stream of plasma at *White Zombie*.

The artillery shredded the bug's armor, with thirty-centimeter wide gaps appearing across its surface, and *Eclipse* added to the weight of fire with its twin chain guns. Two hundred rounds per second poured into the unprotected holes in its armor, and *Cave Troll* soon added its own coilguns to the mix and poured thousands of rounds into the thing before it shuddered, fell over, and died.

The two bugs that had been hanging back scurried down their holes, disappearing before Xi could react to their flight. "Dammit," she growled, but even as she spoke, the last remaining bug squared off against her.

Again, there was something about its posture which gave her pause, and she suddenly suspected the thing was trying to communicate something with its posture.

The ground beneath *Elvira*'s legs began to thrum, and it took her a fraction of a second too long to realize *Cave Troll* was prepping to fire.

"No, wait—" she began, only to be silenced when *Cave Troll*'s plasma cannon incinerated the last bug vehicle on the field.

"Repeat your last, *Elvira*?" *Cave Troll*'s Jock asked after the steam had dissipated, leaving nothing but the smoking ruin of the fourth bug vehicle behind.

Xi bit her tongue, knowing that to explain what she had meant to say would compromise the mission's secrecy. "Nothing, *Cave Troll*," she replied as lightly as possible. "I was just going to say that one was mine."

"I think you've notched more than your share of kills down here, Captain," *Cave Troll* chuckled.

"This is *Elvira*," she raised HQ, "requesting R&R at current position."

"R&R inbound, *Elvira*," acknowledged Styles. "ETA: fifty-three minutes. Will you need medevac?"

"Negative, HQ," she said firmly. "*Widowmaker* was lost with all hands, but the rest of us are alive and well. We'll be limping back to the barn."

"Copy that, *Elvira*," Styles acknowledged. "Good work out there."

In spite of the obvious fact that he was right, Xi couldn't help thinking that she had just made a catastrophic error by not stopping *Cave Troll* in time to investigate the bugs' strange behavior.

She could only hope she would get a chance to redeem herself. But first, she needed to figure out if she was jumping at shadows or if the bug had been attempting some form of communication.

13

COMMAND DECISIONS

"After the Jemmin Assault destroyed thirty percent of our radiation meds," Doc Fellows reported in the privacy of Jenkins' cabin, "we're down to just three days before the exposed men and women start suffering permanent radiation damage."

"We can't extract the infantry to the *Bonhoeffer*..." Jenkins shook his head bitterly. "Not with the Jemmin lurking out there."

Fellows' expression darkened. "Then unless you can neutralize their anti-aircraft capability, men and women are going to start dying within the week, Colonel. And when they do, it's not going to be pretty."

Styles leaned forward. "We're working on some theories for neutralizing the Jemmin, Doc."

"It's time to put them into action." Fellows snorted. "You don't want men and women dying on this rock from rad poisoning...and you don't want pictures of their deaths making their way back home," he added pointedly.

"Frankly, fuck the political fallout," Jenkins grunted, slicing a look over at the cramped room's lone silent occupant, Sergeant

Major Trapper Sr. "But you're right...something has to give down here. Soon. Is there anything else?"

"The mech crews should be able to stretch their deployments out to another ten or twelve days before they start suffering effects." Fellows nodded. "If you could somehow extract the infantry, you could stretch that timeline out to two or three months with our remaining supply of meds."

Jenkins was not about to put Trapper on the spot, but he needed some kind of input from his infantry commander. "Your thoughts?"

Trapper smirked, looking precisely like his son as he did so. "I'm just here to fight, Colonel."

"I know you don't outrank me, Sergeant Major," Jenkins retorted mildly. "Combined with the difference in our respective field experience, I have greatly appreciated your deference to this point when it comes to my command decisions. But right now, I need the best counsel available to me to make my next call, and that counsel includes the honest opinion of the most experienced soldier on this hunk of ice."

Trapper nodded in thought for a long while. "My boys and girls aren't plagued by the targeting problems your mechs have had. We only had a twenty percent miss rate when those Jemmin hover-fighters ambushed us from inside HQ," he finally said. "To remove the infantry, even though we're fatally wounded to a man, would be to abandon you and your clankers to an enemy that has the tactical upper hand." He shook his head with finality. "We knew what we signed up for when we came down here, and we're going to stand our posts until ordered to do otherwise. That's not some veiled plea for you to give me an out," he added, his eyes as hard as diamonds. "As long as Armor Corps shares this rock with hostiles, my troopers are staying put."

"I appreciate your stalwart support," Jenkins said with feeling.

"Besides..." Trapper's smirk turned mischievous. "We're not about to walk off the line in front of the brass."

Jenkins chuckled, recalling his brief but important meeting with General Akinouye. During that meeting, the general had made two things abundantly clear: Armor Corps was here until this situation was resolved, and he had no intention of assuming operational command. The first bit had been expected since their last conversation prior to *Bahamut Zero*'s arrival, but the second was a shock. How often did the longest-tenured officer in the armed forces abdicate operational command to a lieutenant colonel on his first official deployment under his branch's banner?

It was a hell of a recommendation, and Jenkins felt every pound of pressure that recommendation placed upon his shoulders.

"All right." Jenkins nodded approvingly. "Then for the time being, we're staying put." He turned to Styles. "But I want our best extraction packages presented for my review in twelve hours."

"You'll have them."

"Good. Thank you, Doctor." Jenkins nodded to Fellows, then stood to salute the older man. "Sergeant Major."

Trapper returned the salute, and the two departed the cabin.

"My simulation packages can't produce better than a sixty percent withdrawal success rate," Styles said grimly after they had gone.

"Which means that, with three heavy lifters aboard the *Bonhoeffer*," Jenkins grumbled, "the odds are we'll only get the troopers off this rock before the last of our lifters is shot down."

"Leaving us stranded unless or until the *Bonhoeffer* can go get fresh lifters." Styles nodded knowingly.

"During which time, the Jemmin will doubtless return and finish us off from orbit." Jenkins rubbed the bridge of his nose before moving his fingertips to the dark semicircles beneath his eyes. "The only reason they haven't already done so is because of the political fallout they'd suffer."

"It seems their control of the Illumination League is a lot more tenuous than most people believe," Styles observed. "Otherwise why not just drop a nuke on us from orbit and then claim we violated some obscure law, before offering the Republic a token of contrition?"

"They're afraid of something..." Jenkins agreed. "And whatever they hoped to find down here is part of it."

"It has to be evidence of something. But what?" Styles asked frustratedly.

"We don't have time to indulge in further speculation," Jenkins said, feeling his resolve strengthen now that he had a new clock to work under. "Let's see your latest idea on neutralizing the Jemmin."

"All right..." Styles hesitated before producing a data slate and sliding it across the table. "But you're not going to like it."

Stifling the urge to groan, Jenkins picked up the slate and began to examine its contents. A few minutes later, he muttered, "I'm starting to hate how often you're right."

"Lu, Staubach," Xi called after parking *Elvira* following their latest patrol and disconnecting the neural link, "to the cockpit."

Her mech's crew reported, with Staubach predictably arriving first in spite of having farther to come from the rearmost seat in the mech's cabin.

"Reporting, Captain," Staubach declared, bracing at attention.

"At ease," Xi said, resisting the urge to smile at his infectious enthusiasm while Lu made his leisurely way to the cockpit. "All right," she declared, "I think it's time to switch things up a bit. Chief Lu—" She turned to the middle-aged mechanic. "—you've done everything I've asked of you since joining my command."

"Thank you, Captain," he replied in his usual, flat fashion.

"Also," she continued neutrally, "Private Staubach has gone above and beyond on multiple occasions, including live-fire hull walks to expedite repairs."

Lu stiffened. "Captain, you can't order me to take those kinds of risks. The Uniform Code..."

"I'm well aware of the Code, Chief," she interrupted. "I'm also well aware that, as the ranking officer in this company, it is my prerogative to confirm duty posts and roster assignments. I think *Elvira* will function better in combat if we had you and Blinky switch posts for a deployment or two. I know you're capable of being my Wrench," she continued, ignoring the growing look of resentment on Lu's face, "but I want to see if Blinky is as well. With all the casualties and material damage the battalion has suffered on Shiva's Wrath, it's going to be critical going forward to examine who can and can't demonstrate flexibility under fire." She drew a short breath. "To be blunt, you're a known quantity. You're predictable. You're reliable. I appreciate reliability. But Blinky has picked up the slack for you on several occasions and has gone out of his way to make your job easier. I haven't seen you reciprocate, and that's concerning to me. This is your chance to pay him back," she finished, pointedly not adding, "to say nothing of actually trying to impress your CO for the first time in your service together."

Lu braced to stiff attention. "Yes, Captain."

"Carry on," Xi acknowledged, returning the salute and

subtly gesturing for them to exit the cockpit. While she had spoken the truth to Lu about his change in assignment, Xi knew that some part of her decision had been due to the nagging thought that Lu simply couldn't measure up to Podsy. And judging from the early returns, it was possible that Blinky could. Xi and Podsy had completed Durgan's Folly together, just two people in a mech designed to be run by a crew of three. She missed that efficiency almost as much as she missed Podsy himself.

A few seconds after Lu had departed the cockpit, Ms. Samuels entered through the open door and nodded approvingly. "I was wondering when you'd do that."

"Excuse me?"

"Oh, come on." Samuels lowered her voice to just above a whisper. "It's plain as day that Lu's been sandbagging, doing the bare minimum. It must be a relief to snap him up after all this time. I've seen the way your jaw muscles bunch when he shows less enthusiasm than Private Staubach."

Xi shook her head in amazement. "How can you be the Fourth Estate's spear-tip if you can't see what's going on here?"

"Help me understand," Samuels urged, leisurely propping herself against the bulkhead.

"We're in the middle of a fight, Ms. Samuels," Xi said, fighting to keep her emotions reined in. "Now is not the time for upbraiding or public floggings. Wars are won and lost in the temples. They just play out on the field like a Rube Goldberg machine."

"I don't think that's *quite* what Sun Tzu meant." Samuels offered the hint of a smile.

"I think it is." Xi shrugged. "There's no sense arguing with the laws of physics, and there's no sense trying to make someone into something he'll never be. I'm not being punitive with Lu, I told him the truth. I need to see how Blinky performs for a few full shifts as a dedicated Wrench, and I'd like to see how Lu responds to what he probably sees as a demotion. Staubach's obviously over-qualified to be a Monkey, and both his neural batteries and tactical reasoning show enough promise that he might even make Jock soon. As a potential bonus, I *might* also reignite the same passion in Lu that saw him enlist two days after the atrocity at New Australia became public knowledge. But that didn't factor into my decision," she said with conviction she didn't entirely feel. "Any commander who lets personal feelings or grudges influence her command decisions doesn't belong in the big chair. This is the best move not just for *Elvira* and her crew individually, but for the battalion as a whole, and I'll stand by it if and when Chief Lu submits my order for official review."

Samuels' grin faded and was replaced with her professional veneer of detachment. "Thank you, Captain Xi."

Xi suspected Samuels had been recording the conversation, so she had purposefully failed to mention the handful of times Lu had been mildly insubordinate. And her reason for leaving that part out was simple: she *needed* Lu, just like everyone else in the battalion needed him. And if she stabbed him in the back by airing those issues in public, she could kiss her hope for *Elvira*'s improved performance goodbye.

Xi hesitated for a long moment before closing the cockpit's door and hailing *Roy* on the P2P. She was ready to discuss her theory about the bug vehicles with the smartest man in the battalion.

"*Roy* here," greeted Styles. "What can I do for you, *Elvira*?"

"I need to run a *theory* by you," Xi said with deliberate emphasis on the word "theory."

He recognized her coded message indicating that she needed to discuss the bugs, evidenced by his next, "Stand by." A few seconds later, his voice returned, and it was clear he had switched mics—and probably rooms. "Go ahead, Captain."

"If I'm right about this," she began, "then I think I know how to complete our secondary objective."

The "secondary objective" was a coded reference to the diplomatic mission they had come to Shiva's Wrath to conduct. Styles, ever the bright spark, replied, "I'm all ears, Xi."

She explained her theory and, to her surprise, found very little in the way of criticism from Chief Styles.

Not long after Styles ended the call, Xi's comm board showed an incoming missive summoning her to *Roy*.

Styles had apparently recommended she join them to discuss her budding theory, so Xi donned her rebreather and made her way to the battalion's command vehicle.

This wasn't the kind of thing to be discussed in the open, even on a nominally-secure P2P line.

"All right, Captain," Jenkins said after Xi had closed the cabin door behind her. "Start at the top."

Xi stood opposite from the seated Jenkins, while Styles sat beside Xi as the young woman replied, "I think I know how to make contact with the bugs, Colonel."

"So Mr. Styles tells me." Jenkins nodded toward the technician. "But I need details, Captain Xi, and I need them now."

"Vorr are an aquatic species largely similar to the octopus," Xi explained. "They regenerate their limbs, and part of their customary greeting posture is to willingly surrender a portion of one of their own limbs in order to allow the faction they are greeting to appraise it, usually via consumption."

"I'm aware of Vorr social quirks." Jenkins' eyes narrowed. "But we're here to talk about the bugs, not the Vorr."

"I'm aware of that, Colonel," she said, firmly holding her

ground. "But I think Vorr greeting rituals informed this species as to how they're supposed to greet others."

Jenkins cocked his head in mild confusion, flicking his eyes to Styles, who nodded approvingly. The colonel leaned back. "I don't follow."

"The Vorr have some kind of diplomatic relationship with the bugs," Xi explained. "It stands to reason that during first contact, they probably greeted these new aliens according to some modified version of their cultural practices."

"They fed them parts of themselves—" Jenkins nodded, having followed that much. "—or surrendered tech or some other valuable resource as an opening gesture of goodwill."

"Yes, sir," she agreed. "Now, these aliens are largely unknown, but it seems that both the Vorr and the Jemmin are familiar with them. I base that on the orbital strike the Jemmin warship sent down after the lone survivor of my engagement with the bugs. Why send an orbital strike down on a lone, wounded vehicle and risk aggravating the situation with us? It doesn't make sense unless the Jemmin already know about this species and, unlike the Vorr, *don't* have a working relationship with them."

Jenkins' eyes flicked over to Styles, who was nodding slowly. "Go on, Captain." Jenkins gestured invitingly.

"I think the Vorr knew enough about human social customs," Xi continued, "that they intended to act as intermediaries to facilitate a smoother introduction between ourselves and these bugs. The Jemmin, knowingly or not, interrupted that by driving the Vorr off this rock and leaving both us and the bugs to figure each other out without a manual."

"Nearly every first contact situation in recorded history involving unknown species has ended catastrophically," Styles interjected in support of her supposition.

"I don't think the Jemmin knew about the bugs before they

withdrew the bulk of their fleet, sir," Xi said confidently. "Otherwise, I doubt they would have left just one ship in orbit. When they fired on that fleeing bug, they were making it as clear as a Solarian's conscience that they didn't want us meeting these new aliens."

Jenkins nodded, having already arrived at much of this behind closed doors with Styles. "What is your recommendation, Captain?"

"Look at these after-action reports, Colonel," Xi urged, proffering a data slate. "The highlights are mine."

Jenkins scrolled down the record, finding the indicated passages that compared the number of mechs on battalion patrols when they encountered the bug vehicles. His eyebrows rose in genuine surprise. "They're all perfect matches..."

"Four vs. four, three vs. three, four vs. four." Xi nodded eagerly. "Even in my last engagement, I had six mechs before the Jemmin attacked. I lost two mechs, but six bugs appeared..."

"And two held back," Jenkins finished, more than slightly alarmed that no one else had noticed this fact earlier.

"Making that engagement four vs. four," she finished emphatically. "And twice these bugs have gone head-on to me near the end of the engagements. I didn't understand it before, but I think I do now." She squared her shoulders and stiffened her posture. "I think they were attempting to initiate a social exchange of some kind."

"If so, why the ambushes?" Jenkins pressed. "If they wanted to talk with us, why attack us and tear our mechs down?"

Styles leaned forward intently. "Xenopsychology is anything but intuitive, Colonel. Even anthropologists have trouble coming to a consensus on the root meaning of a simple gesture like the human smile. We think of it as a universally pleasant display, but think about it for a second: you're baring your teeth at someone when you smile. When do most animals on Earth bare their teeth?"

"It's a threat display." Xi nodded in seeming agreement.

"Which means it's possible," Styles continued, "that humans are such aggressive and violent creatures that we consider certain teeth-baring displays to be friendly. And think about handshakes. Few people stop and consider what you're doing by shaking someone else's hand, but it's usually right-hand-on-right-hand," he explained, picking up steam as he went, "and since most people are right-handed..."

"It's a gesture of temporary mutual disarmament," Xi finished with certainty. "Like a salute harkens back to knightly visors needing to be raised while approaching on horseback."

"And salutes are done with the right hand." Styles nodded approvingly. "Which, again, is a tacit agreement to mutually disarm long enough to attempt a peaceful exchange. But we take *all* of those gestures for granted because they're based on our physiologies and social traditions."

"It's possible the bugs are just following their social programming the same way we do with salutes and hand-shakes." Xi shrugged. "Maybe they view an ambush like we view a smile? It's a threat display, yes, but it's obviously got limits. And maybe—" Her visage hardened as she finished. "—just maybe, we're failing to observe those limits because we don't yet know what they are."

"And if the Jemmin thought we couldn't crack the code," Styles said pointedly, "they wouldn't have fired on the fleeing bug. They'd have just let us keep beating our forces against each other."

"The Jemmin are nervous, Colonel," Xi declared without reservation, "and I think I know how to move this social exchange with the bugs forward a step or two."

"Let's say you're right," Jenkins allowed, "and let's say that the bugs do ambush you again, giving you a chance to test your theory. What about the Jemmin? They're not going to lie down while you try to introduce the Terran Republic to this new species."

"If I'm right, Colonel," Xi said heavily, "then the only way we get off this rock alive is by contacting these bugs and initiating diplomatic overtures. Together we can probably defeat the Jemmin and clear an exit path from Shiva's Wrath. But without help..." she trailed off grimly.

Unfortunately, Jenkins knew she was right. The conflict on this frozen ball had boiled down to a war of attrition, and it was clear that the Jemmin still held the upper hand in numbers and lethality. All the Jemmin had to do was wait long enough for the radiation to kill the human intruders.

"All right..." Jenkins leaned forward, clasping his hands together. "Let's hear your plan."

14

SYMMETRY

The next day, as Shiva's Wrath slowly passed into the shadow of its parent planet, Xi was out on patrol attached to 7th Platoon attached to 3rd Company. In another day and a half, Shiva's Wrath would be plunged into a dark, eclipse-driven "night" that would last for four standard days. That meant Xi needed to get lucky if she was to execute her plan under better conditions.

Part of her plan required her to be with a new unit, and Lieutenant Jesse Winters' company-command platoon was down a mech after the latest Jemmin attack. She thought it an ideal candidate for her first test. Also unbeknownst to her current patrol mates, she had canceled all direct fire support from HQ, authorizing nothing but missile shield support from the rest of the battalion.

She needed to be at her best to pull this off. Thankfully, and true to form, Podsy had been able to deliver a badly-needed replacement leg for *Elvira*, which Koch's people had finished installing mere minutes before Winters' patrol left HQ.

"All right, *Generally*," Xi called as the group reached its zenith, "they didn't hit us, so it's time to pay up."

"We haven't reached the patrol's apex yet, Captain," protested Winters, *Generally*'s Jock.

"Come on, Winters," Xi quipped. "You've been bragging about out-flanking me since you transferred over from Terra Han PDF. You lost, so pay up."

"C'mon, Captain," Winters pleaded as they officially reached the patrol's farthest point, "double or nothing."

"Better back off, LT," interrupted *Colossus'* Jock with a chuckle. "I heard she rearranged *Forktail*'s face but good back on Durgan's Folly. Rumor has it she's long on temper and short on mercy."

"I'm a woman, *Colossus*," Xi quipped, "what'd you expect? *You* try playing with the physicality short stack in every single fight of your life and see how merciful you are."

"Brutally honest," Lieutenant Winters mused. "I like that in a woman. Even more in a CO."

"Luckily for both of us, I'm neither to you, *Generally*," Xi said with a grin. "Consider this a one-off walk around the block so I can get to know Last Company a little better."

"Ouch," *Colossus* laughed at the "Last Company" insult, which had grown in popularity after Winters had demonstrated himself a more-than-capable unit commander. "You gonna stand for that, LT?"

"Doesn't sound like I'll be taking it lying down." Winters sighed.

"You take it however you can get it, *Generally*," Xi snickered.

"You got me there, Captain."

She enjoyed the banter beyond the pale. It was one of the few ways she felt connected with her comrades. No matter how dank or queasy the subject became, she always felt like it was in those moments that she was most connected with the men and women who fought alongside her.

"Hold up," *Leapfrog* interjected. "I'm reading seismic disturbances."

"Defensive posture." Xi felt a thrill as the moment of truth approached. "Do not fire unless fired upon."

"What?" Winters blurted in alarm. "Say again, *Elvira?*"

But before she could reply, the ice-field around them erupted as four breach points appeared. Showers of icy shards flew upward amid roiling clouds of steam, behind which a quartet of bug vehicles appeared.

The bugs had appeared in a picture-perfect diamond pattern near-perfectly centered on her mech. That display of geometric precision meant they had once again precisely predicted her patrol's path well in advance.

The bugs unleashed a quartet of plasma streams at the towering, humanoid *Colossus*. Two beams splashed off the mech's robustly-armored shoulders while its legs were struck by one apiece. The largest mech in the patrol staggered, teetering on the very edge of its ability to balance, before righting itself and squaring to a bug vehicle.

Generally's artillery roared, sending HE shells into one of the bugs while *Colossus*' coilguns sent hundreds of rounds per second at the nearest target. *Leapfrog* sent a dozen missile-intercept drones into the sky while engaging its own target with a pair of chain guns.

Xi admired the platoon's ferocity and fast response, but for her plan to work, she needed them to do the unthinkable.

"Cease fire! Cease fire," she repeated over the 7th Platoon channel. "7th Platoon, cease fire!"

Slowly, 7th Platoon complied, and a few seconds later, all guns were silent. "Captain?" Lieutenant Winters demanded. "What are you doing?"

"Hold your fire, 7th Platoon," Xi commanded. "As battalion

XO, I'm temporarily assuming operational command of this patrol."

"You're what!?" he asked in mixed confusion and anger.

"Under no circumstances are you to open fire, Lieutenant Winters," Xi continued, walking *Elvira* forward while ignoring his somewhat-understandable bout of insubordination. "7th Platoon, fall back on heading one-seven-five at twenty KPH. Acknowledge."

"I'm not about to surrender operational command without an explanation, *Elvira*," Winters snapped, bristling just as she had expected he would. "What the hell do you think you're doing?"

"Stand down, *Generally*," she barked as the insect vehicles continued to circle, but thankfully did not open fire.

Yet.

"Negative, Captain," Winters refused. "This patrol's orders are to engage hostile targets. These things have opened fire without provocation, and I am authorizing my people to—"

As he spoke, Xi pivoted *Elvira* so that her right-flank chain guns were trained on the heavily-armored *Generally*. She unleashed those guns against *Generally*'s formidable forward hull, stabbing sixty slugs into his composite armor before ceasing fire.

"You have your orders, Lieutenant," she growled. "Move off on heading one-seven-five at twenty KPH. Now!"

"You have just opened fire on an allied vehicle," Winters sneered. "You'll lose your command over this!"

"Acknowledge your orders, *Generally*," Xi said through gritted teeth, knowing that much depended on his compliance.

Several taut seconds passed before Winters replied, "7th Platoon, fall back on course one-seven-five. Speed: twenty KPH."

The trio of mechs began to withdraw, and for a moment, Xi

was afraid she had erred. All four of the bugs remained on the field, maintaining their perfectly-symmetrical diamond pattern as they circled her position.

Then it happened.

The nearest bug, which was as-yet undamaged, turned to face her while the others made for the icy tunnels from which they had sprung mere minutes earlier.

Seconds after they had shifted their posture, the three bugs disappeared down the holes.

"I'll be damned..." Winters muttered.

Then, just as Xi had predicted, the tactical plotter lit up with dozens of missile signatures.

Jemmin missile signatures.

"7th Platoon," she called, "you are authorized to engage inbound missiles only. Do not, I say again, do not under any circumstances interfere with my engagement. Acknowledge."

"7th Platoon acknowledges," Winters agreed, his former anger and surprise replaced with professionalism. Just as Xi had hoped it would be.

Leapfrog and *Generally* sent anti-missile rockets into the sky, while *Colossus'* trio of railguns stabbed at inbound missiles. The early miss rate was concerning, but Xi had more important things to worry about than dealing with a few missiles that might kill her while she wasn't looking.

She had a fight to win.

"Eighty-four Jemmin missiles inbound on *Elvira's* position, Colonel," Styles reported.

"Coordinate with *Bahamut Zero*," Jenkins ordered. "I don't want a single strike within five hundred meters of *Elvira's* position."

Rockets soared into the sky and railguns stabbed upward, scrubbing no more than a quarter of their targets. But as had been demonstrated amply throughout human history, quantity had a quality all its own.

Bahamut Zero's anti-missile shield went hot, splitting the sky and melting the ice around it as rockets shot from their mounts and railgun capacitors discharged. Unfortunately, *Bahamut Zero*'s targeting systems were no more accurate than the rest of the battalion's, which was bad news in more ways than Jenkins cared to think about.

Luckily, Styles had planned for that eventuality.

"Styles..." Jenkins drew a steadying breath. "Execute program Bloodmoon."

"Program Bloodmoon, aye," Styles acknowledged before raising *Eclipse* on the P2P. "*Eclipse*, this is *Roy*. Execute Bloodmoon. I say again: execute Bloodmoon."

"Bloodmoon order confirmed," *Eclipse* acknowledged, and all of *Roy*'s sensor feeds briefly went dark. "Blanket interference initiated," *Eclipse* declared. "Uploading new targeting solutions throughout the battalion via chained P2P linkage."

Precious seconds ticked by while missiles soared through the air. The battalion stood by, every man and woman on edge as the special operations mech, *Eclipse*, did what it did best.

Then the sensor fog suddenly disappeared, followed by *Eclipse*'s report. "All targeting systems slaved to *Eclipse*. Bloodmoon is online."

"Copy that," Jenkins cut in across the battalion-wide comm. link. "This is *Roy*. Re-engage anti-missile shield under pattern aegis six. I say again: aegis six."

The acknowledgments flickered across *Roy*'s comm panel, and this time when the battalion unleashed its anti-missile arsenal, it did so with devastating effect.

Railguns struck missiles at an accuracy rate greater than

ninety percent, while anti-missile rockets managed to clear the seventy percent mark. Hundreds of outbound rockets scrubbed their targets as the Jemmin sent up a second, larger wave of a hundred and fifty missiles in reply.

Jenkins had just played his last major card in authorizing Bloodmoon. By rebooting *Eclipse*'s entire computer system, he had relegated it to a purely support role from which it, and it alone, would provide live telemetry and targeting solutions to the rest of the battalion.

With a fresh, uncontaminated targeting computer, *Eclipse* could temporarily neutralize the Jemmin virus's effects on Terran targeting systems. It wouldn't take the Jemmin long to triangulate on *Eclipse*'s newfound importance, and when they learned of it, they would attack with a vengeance to once again neutralize the Terran missile shield.

But for those few seconds following Bloodmoon's activation, Colonel Lee Jenkins couldn't help but smile as Jemmin missiles were torn from the sky with clinical precision. The entire first wave was eliminated long before it could interfere with Xi's bizarre attempt at diplomacy.

Sure enough, and quite a bit faster than Jenkins would have liked, the Jemmin responded to this latest shift in battlefield conditions.

"Two hundred Jemmin missiles inbound on HQ," Styles reported urgently as a fresh volley of inbound ordnance appeared on the screen. Making little attempt to hide their position, the Jemmin authors of those missiles suddenly became visible on the screens.

"Authorize anti-personnel weapons to engage inbound missiles," Jenkins ordered. "But under no circumstances are we to compromise *Elvira*'s shield."

"Copy that, sir," Styles acknowledged.

"*Preacher*, this is *Roy*." Jenkins raised the company's main missile-mech. "You are cleared to engage Jemmin targets at your discretion."

"*Preacher* here," the missile mech's Jock acknowledged with relish, "spreadin' the word."

Missiles screamed out of *Preacher*'s launch tubes, locked onto a handful of distinct Jemmin targets that *Eclipse*'s ultra-powerful sensors were finally able to locate after the purge of its sensor computer.

The Jemmin targets scrambled, looking every bit like spooked rabbits as the precision projectiles hurtled toward them on low trajectories.

"Incoming!" Chaps called out before *Roy* was rocked by a Jemmin near-miss. A dozen missiles struck the icy field of the battalion's new HQ, with two striking targets directly and the rest missing by less than five meters.

"Their targeting systems aren't any better than ours," Jenkins realized, as *Eclipse* and the anti-missile drones now hovering above HQ created a partially effective sensor barrier to Jemmin targeting systems.

"Not so tough now, are you?" Chaps sneered, sending SRMs streaking toward a fresh Jemmin target twenty-one kilometers from HQ. *Roy*'s chain guns whined on full-output, and they actually managed to snipe a pair of missiles a hundred meters above the surface. Their mid-air explosions showered HQ with shrapnel, some clattering off *Roy*'s topside. "I love it when it rains!" Chaps howled gleefully, turning *Roy* toward a fresh Jemmin signature as his previous flight of SRMs pulverized the twenty-one-kilometer target.

For the moment, the tide was in their favor, and Jenkins knew they needed to take as much advantage as possible.

Because if there was one thing he had learned in his career about momentum, it was that the pendulum never stopped swinging until the last enemy was off the board.

Podsy knew what he was about to do could get him court-martialed. There was no question. And frankly, he couldn't blame them.

A firefight had just erupted on the surface, and it looked like this one would be for the whole kit and kaboodle. He had done a monumental amount of work on the *Bonhoeffer* to ensure a constant flow of supplies made its way planet-side, but he knew there was one more move he could make that might prove decisive.

Then again, it might blow up in his face. And not just *his* face, but in the face of everyone on the *Bonhoeffer*.

He had secretly coordinated with Styles to work up a program which, if introduced directly to the *Bonhoeffer*'s computer core, would do two things. First, it would confirm if the Jemmin had somehow managed to sneak their sensor virus into the *Bonhoeffer*'s systems. And second, if the Jemmin *had* achieved that unlikely feat, the upload would purge it just as it had done for *Eclipse* in preparation for Bloodmoon.

Of course, all of that sounded well enough until one realized that in order to upload the antivirus, one would need to directly insert it into the *Bonhoeffer*'s computer core. If it worked, it would permit the warship's powerful sensors to easily locate the Jemmin forces on Shiva's Wrath, enabling orbital strikes to eliminate them from the surface of that frozen world.

If it failed, it could potentially mean taking the *Bonhoeffer*'s entire sensor grid offline while the data techs worked to restore the system. Styles had been clear that the reboot process could take up to three hours, during which time the ship would be unable to contribute in any meaningful capacity.

So even the normally devil-may-care Podsy hesitated as he reached toward the control icon which would insert the antivirus into the *Bonhoeffer's* systems. The best-case scenario was that it worked, the Jemmin suddenly appeared on the *Bonhoeffer's* scanners, and they were eliminated without anyone tracing the insertion back to Podsy.

Fat chance of that. He smirked.

"Okay, Podsy..." He exhaled steadily. "Time to earn your keep."

Striking the icon, he inserted the program into the *Bonhoeffer's* computer core. At first, nothing seemed to happen, and he felt the pit of his stomach fall away in the ensuing ninety seconds.

During which time, absolutely nothing happened.

He laced his fingers behind his head and closed his eyes, wondering precisely how many days they'd keep him alive in the brig before they spaced him for mutiny and a dozen other charges.

The bitch of it was, he'd do it all again given the chance.

15

THE DUEL

Xi flattened *Elvira* to the ground just as the bug spat a bolt of blue plasma at her cockpit. The plasma struck her topside, gouging a red-hot, thirty-centimeter-deep groove that stretched a third of the mech's length.

"You want to dance?" Xi growled, crab-walking and raising her stern to train the fifteens on the bug-thing. AP shells loaded into the fifteens, with both guns going green on her HUD as she lined up a shot. "Let's dance."

The shockwave of the deafening reports sent icy debris scattering in a rapidly-expanding disc. Both shells struck true, but neither pierced the thing's robust hide.

"Fine, you like it rough?" she quipped, loading HE shells as she continued crab-walking in a clockwise pattern. "I can do rough."

The bug spat another bolt of plasma that struck her front-left leg, slagging much of its armor but failing to damage the limb's internal workings. Crab-cakes skittered out from beneath the thing's bulbous form, and with single-minded purpose, the mobile grenades surged toward *Elvira* with chilling unity.

"On the way!" she barked, authoring another pair of reports

from her fifteens. The HE shells struck home, one head-on and the other a near-miss that blew a three-meter-long gash open on the very top of the thing's "back."

Strangely, the head-on impact seemed not to have much effect. She loaded another pair of HE shells with the intention of putting the overgrown bug down. *Hard.*

She presented her left flank to the line of crab-cakes, raking up and through the tide of explosive drones-slash-creatures and causing more than half of them to explode on impact. No matter how good she aimed, a few snuck through and began latching onto her limbs, where they exploded with such intensity that plumes of steam wafted up around her mech.

Her board registered a pair of the bizarre, mortar-like projectiles, and she was unable to re-train her guns before they struck near her stern. Warning lights sprang to life, indicating her right fifteen had suffered severe damage to its aiming mechanism. Snarling in frustration, she removed that gun's shell and quickly fired the left gun's HE round, where it exploded with a violent crack against the bug-thing's carapace.

"Come on," she muttered, "give it up. You're tough, I'm tough, *everybody*'s tough. Let's make nice and grab some tacos—"

Another bolt of plasma fire struck her, this time hitting the left fifteen and causing similar warning alarms to sound.

"Lu," she snapped, "see if you can do something about Righty's aiming mech."

"Yes, Captain," he acknowledged.

"Blinky," she continued, increasing her lateral speed as her chain guns tore deep divots in the icy shell of Shiva's Wrath while steadily picking off the crab-cakes, "I need you to remove the safety interlocks on the primary drive hydraulics."

That last order was one of the many reasons she had switched Lu and Blinky for this particular op. She expected Lu would argue, or at least delay carrying out such an order, but Staubach was ever-eager and would likely not hesitate to follow such a dangerous command.

True to form, Blinky replied, "Safety interlocks disengaged. Increasing system pressure to one-hundred-twenty-percent of maximum."

"That'll do," she grunted, careful not to overdrive the suddenly super-powered ambulatory system. "All right..." she muttered as the tide of crab-cakes drew steadily nearer, during which time she waited for the opportune moment to mute her chain guns. "Hang on!" she yelled when that moment arrived.

She cut her chain guns and, using *Elvira's* briefly super-powered legs, jumped her mech a full two meters off the ground before bringing it back down with precisely the desired effect.

Every crab-cake within thirty meters of her position exploded when a chain reaction took place as a few of the nearest crab-cakes were crushed by her mech's legs. Their explosions rippled down the line of encroaching critters, killing at least three-quarters of them in the most satisfying version of the domino effect that Xi had ever instigated.

She howled with delight, re-lighting her chain guns and tearing into the few remaining grenade bugs with surgical precision.

It wasn't until she had cleared the ground of the destructive little drones that she realized how bad the damage to her drive system was. Three of her legs were seriously damaged, with Leg Two knocked completely offline.

Gritting her teeth in irritation, she called, "Blinky, I need you to get Two Leg back online."

"Working on it, Captain. Give me twenty seconds," Staubach acknowledged, neither frantic nor muted in his tone. He was proving himself worthy of full-time assignment as a

Wrench with his combination of a steady hand and eager demeanor.

"How's that gun coming, Lu?" Xi asked as she prepared to fire SRMs at the wounded bug-thing, which circled clockwise opposite her position on an invisible circle nearly a hundred meters across.

"Right gun's out, Captain," Lu replied, his voice strained. "Left gun's...questionable. Give me thirty seconds."

"We might not have it." She grimaced, recoiling in sudden surprise when the bug-thing shuddered.

She narrowed her eyes as its chitinous plates began to fall away one by one until something entirely different took shape beneath.

"Oh, you have got to be fucking kidding..." she swore, firing all of her SRMs simultaneously as the bug-thing split in two smaller creatures. One of them slithered out like some kind of centipede, complete with a pair of horn-like apparatuses at its head and a long, articulated spike at its tail.

The other unfurled yellow, wasp-like wings from a slender, teardrop-shaped body and took to the sky.

The SRMs destroyed what was left of the original creature's hide, and the shrapnel thrown off by the explosions struck both the crawler and flyer. Surprisingly, neither seemed deterred by the impacts even though each began dripping greenish-blue liquid onto the ice.

The flyer shot forward as a rocket-like flame erupted from its rear, propelling it faster than any creature its size had a right to fly. She swept her chain guns up to intercept, but it simply moved too fast for her to be able to do more than rip a dozen holes in its wings before it cleared her firing arcs.

Xi began loading anti-missile rockets into her launchers, but no sooner had she issued the command than both launcher mechanisms registered catastrophic warning alarms as the flying thing dropped some sort of incendiary devices onto *Elvira*'s stern.

A bloodcurdling scream pierced her skull, and she immediately knew what had happened: caught in the tiny crawlspace beneath the left gun, Lu had just been burned by whatever the flyer had dropped on her.

"Blinky," she yelled, "get him out of there ASAP!"

"Already on it," Samuels unexpectedly replied. And if the reporter's voice was filled with abject terror, Xi would die before confirming it. Not now. Not ever. For all her flaws, Samuels had answered the call without hesitation during this deployment. She had earned respect the hard way.

"Good work, Samuels," Xi acknowledged grimly, turning and raking the meter-tall, three-meter-wide, and ten-meter-long centipede-looking thing with her right flank chain guns.

She struck true with over half of her rounds, but somehow *none* of her slugs pierced its skin. It would have taken a mech with fifteen centimeters of solid steel armor to shrug off such an attack.

Xi moved *Elvira* toward the centipede and was pleased to see Blinky bring Two Leg back online while somehow stemming the flow of hydraulic fluid from a dozen different leaks caused by her jump's self-destructive back-pressure.

The flyer swept along a ponderous arc as it lined up for another strafing run, but Xi suspected anything light enough to fly would be less durable than the armored centipede.

With her right flank chain guns pouring fire on the fast-approaching centipede, Xi turned her left chain guns onto the flyer. Three hundred and fifty depleted uranium slugs flew from her rotary barrels each second, and it took her two full, agonizing seconds to sight in on the flyer.

But when she did, it was all over for the would-be bomber.

Gore flew in all directions as *Elvira*'s anti-personnel guns cut the five-meter-long flyer into ribbons. Somehow, it maintained its approach trajectory, even firing its bizarre thruster before finally succumbing to the savage ferocity of Xi's chain guns.

The flying thing's devastated form hurtled mindlessly over *Elvira*, its rocket engine suddenly firing at maximum. The flyer tumbled end-over-end in mid-air again and again before its chaotic death throes finally ripped the thing completely apart in a shower of fiery gore that spread across the ice-field just under a hundred meters from *Elvira*.

"One down." She smirked. "One to go."

But without her artillery or missile launchers, Xi was seemingly unable to deter the oncoming creature. Its twin "horns" belched fire when it came within twenty meters, and those streams of liquid flame covered *Elvira*'s hull from stem to stern.

Steam boiled up all around *Elvira* as the burning fuel dripped onto the ice, and for a brief moment, Xi imagined her mech, surrounded by both ice and fire, as a metaphor for the Terran contingent on this world. Surrounded by forces that wanted to destroy them, it seemed their only hope was to master one before the other could kill them.

Then the centipede came within five meters, and Xi lowered her right legs at the last second, hoping to crush the thing before it reached the lightly-armored undercarriage of her mech.

That undercarriage would almost certainly fail to protect *Elvira*'s crew from any anti-vehicle ordnance the centipede might be carrying.

As her legs struck the ice, Xi experienced the phenomenon of her life flashing before her eyes.

And she was proud of what she saw.

"Colonel," Styles called out in a raised voice as the Terran missile shield continued to scrape Jemmin missiles from the sky, "I'm receiving telemetry from the *Bonhoeffer* forwarding fresh target locks on nine Jemmin Specters...and one Jemmin Poltergeist."

"A Poltergeist?" Jenkins repeated in surprise as heads turned all around the compartment.

Jemmin Poltergeists were the rarest of Jemmin vehicles, rumored to be the command vehicles for planetary-scale invasion forces and only cataloged once before in Terran history. Many Terran military theorists suggested that a Poltergeist was worth more than three of their standard Wraith-class warships, like the one the *Bonhoeffer* had destroyed. If a Poltergeist was here, then destroying it would certainly prove decisive in the outcome of this engagement.

It might even end the conflict outright, depending on which theories of Jemmin society were correct. Jenkins and his people were about to put some of those theories to the test.

"Chaps, engage those targets with priority on the Poltergeist," Jenkins ordered. "Styles, forward all target locations to the battalion and put all of our Owls on that command vehicle. Request orbital strikes from the *Bonhoeffer* on all locations, with priority on that Poltergeist," he finished eagerly.

"Negative on orbital strikes, Colonel," Styles said with disappointment as the battalion unleashed its fury on the enemy command platform. "*Bonhoeffer*'s weapon control systems are on temporary standby following some sort of core computer breach."

"Acknowledged." Jenkins grimaced, hoping that he and his people could bracket and scrub those targets before they lost the *Bonhoeffer*'s target locks.

Shockingly, the Poltergeist was just sixteen kilometers from Terran HQ. It seemed to be nestled beneath a two-meter-thick layer of ice lined with sensor-disrupting materials. How the *Bonhoeffer* suddenly located ten high-value targets was beyond Jenkins, but whoever was responsible would earn himself Jenkins' undying gratitude.

"Missiles away," Chaps declared, sending missiles downrange while *Preacher* and several other mechs did likewise. Even the fortified Beta and Charlie Sites, over thirty kilometers from HQ, sent their limited supplies of mid-range missiles at the Poltergeist.

The Poltergeist, apparently aware of its pending demise, broke cover and sped off at nearly three hundred KPH. MRMs and LRMs tore after it, while artillery mercilessly pummeled its recently-vacated foxhole. Some of the SRMs struck the foxhole as well, but others adjusted course and pursued the accelerating vehicle as it passed the six hundred KPH mark.

Burning ordnance pursued the fast-fleeing Jemmin vehicle, and for several seconds, all eyes were on the tactical plotter as a dozen missiles slowly converged on the Poltergeist's location.

The first missile struck true, slowing the enemy platform to just under four hundred KPH before it resumed its breathtaking acceleration.

Unfortunately for the Jemmin commander, that dip in velocity proved decisive.

Three more SRMs slammed into its stern in rapid succession while five were torn from the sky by Jemmin countermeasures. An MRM impacted on the ground in front of the Jemmin vehicle, which passed through the flaming steam cloud and cut a stunning visual worthy of a top-shelf action holo-novel. An LRM was ripped from the sky by some sort of Jemmin drone, but a final SRM snuck underneath the briefly-tilted Poltergeist and exploded.

The Poltergeist's hover-drive system was destroyed, causing the roughly disc-shaped vehicle to career into the ice and tumble like a rolling coin, going end-over-end and scattering hull debris as the vehicle started to come apart.

Just before the Poltergeist came to a rolling stop, four MRMs sent by the Beta and Charlie Sites slammed into it. In a cataclysmic release of energy that equaled roughly two megatons, the Jemmin command vehicle ceased to exist. The steam cloud from the blast site tore skyward, preceded by the multi-layered mushroom cloud that seemed to clear a path for the boiling, seemingly volcanic jet of steam released from the immense explosion.

Roy's command center erupted in cheers, but Jenkins knew this fight was far from over.

"There are still at least nine Specters out there," Jenkins bellowed, quickly quieting the compartment. "Let's deal with them before we break out the champagne."

But the truth was he felt every bit as exhilarated as they did. His people had just done the unthinkable: they had destroyed the most valuable and potent Jemmin ground platform known to humanity.

Unfortunately, as with the Arh'Kel on Durgan's Folly, he suspected no one would learn about their victory until everyone in the unit was well into their grey hairs.

"Maintain focus, people." He swept the room with a hard look. "We're not out of the woods yet."

16

FRIGID FURY

Xi shook her head in confusion. She remembered shooting down the flyer, and being unable to hurt that Goddamned centipede thing, but after that, nothing seemed to make sense.

She looked down at her console, seeing that only a quarter of the indicators and interfaces were online. Her neural link was severed, and after looking down at her chest, she realized she had emptied the meager contents of her stomach at some point in the last minute or so.

She tried to speak, but nothing came out. She worked her jaw up and down for several seconds, cleared her throat, and repeated the attempt.

"Podsy?" she asked, belatedly realizing he was no longer part of her crew. She shook her head again, causing a wave of vertigo to wash over her that made her grip the arms of her pilot's chair until it had passed. "Blinky?" she said, this time more loudly. "Lu?" she demanded, unstrapping her harness and falling out of the chair, only realizing after she hit the deck that *Elvira* was tilted twenty degrees starboard.

She got to her hands and knees and reached for the door, relieved to find that it quickly opened at her command.

The rear cabin was in shambles. Scorch marks covered the walls, and a fire had apparently broken out near the left power coupling. Sarah Samuels was normally strapped in near that coupling, but Xi saw no sign of the reporter.

"Blinky?" she called, staggering to her feet and gripping the smartly-positioned rails along *Elvira*'s ceiling. The rails allowed her to balance, despite her vertigo, her progress slower than she would have liked as she made her way through the compartment. She only remembered the fire that had burned Lu after she had traversed half the cabin. "Samuels?" She raised her voice, wondering if she was the only survivor of the bizarre fight.

"I'm here..." Samuels replied weakly. "But I...I hit my...ear."

"Stay down," Xi commanded, her focus sharpening after hearing the woman's voice. "I'm coming."

The rearmost section of the cabin was where the gun mechanisms were accessible. They were secured behind a thick bulkhead that featured a single, narrow hatch situated along the starboard side of the compartment. Xi moved through that hatch and was relieved to find all three of her fellows alive.

Blinky was breathing but unconscious, lying across Sarah Samuels whose eyes rolled around aimlessly. Lu, on the other hand, looked even worse than Podsy had back on Durgan's Folly. The back of his head was scorched, bloodied, and rough. The left side of his face was badly burned as well. His left arm dangled at an unnatural angle, but he too was breathing, and it appeared that Blinky had managed to put tourniquets on his arm to stop the bleeding.

Xi performed a quick inspection of the trio, finding none of them in immediate danger of dying from blood loss or asphyxiation, so she reached for the med-kit Blinky had used to bind Lu's wounds.

She produced a pair of stim syringes, rolled Staubach over

onto his back, and injected the high-powered cocktail directly into his heart.

For a few seconds, nothing happened. Then he gasped, sitting bolt upright as his eyes snapped wildly around the room.

"Blinky, focus," she said, placing a hand on either side of his face and locking eyes with him. "Where are you?"

His eyes darted left and right several times before settling on Xi, and after a few short, panicked breaths, he said, "Shiva's Wrath?"

"Good enough." She nodded. "Listen, Lu's hurt—" She gestured to the burned Wrench-turned-Monkey, then the reporter. "—and so is Samuels. Can you drive the ATV?"

Blinky, true to his nickname, worked his eyelids up and down a dozen times in rapid succession before nodding. "I...I think so. I'm a little wired, though."

"I know," she said apologetically, gesturing to the empty syringe. "It'll wear off in about twenty minutes. You need to rendezvous with Winters and his platoon. They're due south of here. Where are you going?" she asked when his attention seemed to drift.

"Due south," he replied, his words coming faster than normal, "gotta chase the winter."

"Close enough," she agreed, helping him stand. "Take Lu," she urged. "I'll get Samuels."

Together, they brought the pair of injured to the hatch where they strapped rebreathers onto everyone. She pulled the emergency lever and the hatch swung open, clanging against *Elvira*'s hull as the flames on the ice-field where the flyer crashed were still burning, though less intensely than before.

With the thankfully-slender Sarah Samuels' arm around her neck, Xi carefully walked down the ramp to the icy ground and found the ATV's deployment switch. She was rewarded by the hiss of pneumatic cylinders which released the sparse, six-wheeled vehicle, dropping it to the ice beneath *Elvira*'s stern.

"Ms. Samuels," she said, propping the woman up in the vehicle's right-rear seat and strapping her in, "you need to stay awake, okay?'

Samuels was still groggy, suggesting she might have suffered a severe concussion. Deciding against further attempts to communicate with the reporter, Xi helped Blinky strap Lu into the ATV's left-rear seat.

"Fire it up, Private," Xi said, gesturing for him to take the driver's seat.

"I can't do that, Captain..." he began to protest.

"You can, and you will," she snapped. "I have to complete this mission alone. Hook up with Winters to the south. That's an order," she said, her voice cracking like a whip on the last words.

Blinky looked like he wanted to argue, but reluctantly nodded and boarded the vehicle. Its capacitors were green, and a test of its motors showed it was ready to roll. "Good luck, Captain," he said, his hands trembling slightly from the stims.

"Move out," she clapped him on the shoulder. He pulled his hood over his head, checked that his passengers had no exposed skin, and sped off to the south.

Xi eyed the flaming wreckage of the flyer, seeing only a few pieces larger than a meter in diameter. She then turned her focus to the right side of *Elvira*, where she and her people had just disembarked, and appraised the damage.

The front and middle legs on that side were almost completely destroyed, with the middle leg's joint annihilated. It was a miracle the blast hadn't gone completely through her mech's armor and vaporized everyone inside.

Bits of the centipede's carapace were strewn about, embedded in the melted ice, which was the main culprit for

Elvira's aggressive rightward tilt. A meter of ice had melted away beneath the mech, likely from a combination of the explosion and the burning liquid the centipede had covered her with prior to that.

"Damn..." she muttered, bracing herself on the gangway's rail before hearing a faint noise from behind her. She set her jaw and slowly turned toward the source of the sound, which perhaps unsurprisingly originated from the dying flames of the flyer's wreckage. "Of course..." She grimaced as the sound of chitin scraping against the ice was accompanied by a flicker of movement beyond the flames.

Knowing that her fight was not yet over, she regained *Elvira*'s interior and made for the small arms locker. Inside was a collection of weapons, some of which she was rated on and others she was not. She strapped a sidearm to her uniform, clicking it into place just below her hip as she took a tac-vest and visored helmet from the rear of the locker. Strapping the protective gear on, she reached for a handful of micro-grenades, a combat knife and, finally, the locker's anti-material rifle with collapsible tripod.

"I don't play to lose," she declared, snapping a ten-round clip into the rifle and hefting it before her chest as she made her way to the mech's exterior hatch.

Once she was there, she peered through the portal and saw something that was both completely unfamiliar and still expected.

The thing stood a head shorter than Xi, with a stooped posture and half-insect, half-crustacean-looking physique the basic shape of which resembled nothing so much as a mythological centaur. It had no proper head, but its four legs supported a medium-long body. At the front of the body was a pair of long, double-elbowed "arms" ending in four-pronged pincers. Those arms protruded up from a short "torso" affixed to the front of the thing's main body, and seemed remarkably thin and wiry considering the thick, blade-like proportions of the lower limbs.

The creature passed through the flames as though they were not there, making a bee-line for her position at a pace equal to a brisk walk.

And while it was possible the thing meant her no harm, she wasn't about to risk being wrong about that.

Moving down the gangway, she nearly lost her footing on the last step but managed to save both herself and the rifle from a fall to the ice. Gritting her teeth in annoyance, she unfolded the rifle's tripod and ducked beneath *Elvira*'s hull, slipping her body back a couple meters before laying her rifle on the ice and sighting in on the thing.

The range-finder showed it was forty meters away. Point-blank range for such a potent weapon. Jacking a round into the chamber, she pressed her finger against the trigger and put the thing in her crosshairs.

"Nighty night," she whispered, squeezing the trigger and sending a fifty-caliber slug downrange. The gun's report was deafening—especially since she had chosen to fire it beneath *Elvira*'s tilting hull, where the sound waves immediately reflected back at her with near-full intensity.

The bullet struck just a few centimeters from where she aimed, and the impact sent the thing skittering across the ice as its chitinous legs failed to find purchase on the frozen surface. But just as quickly as it had been knocked off-target, it resumed its forward progress with machine-like focus.

"Seriously?" she muttered, her ears ringing as she centered the oncoming thing in her crosshairs and squeezed the trigger a second time.

Amazingly, the thing somehow dodged the second bullet and barely broke stride while doing so.

"Oh no, you don't." She grimaced as it passed the twenty-five-meter mark. Switching the gun to full-auto, she was counting on its impressive, active recoil-dampening system to keep her from spraying all eight remaining bullets high and wide.

Xi drew a short breath and exhaled as the thing reached the seventeen-meter mark, at which point she unloaded the rifle's remaining ammo.

The insect-looking thing evaded the first round, but the second and third struck it just above where she had wanted. One of its arms was blown off by the third round, and its rear leg was luckily crippled by the last.

But the creature's focus was incredible. In spite of its terrible wounds, it tossed some sort of grenade at Xi even as it skittered back from the force of the fifty's multiple impacts.

Xi log-rolled as fast as she could away from the rifle, but the grenade-like device still caught her in a spray of acid that caused her helmet and vest to hiss as smoke poured off them.

She kept rolling toward *Elvira*'s relatively-raised stern section, feeling angry burns begin to erupt across her left shoulder and back. Her neck soon felt as though a thousand needles were stabbing it, and she knew she needed to get her vest and helmet off.

Before leaving the relative cover of *Elvira*, she tore her helmet off and tossed it aside. Unstrapping her vest, she screamed in pain as her right hand was burned by a thick clump of flaming material that was actively eating into her protective armor.

Her head was on a swivel as soon as she doffed the ruined armor, and her hand went to the micro-grenades stuck to her belt. The barest flicker of movement beneath *Elvira* prompted Xi to toss the first of her three grenades near the abandoned rifle, where it exploded with a blinding flash and ear-splitting crack. Shrapnel flew outward as the rifle was destroyed by the explosion, but Xi could not see whether the bug had been caught by the blast.

Acting purely on instinct, she drew her sidearm and looked up to *Elvira*'s badly-damaged topside just in time to see the creature appear between the dual fifteens. The same place Sergeant Major Trapper and his Pounders had nested during the last push on Durgan's Folly.

Snarling in primal anger at this thing somehow transposing itself on Trapper's memory, Xi fired her sidearm a dozen times at the bug-looking beast. The rounds were surprisingly more effective than she expected, with the repeated impacts causing it to lose its footing atop the derelict mech's hull. The creature's legs splayed as it struggled to keep something approaching a combat-ready posture, but Xi kept it off-balance with well-timed shots that struck its body near the lower leg joints.

Using a one-handed grip, Xi emptied her thirty-round clip at the thing. As she fired, she drew the second grenade from her belt and tossed it on top of *Elvira*. Ducking beneath the mech's raised stern, Xi was protected from the blast while she drew the third and final grenade from her belt.

"All or nothing," she hissed, discarding her sidearm and drawing the last weapon at her disposal—the combat knife. Whirling out of concealment, she barely managed to avoid the thing as it leaped toward her. Less a matador and more an unpracticed ice skater, Xi's feet slipped out from under her, and she crashed to the ground a meter from where the centaur-bug did likewise.

Raising her knife, she stabbed down on the creature's lone-remaining arm as it flailed in her direction. She hesitated, wondering whether she should use the last grenade or not, but suddenly, something happened.

The creature's body relaxed, but not in anything like a death rattle. Its lower limbs splayed wide while its upper limbs spasmed, twitching left and right in search of something to grapple.

Muted whumps and brilliant flashes pierced the sky above as Terran anti-missile fire scraped inbound ordnance from the air. And beneath that ongoing battle to protect this historically unprecedented first contact situation, Captain Xi Bao did the nearly unthinkable.

She dove knife-first on top of the creature, plunging her weapon deep into its torso. Xi twisted the blade left and right, digging the blade deep and wrenching like she was attacking a lobster with dinnerware. She knew even as she did it that she might have just made the most catastrophic mistake of her life, and that she might have just cost the Terran Republic the chance to form a productive relationship with a new species.

But she had to go with her gut, and her gut told her to show no mercy since that was precisely how the bug-things had behaved.

The six-limbed thing finally spasmed, but as it did so, something remarkable happened: its limbs splayed outward in a symmetrical display that was certainly unnatural given the damage it had sustained.

Xi felt a surge of hope that she had chosen the right path and quickly disarmed the grenade before tossing her knife to the ground. Now disarmed, she did her best to assume a symmetrical posture while remaining upright. Her arms at ninety-degree angles to her sides, and her feet spaced as far apart as her shoulders, she straightened her head as much as she could manage considering the continued vertigo.

The ruined creature held its own posture for a long while before its limbs fell limply to the ice, and Xi fell to her knees as mixed waves of victory and despair washed over her. She had survived the battle, but if this thing had died, then how in God's name could she complete her mission and establish some kind of dialogue with the things?

She wanted to cry in frustration, but her brain was apparently too rattled to behave in what she thought would be its usual fashion.

Then suddenly, fifty meters from her position, the ice split apart with the sound of a glacier tearing through rock. The cracking of frozen water tearing apart continued as an undamaged version of the hunchbacked alien vehicles emerged from the ice.

She was on her knees and decided now was not the time to adjust her posture. With her heart pounding in her ears, she remained as motionless as she could manage while the vehicle's crab-like legs brought the lumbering vehicle close to her.

When it was about twenty meters from where she knelt, the giant insect-like thing stopped. For a long moment, nothing seemed to happen. She wondered if she was about to die, on her knees and bathed in plasma fire. Hardly a pleasant end by any measure.

Then the forward-most layers of metallic, chitinous armor folded back into themselves, and a centaur-like creature identical to the one she had just fought emerged.

It approached with its arms splayed outward at near-ninety-degree angles from its body, seeming to approximate her previous posture. She responded by mirroring the pose, and the creature's blade-shaped, crab-like legs brought it to a stop less than three meters from Xi.

Slowly, with obvious deliberation, the thing reached behind its torso section and produced a small, triangular device approximately ten centimeters long on a side. It was of decidedly non-human design, and if Xi had to guess, she would have said it was Vorr technology.

The triangular device began to glow with a faint, blue light, and a tinny voice crackled to life from within it. "You brave. We brave. Symmetry."

She felt her heart leap into her throat as a wave of relief washed over her. She had been right! All of this was some sort of inhuman greeting ritual.

She nodded, repeating the phrase. "You brave. We brave. Symmetry."

"No harm," the thing's translator box said, though it lacked inflection, so she had difficulty understanding what it meant.

She cocked her head in confusion. "I don't understand."

"No harm. We no harm you," it clarified as it stepped closer to its fallen comrade.

She nodded unthinkingly. "Yes, tend to your wounded."

"No harm," it repeated as it stooped down and, using its one free four-pointed pincer, performed a strange sequence of movements that saw the fallen centaur-thing's body burst open on the underside.

Xi watched in fascination as the living centaur-thing reached purposefully inside its dead comrade and, with evident care and tenderness, removed something that looked like a cross between a slug and a grub. It was a half-meter long and appeared incredibly delicate.

But the grub-slug thing was still moving, and Xi dimly realized it was the real creature. The centaur-like exoskeleton was some kind of removable armor!

The new insectaur's armor opened on the underside, where it tucked its suit-less comrade before the armor folded back into itself.

"You brave," the box reiterated, "we brave. You not food. We not food."

"Yes." She nodded eagerly. "You brave. We brave. You not food. We not food. We wish reciprocity...symmetry," she clarified before gesturing to the translation device, "like you and Vorr."

"Vorr brave. Vorr food," the thing unexpectedly said. "Brave food not symmetrical."

She laughed in spite of herself, concluding that this species was confused by the concept of "brave food." The confusion was understandable since most prey animals humanity had encountered were not, in fact, "brave" by any human-recognized definition of the word.

"All brave?" the thing asked, clearly posing a question despite the translator's emotionless delivery.

"Yes." She nodded, placing both hands on her chest. "All Terrans are brave." She tapped her chest. "We Terran. Not Vorr. You?"

"You Terran. Not Vorr. We Zeen," it replied through the translator before the armored exoskeleton emitted a sound that actually sounded like a particularly lengthy enunciation of the word "Zeen." While it spoke, the vehicle behind it withdrew back to its originating tunnel where it soon disappeared.

"You Zeen..." She nodded, wary of why its vehicle had withdrawn. "We Terran."

"Terran hierarchical," the Zeen said before uttering a variation on the most cliched phrase in the history of science fiction. "Take Zeen to Terran leader."

17

BATTLEFIELD DIPLOMACY

The live feed from *Leapfrog*, assigned to the same patrol as *Elvira*, showed the last seconds of the fight between Xi and the alien soldier as Lee Jenkins watched with bated breath. It wasn't until the lumbering bug vehicle emerged from the ice and came to a stop nearly on top of her position that Jenkins knew Xi had been right. Her whole theory had just been proven out, and he watched with eager anticipation as a second creature emerged from the larger bug and approached Xi.

The two seemed to converse for several minutes before Styles urgently declared, "New contacts, Colonel."

Jenkins looked up to see *Roy*'s tactical viewer show dozens of fresh contacts, none of which seemed interested in hiding themselves. Groups of four to six fresh icons appeared right on top of the remaining Jemmin targets, and in a span of twenty-one seconds, all Jemmin targets were wiped off the face of Shiva's Wrath.

And the fact that they didn't react nearly as quickly or intelligently to the ambush as they had done prior to the Poltergeist's destruction was not lost on either Jenkins or Styles.

"Jemmin targets neutralized, Colonel," Styles reported

ominously as the entire command center came to terms with what just happened. Over two hundred of the bug vehicles had just popped out of concealment and erased the entire Jemmin presence on Shiva's Wrath.

Which meant that they probably could have done the same thing to the Terrans.

"Verify all Jemmin targets are down," Jenkins ordered as the bugs returned to their icy tunnels, where they remained visible for several minutes before their thermal signatures were occluded by the ice. "And, Styles, I need you to personally take an APC out there to collect the captain and her package."

"APC en route," Styles acknowledged, standing from his station and making for *Roy*'s cabin door.

Jenkins raised the *Generally* on a secure line and forwarded a classified order signed by General Akinouye. "Lieutenant Winters, this is Colonel Jenkins. Hold your position and verify receipt of new orders."

The orders were clear: Winters' people had just observed a classified encounter and were now under explicit orders not to discuss it, or even to surrender their mechs' data storage system contents to anyone but Colonel Jenkins.

A lengthy pause ensued while Winters presumably read the order, and eventually the young officer acknowledged, "Copy that, Colonel. Orders received and executed."

"Good work, 7th Platoon," Jenkins replied. "*Roy* out."

"Colonel Jenkins," greeted Captain Xi Bao after disembarking the APC. The vehicle had been dispatched to retrieve her less than two hours earlier and had just arrived back at HQ bearing its all-important guest. Driven by Chief Styles, the APC was empty of other crew, which made this meeting as secretive as it could possibly be given the circumstances. Xi looked around with concern. "Where's General Akinouye?"

Jenkins shook his head. "This needs to remain compartmentalized for the moment. Are you all right?" he asked, gesturing to the angry, blistered burns running from beneath her rebreather's jaw-line down her neck. The burns seemed to extend well beneath her new enviro-suit, which covered her pilot's jumpsuit and nearly all of her body to protect it from the extreme cold.

"I'm fine, sir," she said dismissively. "It took me a while to master the secret handshake, but I got it." She gestured deferentially toward the APC's interior. "This way, Colonel."

Jenkins walked up the boarding ramp and entered the vehicle where his eyes soon fell upon a truly bizarre-looking creature.

It had four multi-jointed, blade-shaped legs situated beneath its more than meter-long body. Situated over the front legs and protruding from a half-meter tall "torso" was a pair of delicate-looking arms ending in four-clawed pincers. The thing had no discernable head, or any other recognizable organs for that matter, but Xi's initial classification "insectaur" did a good enough job describing its shape.

Gripped in one of those clawed "hands" was a triangular bit of metal that glowed with a soft, blue light. That light pulsed as it emitted English words. "We Zeen. You Terran leader."

Jenkins nodded. "I am a Terran leader."

"Clarify singular," the Zeen said in its strange, inflectionless tone. Jenkins had heard dozens of auto-translation devices, and none of them projected the strange, hollow, seemingly emotionless tone that this one did.

He cocked his head in confusion, looking at Xi for an assist. She gestured toward the Zeen insectaur. "It's asking why you said you are 'a' Terran leader, Colonel."

He nodded, recalling her brief message that had summoned the APC. "Hierarchical structures...right. I'm the commander of the Terran ground forces deployed on this world," he explained.

"You apex leader here?" the Zeen pressed.

"No..." Jenkins replied firmly. "But I am the highest-ranking officer you can communicate with."

"You not apex leader. Preserve hierarchy fundamental hierarchical feature. Limit sensitive component exposure. Terran hierarchical structures symmetrical," the Zeen intoned.

Jenkins was confused, but thankfully, Xi stepped in. "The Zeen is saying it understands the 'apex' leader isn't here because of security concerns. When it says something is 'symmetrical,' it means that it understands and approves of its function or the logic behind it."

Jenkins nodded, impressed by how quickly Xi had picked up the thing's fragmented speech patterns. "Why are the Zeen here?" he asked, diving straight at the heart of the matter.

"Vorr help Zeen," the Zeen replied. "Zeen help Vorr. Vorr brave. Vorr food. Brave food not symmetrical."

Xi giggled, drawing an alarmed look from Jenkins before she explained her outburst. "Apparently, the Vorr don't make much sense to the Zeen, who think they act too much like prey. But the Zeen still seem to like them well enough. That's the fifth time it's described the Vorr like that. I'm sorry, Colonel." She schooled her features into something approaching a professional expression. "It just sounds funnier every time I hear it."

"Zeen not food," the Zeen continued. "Terran not food. Vorr help Terran. Vorr help Zeen. Zeen help Vorr. Zeen help Terran. Terran help Vorr. Terran help Zeen. Mutual help symmetrical."

"We would like that..." Jenkins nodded warily. "But I need you to understand that this is a preliminary meeting."

"Define 'preliminary,'" the Zeen requested.

"We can't complete any agreement here," Jenkins explained. "We need to take what we learn here back to the Terran government."

"Hierarchical structures symmetrical," the Zeen said in what sounded like vaguely reassuring tone. "Zeen help Terran. Zeen not help Terran government. Terran government not symmetrical."

"What do you mean?" Jenkins felt his neck-hairs rise in alarm. "Why do you say 'Terran government not symmetrical'?"

"Terran government subordinate," Zeen replied simply. "Vorr help Zeen. Vorr help Terran. Zeen help Terran. Vorr not help Terran government. Zeen not help Terran government. Terran government not symmetrical."

Of all the possible ways this meeting could have gone, this was not among those which Jenkins had prepared for. "I'm not sure I understand," he eventually said.

"Terran government subordinate," the Zeen serenely repeated.

"Subordinate to who?" Xi demanded.

"Terran government subordinate to Sol," replied the insect-like creature. "Sol subordinate to Jemmin. Jemmin not brave. Jemmin not food. Jemmin not symmetrical. Zeen not food. Zeen brave. Jemmin eat Zeen. Zeen not help Jemmin. Zeen not help Jemmin subordinates."

Jenkins nodded as he sorted through what the Zeen representative had just said. "I need to confer with my subordinate." He gestured to Xi.

"Hierarchical structures symmetrical," it approved.

"Captain..." Jenkins gestured for her to come over for a brief conference. "What else have you learned from the Zeen?"

"One thing that came through loud and clear on the trip here is that they *really* don't like the Jemmin," she explained. "And it seems like the only reason they're on Shiva's Wrath is that the Vorr needed their help with something here. The Vorr asked them to meet with us and see if we could come to some kind of understanding, and it sounds like it took some convincing before the Zeen agreed. I think the main sticking point is that the Zeen insisted on meeting us on their terms rather than in some kind of formalized summit orchestrated by the Vorr," she explained, her words quickening as she made her report. "Just like we thought, those terms include a combat ritual which the Vorr disapproved of but ultimately decided not to interfere with. The Zeen liked what they saw in how we conduct ourselves under fire, and in how we fought against the Jemmin, so they've decided we're 'not food.' As far as I can tell, that's as much respect and regard as we can hope to get from this species."

"Do you know why they don't like the Jemmin?"

She shook her head irritably. "I haven't been able to get any further than 'Jemmin eat Zeen' and 'Jemmin not brave' on that front, Colonel. It seems like the Zeen is being more guarded on the subject of the Jemmin than on just about any other."

He nodded contemplatively before turning back to the Zeen. "Why do you think Sol is subordinate to the Jemmin?"

"Technology symmetrical."

Jenkins quirked an eyebrow in surprise, seeing a look of confusion on Xi's face that matched his own. "Clarify," he urged.

"Sol technology and Jemmin technology symmetrical," the Zeen explained. "Symmetry indicates union. Sol unified with Jemmin. Terran technology and Sol technology asymmetrical. Asymmetry indicates disunion. Terran not unified with Sol. Terran not unified with Jemmin. Terran eat Jemmin. Zeen help Terran."

"But you think Terran government unified with Sol?"

Jenkins pressed, realizing only after he had spoken that he was aping the Zeen's speech pattern.

"Sol and Terran government partially symmetrical," the Zeen agreed. "Vorr and Zeen analysis symmetrical."

"The Vorr and Zeen both think that the Terran government is secretly in league with Sol?" Xi clarified.

"Symmetrical."

Jenkins had no idea what he could do with this information. It was possible the Zeen were overreacting to similarities between certain factions within the Terran government and humanity's parent system of Sol.

But the Vorr were the second-most powerful species in the known galaxy, and if they concurred with the Zeen appraisal of the situation, that gave him serious pause when it came to dismissing their theory.

"Zeen help Terran," the Zeen said into the growing silence. "Terran help Zeen."

"Yes," Jenkins affirmed. "We would like to help each other."

"Symmetry," the alien made a peculiar, mirrored gesture with its arm-like appendages.

"Symmetry," Jenkins agreed, closing the hatch and sitting down on one of the benches normally used to seat troopers in transit. "Captain?" He gestured for Xi to sit opposite him. "Let's continue this dialogue with our new friend."

Colonel Jenkins sat in *Bahamut Zero*'s conference room while General Akinouye reviewed his report on the Zeen meeting. Jenkins had excluded nothing from that report, though it had been tempting to do so with some of the more sensitive bits of information.

Fifteen minutes of total silence passed before the general

finally looked up. "I don't know how actionable any of this is, Colonel. But it seems unlikely the Vorr would bring us here to present a convoluted smokescreen."

"I agree, General." Jenkins nodded. "And given the complexity of establishing a dialogue with them, it seems even more unlikely that the Zeen would willingly participate in such a scheme."

"On that note, the Zeen seem to have taken a liking to Captain Xi," Akinouye mused.

"They have indeed, sir. They made clear toward the meeting's end that they consider her their lone point of contact with Terran humanity," Jenkins explained as a grin tugged at the corners of his mouth. "They tried telling her that she needed to pull back from active duty to protect herself and facilitate future Terran-Zeen interactions."

Akinouye returned Jenkins' grin. "Didn't go over too well, did it?"

"No, sir," Jenkins agreed with a chuckle, "but I think the way she rejected that particular overture only served to endear her to them even more. In any event, they've made it abundantly clear that they don't want their meeting with us to be made public. Not yet, anyway."

The general sighed irritably. "They're rather vague as to why they distrust our government."

"I tried to dig for specifics, but I don't think this particular Zeen has access to them," Jenkins explained.

"If this is a designated Zeen representative, it seems impractical to keep such information from it," Akinouye said pointedly.

"I don't think the Zeen work that way, sir," Jenkins said hesitantly. "From what Styles and Xi have worked out, the Zeen don't have a standard hierarchical society like ours. And they don't have a totally distributed social system like the Arh'Kel, whose lack of formal leadership is one of the only reasons we've managed to stay ahead in our ongoing conflict with the rock-biters." He shook his head in mild frustration as he tried to relay his experts' best theory. "It seems like the Zeen operate in some kind of interdependent caste system."

"Castes are innately hierarchical," Akinouye said flatly.

"Human castes are, yes, sir. But my people think *this* variant isn't," Jenkins explained. "The Zeen appear to have mastered bio-tech so completely that they've integrated multiple organisms into interdependent configurations which, for all intents and purposes, look like a single 'Zeen.' For example, each of the vehicles we previously engaged houses no fewer than eight distinct life forms, each of which has been specifically cultivated to serve a relatively narrow purpose. The 'main vehicle' is primarily an armored transport equipped with a mid-grade plasma cannon, and is controlled by a grub-like facilitator life-form responsible for coordinating communication between the various Zeen caste members assigned to that vehicle. Inside the vehicle are two smaller vehicle-grade creatures, each of which bears a centaur-like exo-suit, which in turn houses a grub-like facilitator that controls both the vehicle and the exo-suit-like organism it rides. As far as we can tell, Zeen work together in relative harmony to produce a kind of gestalt organism. And while the communicator bugs are the most sensitive and critical to the performance of complex tasks, each organism in a given Zeen configuration is fully self-aware and actively participates in group actions and decision-making. Each organism is an individual, but linkable to adjacent Zeen, with the facilitator 'grubs' doing the heavy lifting of keeping everything moving smoothly."

"It still sounds like the brain bugs are running Zeen society," the general grunted.

"The Zeen might be misrepresenting the facts, or we might have asked the wrong questions," Jenkins allowed, "but we've already seen just how differently the various League species are from one another. The Zeen don't seem to deviate any further from the League norm than any other known non-human species."

"Probably not," General Akinouye grudgingly agreed.

"In fact," Jenkins continued, "I think the concept of hierarchies disturbs the Zeen because they see the opportunity for catastrophic systems failures in hierarchical structures. When a relatively small group at the top of a hierarchy works against the good of the whole system, it's difficult to counter their efforts."

"I do recall my basic sociology, Colonel," Akinouye rebuked his subordinate.

"Of course, General." Jenkins nodded. "But the Zeen don't have ready access to our same perspective. Think about this from their point of view. If they're telling us the truth about how their society is organized, how could they view a hierarchical society as desirable? Or, even more importantly, how could they see it as *trustworthy*? When the potential failure points of a system are so blindingly obvious, it's difficult to justify investing in that system," he explained, seeing a look of comprehension dawn on the general's aged features. "I think the Zeen mistrust our government because they've seen its failures, and those failure points are related to the way we structure our society. They dislike the Jemmin and are convinced that Sol is currently moving in lock-step with the Jemmin. It seems to me, while considering their perspective, that they're taking an enormous risk by introducing themselves to us even though we are fundamentally identical to Solar humans."

"What are you saying, Colonel?"

"I'm saying," Jenkins replied with conviction, "that the Zeen see contacting us as a serious risk, but one worth taking. Why?" he asked earnestly. "The most basic rules of self-preservation dictate that, when given two options, you generally pick the less dangerous one."

Akinouye's eyes narrowed. "You think the Jemmin are plotting some kind of major offensive?"

"I think it's possible," Jenkins agreed, "but it's almost certain that they've *already* got something underway that both the Vorr and Zeen are opposed to. And for whatever reason, the Vorr think the Terran Republic can help them. But more importantly from our perspective, they think that *they* can help *us*."

The general leaned onto the arm of his chair. "I'm not a fan of all this cloak and dagger, Colonel...but it's what we came here to do, and our primary objective is now complete. We made contact with an unknown alien species and negotiated an introduction while protecting Terran interests. But," he said pointedly, "we can't leave this rock until we know *exactly* what the Vorr, Jemmin, and Zeen were so interested in. I need you to realize just how bad the shitstorm will be when we return to Terran space, Lee."

Jenkins knew that Armor Corps' political enemies would have a field day with the fact that they engaged and destroyed a Jemmin warship in a relatively unimportant star system. A star system to which the Terran Republic had no primary claim.

"I'm aware there will be blowback, General," Jenkins said firmly.

"And with my ship blown to hell," Akinouye continued grimly, "we're going to need to get creative if we want to keep your unit on active-duty where it can continue demonstrating the Metal Legion's worth." He sighed in resignation. "On top of which, I doubt Fleet's going to prioritize the *Bonhoeffer*'s repairs in any of their shipyards. And the Legion doesn't have the facilities to conduct those repairs ourselves."

"Understood, General," Jenkins said, knowing that the general's preamble pointed to the necessity of another meeting with one of the wealthiest humans who ever lived: Director

Durgan of DIE. "I'll do what I can to secure the Legion's interests via private support."

"Good." Akinouye nodded. "Which leaves us the matter of figuring out why these non-humans came to Shiva's Wrath. Answer that question, and we can get the hell off this snowball."

"Thank you, General." Jenkins nodded, standing and making his way to *Bahamut Zero*'s exit ramp.

"We need to know," Xi said urgently after receiving an update from Colonel Jenkins regarding the importance of solving the mystery of what the three alien races were looking for on Shiva's Wrath, "why did the Zeen, the Vorr, and the Jemmin come here?"

"Symmetry," the Zeen replied simply.

"Yes, I understand the reason was the same," Xi said, working to suppress her mounting frustration after nearly three hours of circling this particular question. "But *we* still don't know what that reason is. What is the purpose of your coming here?"

"Terran and Sol not symmetrical," Zeen said matter-of-factly.

"I understand," Xi said with growing impatience, "but why did *you* come to *this* world?"

"Terran and Sol not symmetrical," the creature repeated.

Xi chewed her lip, stifling a scream of frustration as Styles sat down on the bench beside her.

"I think," Styles mused, "that there's something we're missing about its transmission. I've noticed that it doesn't use the terms 'not symmetrical' and 'asymmetrical' interchangeably. They seem to mean different things."

"I noticed that, too," she said irritably, "but how does it help?"

Styles produced a handheld scanner capable of detecting myriad types of radiation and pointed the device at the Zeen. "Ask it again. We have to be missing something fundamental here."

Xi drew a cleansing breath. "Why did Zeen come to this world?"

"Terran and Sol not symmetrical," the Zeen repeated, and Xi looked over at Styles as he flipped through screen after screen on the scanner's interface.

"Anything?" she asked hopefully.

"Not yet..." He shook his head after scanning through the scanner's settings.

"Wait..." she said, pointing to the translation device. "That's Vorr, right?"

"Right," Styles absently agreed.

"Don't Vorr use a combined audio-visual communication system for person-to-person interactions?" she asked.

Styles stopped fidgeting the scanner instantly, his eyes snagging on the translator. "That's right... They're like octopuses."

"Octopuses use skin pigment changes to communicate sensitive information with each other, and audio to communicate more publicly," Xi continued, thinking they might finally be onto something. "What do we have on file for Vorr translation programs?"

"Hold on..." he said, switching over to a data slate and working to access *Roy*'s main computer. "There it is," he said, pulling up a program designed to translate individual Vorr visual displays. "Help me link these things," he urged, and Xi did as bidden. It took them nearly five minutes to establish a makeshift translator out of the two nearly-incompatible pieces of equipment, but when they finished, Styles pointed the scanner at the Zeen and said, "All right... Ask it again."

Knowing they were near the end of their rope, Xi drew yet another steadying breath. "Why did Zeen come to this world?"

"Terran and Sol not symmetrical," the Zeen replied, and as it did so, the Vorr translator pulsed with the same rhythmic, blue light.

Except this time, Styles' scanner recorded every pulse and wave shift, which came back as a perfect match for short-range information burst codes employed by Vorr to communicate highly-sensitive information.

"Holy shit..." Styles muttered as hundreds of megabytes of data, pre-arranged to be easily understood by humans, streamed across the data slate.

"Are you saving all of this?" Xi asked breathlessly.

"You bet your ass," Styles assured her as a stream of visual images populated the screen. "Wait..." he said in surprise. "Is that what I think it is?"

At first, Xi didn't know exactly what he had seen, but then a schematic flickered across the screen almost too fast to register.

It was a diagram that any self-respecting nerd born after the mid-twenty-first century would recognize.

"I have to show this to the Colonel," Styles said urgently, using his wrist-link to discretely contact their CO.

While waiting for the CO, both Xi and Styles had time to peruse the Zeen's information-rich transmission burst. A few minutes later, Colonel Jenkins arrived at the APC's outer door.

"What have you got?" Jenkins asked, causing Xi and Styles to share a brief but meaningful look. "Captain?" Jenkins pressed when the duo made no reply.

Xi was so utterly dumbfounded by what they had just seen that she could hardly clear her throat.

Thankfully, Styles was better prepared to convey their findings, though his voice trembled with anxiety as he said, "We found what brought the Vorr, the Jemmin, and the Zeen here, Colonel."

"Let's hear it," Jenkins said, giving Xi a muted look of concern as she anxiously rubbed the back of her neck.

Styles handed the data slate to Colonel Jenkins, with the display prominently featuring a handful of nearly-identical images.

"What am I looking at?" Jenkins asked after perusing the series of images.

"One is a technical diagram of humanity's first-generation quantum processor, which has not undergone serious modification since its inception," Styles explained tremulously. "It was first mass-produced two full decades before humanity cracked FTL. It has only seen minor changes made to its supporting architecture over the last two centuries."

Jenkins narrowed his eyes before looking back down at the slate. "The one with English lettering in the top-left is obviously the human schematic," he mused.

"Correct." Styles nodded, and Xi could hardly believe what she was about to hear him say in reply to Colonel Jenkins' inevitable follow-up.

"Then what are the other three images?"

"The others..." Styles trailed off, causing Xi to step in.

"The others were reportedly found in a data storage device," Xi explained, "which, until recently, rested below fifteen kilometers of water and ice beneath our feet."

Jenkins' brow furrowed in confusion. "Why would anyone care about schematics for two-hundred-year-old human technology?"

"That's just it, sir," Styles explained, regathering his wits in time to deliver the most crucial piece of the puzzle. "A header on the Vorr file which those images were packed inside show that at least one of the other three schematics pre-date humanity's first FTL flight by over *six hundred years*."

Jenkins seemed not to take their full meaning, so Xi clarified their findings in a tremulous voice. "Humanity didn't invent the most fundamental piece of technology which ultimately became the backbone of our species' virtual architecture, Colonel."

Colonel Jenkins' brow rose in surprise, suggesting he now understood the full meaning of what they had just learned.

"Put simply, sir," Styles reported, his voice once again steady as he pointed at the data slate, "someone surreptitiously *gave* humanity that technology, and it looks like our species isn't the first one to receive such a 'gift.'"

"There's also bits and pieces of the technology that weren't incorporated. We were given a dumbed down set of keys to the galaxy, or humanity adopted a more restricted version. In either case, we can take this six-hundred-year-old technology to improve our current understanding of FTL engineering."

Lieutenant Colonel Jenkins looked over at the serenely-situated Zeen insectaur while Xi could barely contain her disbelief at the magnitude of what they had just uncovered.

"You knew about this?" Jenkins asked the insect-like creature.

"Symmetry," it replied in apparent agreement.

"Humanity didn't reach the stars on our own feet, sir," Xi said, flushing with anger at the reality of what she said next. "We were technologically uplifted."

Colonel Jenkins' brow lowered thunderously as he gave voice to what Xi considered the absolute worst revelation of all. "And we didn't even know it."

It was a stunning revelation. One which, if true, would reshape the way humanity viewed the cosmos and their place in it.

"Zeen leave now," the Zeen declared. "Zeen help Terran. Terran help Zeen."

Colonel Jenkins nodded slowly. "Thank you for this."

"Zeen help Terran," the insect-like alien repeated, turning to Xi. "You brave Terran. Take."

The thing's frontal carapace slowly spread apart, revealing wire-thin tendrils that produced a small, spiral-shaped object very much like an elongated snail shell.

Xi bent down to examine the object closer before looking to her CO for approval. Colonel Jenkins nodded, prompting her to reach out and pluck the five-centimeter-long object from the Zeen's grasp.

"Show to Zeen," the creature explained, gesturing to the shell-like thing in Xi's hands. "Zeen help brave. Zeen know brave. Zeen leave now," the Zeen insisted. "Return us to Zeen."

Colonel Jenkins nodded approvingly. "Chief Styles, conduct our guest back to the site of Xi's...cultural exchange," he finally said after apparently fishing for the right words. Frankly, Xi couldn't think of a better way to describe their first contact situation with the bizarre species. "Captain Xi," Jenkins said, looking down at the shell pointedly, "I suggest you make no reference to that in your logs."

"Understood, sir," she said, uncertain as to the meaning the token was meant to convey. She turned to the Zeen, holding the shell out between her palms. "Thank you for this."

"Symmetry."

"Are you fit to escort our guest back to where you found it, Captain?" Jenkins asked.

"I am, sir." Xi nodded.

"Good, then do so," the colonel ordered before adding, "and then report to Doc Fellows for a full physical."

She resisted the urge to groan at being ordered into Strange Bed's clutches. "Yes, sir," she acknowledged.

A little under an hour later, the Zeen disembarked the APC and rejoined its comrades aboard one of their large, living transport vehicles.

An hour after that, Xi reported to Fellows and survived the exam with her dignity mostly intact. But rather than succumbing to exhaustion as every cell in her body screamed for her to do, she made her way to Lu's bedside where her Wrench-turned-Monkey was engaged in a critical battle for his life.

18

TIGHT WRAPS

"Colonel Jenkins," Sarah Samuels demanded after somehow escaping Doc Fellows' watchful eye and finding Jenkins in the mess hall, "where are my video drones?"

Since the last of the Jemmin forces were confirmed neutralized, battalion HQ had transferred fifteen hundred kilometers from the irradiated ice-field. As a result, radiation protocols had been relaxed, and free movement was once again permitted throughout the camp.

"I already answered that question, Ms. Samuels," Jenkins said, sighing in frustration at his half-eaten platter of food since he doubted she would let him enjoy the last of his meal.

"I don't need answers, Colonel," the reporter snapped, her head still wrapped with a bandage after sustaining a serious injury that had nearly cost the woman her ear. "I need my cameras. Their data integrity is covered by freedom of the press, freedom of speech, freedom of information, and by my charter approved by the Joint Chiefs of Staff!"

Jenkins closed his eyes, pushing the platter of food away. A soldier got precious little enjoyment on deployment, and Jenkins had worked hard to secure a talented cook to add some vitality to the otherwise-bland foodstuffs. As dozens of his fellow servicemen would readily attest, messing with Lee Jenkins' food was a sure way to find out *exactly* what his bad side looked like.

Still, it seemed that Ms. Samuels' efforts had been integral to saving Chief Lu's life aboard the crippled *Elvira*. As a result, Jenkins grudgingly thought she deserved a little slack.

But only a little.

"Ms. Samuels..." He opened his eyes and stood from the table. "Most of your equipment was destroyed in the fight. Including a pair of cameras you had fixed to *Elvira*'s hull without requesting authorization to do so," he added pointedly. "And I can tell you that most officers in my position would consider bringing formal charges against you for doing that. In combat, information security is critical. Your recording devices were not hardened against enemy takeover attempts, were they, Ms. Samuels?"

Her jaw muscles bunched angrily. "The people have a right to—"

"Again," he interrupted, "I can assure you that most officers in my position would, at the very least, consider your deployment of those data-recording devices to be one of the worst breaches of trust imaginable. And at most," he added casually, "they would recommend the charge of treason be brought against you for knowingly aiding the enemy."

Samuels reared back incredulously, wrong-footed by that last bit. "Are you suggesting I was in league with the Jemmin?" she demanded, quickly regaining her composure.

"No, I'm not." He shook his head firmly. "But there's a saying about stones and glass houses that applies here, Ms. Samuels." He relaxed, giving her a sympathetic look before tapping a series of commands into his link which would summon Styles. "Look, you're here doing your job, and you're doing it as aggressively as you can. I understand that," he said seriously. "But you need to understand that as long as we're on this rock, I also have to do my job, and right now my top priority is safeguarding this battalion while we prep for extraction to the *Dietrich Bonhoeffer*. Once we're in orbit, I assure you that all of your materials will be returned to you along with a verifiable chain of custody which you will be free to formally review with my full cooperation. In the meantime," he continued as Styles made his way through the soft-airlock of the mess hall, "I've had Mr. Styles prepare several items you might find of interest. Included among those items are high-fidelity images of Jemmin war vehicles taken during this engagement. I'm breaking several regs by offering these to you before they get declassified through proper channels, but in my opinion, you've earned them."

The truth was that General Akinouye had unofficially given Jenkins the go-ahead to give her the images since doing so might buy them enough time to get off Shiva's Wrath and keep her from gathering more information on the Zeen.

She was intrigued by the offer, but she was just as versed in the art of negotiation. "You can't brush me off like this, Colonel," Samuels promised.

"I can assure you, Ms. Samuels, that this is no brush-off," Jenkins said seriously, giving the ambitious reporter a knowing look as Styles came to his side and saluted.

"You wanted to see me, Colonel?" the technician asked.

"I believe Ms. Samuels was just expressing her interest in the presentation you prepared for her," Jenkins said, turning back to the reporter with an expectant look. "Isn't that right, Ms. Samuels?"

Samuels shook her head in resignation. "Fine... I'll look at these pictures of yours. But this isn't over, Colonel," she vowed before following Styles to the airlock.

After they had left, Jenkins looked down at his platter and

sighed. But just as he was about to pick up the half-empty tray, the mess hall's lead cook emerged from behind the counter with a fresh platter balanced on one hand.

"Mak," Jenkins greeted with relief, "you're a life-saver."

"Don't mention it, Colonel," the cook said, replacing the cold, half-eaten tray with a full, piping hot one.

Jenkins sat down at the table, and after a few bites, he managed to forget Ms. Samuels and her recording drones.

"*Bahamut Zero* is back aboard the *Dietrich Bonhoeffer*," Styles reported late the next day. With the worldlet of Shiva's Wrath plunged completely into darkness, getting the behemoth off the surface had not been an easy task.

"Good." Jenkins nodded in relief after the first Armor Corps vehicle had been returned to the assault carrier. "We'll complete our withdrawal in three days' time. Have the DIE installations been properly secured?"

"Yes, sir," Styles acknowledged. "All removed or damaged equipment has been replaced, and all four facilities have resumed normal operations."

"Good." Jenkins nodded before lowering his voice. "How about our reporter friend?"

Styles flashed a mischievous grin. "All I know for sure is that she's as kinky as I am."

Jenkins snorted. "Not the kind of intel I was looking for, Chief."

The technician chuckled. "Between our 'calisthenics,' I'm leaving her a trail of breadcrumbs and red herrings to run down while we're still planet-side. She's too smart to be fooled forever, but I doubt she'll catch on until we're out of here. Combined with those exclusive recordings, I think she's leaving Shiva's Wrath with a whole lot more than she expected she'd get. She'll be satisfied," he said confidently before adding on a more bitter note, "but her network's editors are another story."

"We can't control every variable." Jenkins shook his head resolutely. "We were saddled with her before we even accepted this mission, and her presence was always meant to hamstring us. The best we could hope for is to mitigate the PR damage and try to do the Metal Legion proud in the process, and I think that we did that. Keep an eye on her and let me know if it looks like she gets ahead of you."

"Will do, sir." Styles nodded.

"Good work, Chief," Jenkins said with feeling, turning toward *Roy*'s exit hatch. "I'm going to survey the camp."

Xi was tired, weak, and nauseated. But more than just being physically unwell, she was *sick*.

The fight with the Zeen had apparently exposed her to a super-high dose of radiation, and Doc Fellows had kept her on strict bedrest while he pumped her full of drugs and cleansing agents to counteract the damned stuff.

She had never really been sick before. Wounded, sure, but sick? As a nineteen-year-old woman, she was in the physical prime of her life. Even losing half of her liver during the transplant with Podsy had been relatively unremarkable. She wasn't much for drinking anyway, so it wasn't like she would miss out much on the diminished metabolic capacity.

But sitting there, curled up on a cot beside one of Fellows' fancy bio-beds, it was hard to focus on anything but the unrelenting waves of nausea that swept over her. Each felt somehow worse than the last, and it was nearly all she could do to keep from whimpering between the twice-hourly retching sessions she had grown accustomed to.

"Jesus, Captain, you look like dogshit that's marinated in donkey piss for a week," she heard Dr. Fellows say. "You should have let me knock you out for a few days until the worst of this passed."

She smiled weakly. "If you think I'd actually ask you to slip me one of your date rape drugs, you're even stupider than you're perverted."

Fellows laughed, lowering himself to sit on the foot of her cot. "You'll be all right," he assured her with what sounded like genuine sympathy as he gently patted her ankle. "Give it a couple more days, and your stomach lining will be good as new. You'll probably be back on solid foods by the end of the week."

Xi propped herself up, careful not to let the puke bucket stray too far from her lap as she made eye contact with the doctor. "Your wife...Dr. Turney," she began, fighting down the urge to burp since doing so might initiate another full-on retch-fest. "How did you meet?"

Fellows cocked an eyebrow in surprise, "My, my...a polite *question* about my past? Don't try telling me there's an actual *person* under that double-thick layer of dragon-skin you wear around twenty-four-seven."

"Don't deflect, Doc," she urged, remembering what Sergeant Major Trapper had said to her back on Durgan's Folly about letting her guard down more often.

Fellows sighed. "I was working at a frontier clinic in New Africa. Do you know about the Gandel Plague?"

Xi shook her head, having never heard about it.

"It was a mess," he grunted. "Some fucking parasite got dug up on one of the system's colonial moons, and nobody learned about it until two months had gone by and the damned things started showing up on blood slides. By the time the New Africans knew what it was, it had already vectored a dozen virulent strains of the worst shit you could imagine throughout the system. Hemorrhagic fevers, drug-resistant encephalopathics, immunodeficiency strains...you name it, and it was sweeping from one side of the system to the other. Turns out the damned parasite had been coopted by an ex-governor-turned-terrorist named Gandel, which he loaded with every pathogen he could get his hands on before sending them out into the colonies. Three million people died in under two weeks," he said reverently while his gaze fell to the floor.

"Why haven't I heard about this?" Xi asked in alarm, causing Fellows to scoff.

"I knew you were young, but I didn't think you were naïve," the doctor chided. "New Africa's various governments suppressed media outlets from reporting on the calamity, and eventually everyone in power agreed it would be best not to let the truth get out lest inter-system commerce suffer. New Africa grows a lot of specialty foods and the like, but a bio-plague scare would have cut them off from the rest of the Republic due to fear of contamination. So traffic was re-routed to relatively safe ports while the truth was essentially buried. But the aftermath was horrific, with tens of millions suffering debilitating injuries even after surviving the various diseases."

"You went there as part of the relief effort," she said knowingly.

He nodded. "I was a dumb kid, fresh out of med school with the wild-eyed notion that I could make a difference. In the medical community, we knew something was going on in New Africa that was bad, but no one knew the details. I decided that was where I would go and make my mark. I had only been there for a few weeks when I met Mia, and she introduced me to Sarah, Melissa, and Anne."

"Wait..." Xi interrupted. "Mia Turney and your other wives *knew* each other?"

Fellows laughed. "That's the only real way polygamy can work, Captain."

Xi sank back against the cot. "I admit I did *not* see that coming." She gingerly sat back up. "Polygamy is illegal in New America."

"It is," he agreed, "but it's normally more of a 'don't ask, don't tell' policy given the aggressive incentives surrounding procreation. And for twenty-eight years, we lived together, raised eighteen children, and did the things that all married folks do." His mood suddenly darkened. "But when I spoke up about some of the things I'd seen in New Africa nearly three decades earlier, the government decided to make an example out of me for fear that others would do likewise. I was sentenced to sixty-one years in prison, ostensibly just for loving who I love and for supporting them to the best of my ability." He shook his head angrily. "No one should be thrown in jail because they loved too many people, Captain."

Xi was completely taken aback. Never in her wildest dreams had she expected Dr. "Strange Bed" Fellows' prison sentence to be related to marriage laws. He was such a competent surgeon that she always assumed he had killed someone through negligence, or while intoxicated, or that he had actually murdered someone using his advanced knowledge of human physiology.

"So...what you're saying," Xi ventured after a lengthy silence, "is that you would never be satisfied by ruining the life of just *one* woman, so you had to go and marry *four* of them?"

Fellows chuckled before standing from her cot. "That's the long and the short of it, kid."

"Thank you," she said awkwardly, "for...sharing." She felt well enough to sit fully upright, and did so to better see Chief Lu in the bio-bed beside her. "Is he going to recover?"

Fellows nodded with conviction. "There was enough left of his arm that he'll need just three months of rehab to get back to full strength, and by then, the burns will heal as good as Podsy's."

"When will he regain consciousness?" she asked, looking up and down the blood-tinged, medicated bandages wrapped tightly around his upper torso and head.

"I'm keeping him sedated until after he's transferred up to the *Bonhoeffer*," Fellows replied.

"Thank you, Doctor," Xi said just as another wave of nausea slammed into her, forcing her to double over and retch into the bucket.

"Try to keep it off the walls..." Fellows muttered as he moved to the far side of the mobile hospital.

In spite of the dry heaves wracking her body, Xi somehow managed to laugh at the doctor's unflappable persona.

"Captain?" Colonel Jenkins greeted from the foot of Lu's bed.

Captain Xi looked up from a bucket clenched between her legs. Her eyes were sunken and bloodshot, but she was just as alert as ever as she made to stand. "Colonel—"

"As you were," he insisted, and somewhat uncharacteristically, she complied without argument. *She must feel like hell*, he thought as he inclined his chin toward the unconscious Lu. "Dr. Fellows says he'll be ready to transfer Lu to the *Bonhoeffer* with the next can, and he's ordering you to accompany him."

Xi made a distasteful expression. "I'd like to argue the case for keeping me here, but I think it's obvious I won't be any good to anyone for the next few days. I'm just disappointed I left my mech in such a mess," she said with seemingly sincere frustration.

"*Elvira*'s already prepped and ready for retrieval," he assured her. "You've done your part, Captain. Take the down-time while you can get it, because if my read is right, we're going to be under fire again sooner than we'd like."

She straightened in her cot. "Another deployment, sir?"

"Unfortunately, no." He shook his head, pulling a nearby chair over and setting it down beside her.

Xi nodded in silent comprehension. "I'm ready, sir."

Jenkins lowered his voice. "The general's going to give us as much cover as possible, but some of us are going to end up in front of review boards. I won't ask you to compromise your ethics or personal integrity..."

"I'm onboard, Colonel," she interrupted with a measure of conviction that Lee Jenkins doubted he had ever projected, let alone *felt*. "We came here to do a job, and that job isn't done until we've completed our extraction. I understand that going wheels-up off this rock isn't the end of my deployment in relationship to this mission, sir. I'm not going to queer the deal by cracking under bright lights with the finish line in sight. And I fully understand that I might spend my next few birthdays in a cell if I don't stay on my toes and play my cards right."

Jenkins was floored by this latest display of the young woman's resolve and character. As he looked at her, disheveled and in pure agony from the effects of radiation poisoning, she displayed a measure of courage greater than anything he had ever seen in himself.

He looked over at Chief Lu's tightly-wrapped body, and it was that moment when he knew beyond the shadow of a doubt that one day, perhaps very soon, she would assume command of the battalion. If anyone in the Terran Republic could lead the Metal Legion to the rosy future he had pitched to General Akinouye, it was the woman sitting in the cot beside her crippled crewmate.

"This battalion is lucky to have you, Captain," he said, meaning every word as he stood from the chair. He offered a salute, which she returned with a look of surprise before he said, "Now get some rest. That's an order."

"Thank you, Colonel," she acknowledged as he turned to leave.

He was now more determined than ever to keep her out of the pending debriefings and "informal inquiries." Not because he doubted her ability to handle them, but because he couldn't risk the Legion's finest young officer getting caught in the political gears so early in her career.

She was the future of the Armor Corps, and protecting that future was now an objective he needed to keep in mind at all times.

"One more thing, Colonel," Xi Bao said, grabbing Jenkins' arm before he could go. "Did we win?"

"We won because the Jemmin lost and the Vorr lost. We won because our champion rivaled their champion. We won because you convinced the Zeen that we are their equals. Symmetry, Captain."

"I understand, Colonel Li," Jenkins said two days later after learning details regarding Chief Warrant Officer Podsednik's actions during the last engagement with the Jemmin. "I'm not arguing your authority to lock him in the brig."

"The man violated my ship's data core integrity in the middle of combat with an enemy known for committing virtual takeovers," Li said with finality. "He's lucky I didn't space him on the spot, Lieutenant Colonel Jenkins."

Jenkins knew he needed to tread lightly here, and if letting the full-bird colonel rub his nose in their rank differences avoided unnecessary conflict, then that's precisely what he would do. "The logs clearly show, Colonel Li," Jenkins continued evenly, "that the Jemmin were only revealed *after* Chief Podsednik introduced the antivirus to the *Bonhoeffer*'s computer core."

"Antivirus?" Li scoffed. "You call it whatever flowery word you like, but the book calls it an unauthorized attack on the integrity of my ship's information-processing system."

"Unauthorized? Yes, absolutely," Jenkins agreed. "But it's not a 'flowery' word, Colonel Li. It's an accurate descriptor, and we both know it."

"I don't like your tone, Lieutenant Colonel Jenkins," Li said with thin-lipped disdain.

"The only reason Chief Podsednik's program worked was that the Jemmin had already compromised your computer core, Colonel Li," Jenkins said, his voice and visage unyielding. "Without Chief Podsednik's efforts, it's doubtful we would have bracketed that Poltergeist and knocked it off the board. The destruction of that Jemmin vehicle isn't going to be glossed over in some round-filed report, Colonel." Jenkins leaned intently toward the video pickup. "This entire engagement will be examined in excruciating detail for years—no, for *decades*—to come. And right now, you have an opportunity to become part of the narrative that arises from this important first clash with Jemmin forces."

Li sneered at Jenkins with open contempt. "Appealing to my vanity? You misjudged your mark, Colonel."

"Maybe..." Jenkins refused to back down. "But here's the reality: your ship's computer core was first compromised by the *Jemmin*, and Chief Podsednik discovered and neutralized that threat. Now, you are well within your rights to file a report which says that he acted without your knowledge and prior authorization, but I think you and I both know how that will look on your jacket. A ship commander whose data systems were violated not once but twice without his knowledge?" Jenkins shook his head piteously. "Not the kind of thing a promotion board will overlook, to say nothing of the formal inquiries we're all about to face in the coming weeks and months."

Li's sneer had largely melted away and was now replaced with a grim look of distaste. "Go ahead, Colonel," he urged after Jenkins had let the silence linger. "Tell me what you think I should do instead."

"I think you should tell the truth," Jenkins said, diving head-first into a narrative that could very well land him in a cell right beside Podsy. "You should say that you tasked Chief Podsednik with an off-the-books project to secretly investigate whether or not the ship's data core had been breached, following reports from the surface of sensor and targeting system failures. And you should say that he, working under your direct supervision and with General Akinouye's approval, developed an antivirus which he deployed when it would provide maximum effect. Do I need to go on, Colonel?" he asked when it was clear the other man's contentiousness had all but vanished at hearing the general's name invoked.

"The general's approval?" Li repeated.

"Absolutely," Jenkins agreed, having received General Akinouye's go-ahead in an effort to smooth things over with the aggrieved warship commander. He leaned back, careful to keep the triumph he felt from gracing his features. "This is your chance to write your name in the history books, Colonel Li—the first Terran commander to outflank the Jemmin. Not only did you shoot down one of their warships, but you overcame their previously-impenetrable sensor obfuscation techniques and helped clear an entire planet of their presence. Now you tell me —" He shrugged with forced indifference. "—is keeping one reprobate indefinitely confined to the brig for a simple misunderstanding really more valuable to your ship and its crew than having that same man attest and affirm the version of events which will catapult you and your people into the annals of history?"

Li scowled. "You're slipperier than a greased pig, Jenkins."

"Do I take that to mean you'll be releasing Chief Podsednik after he's cooled his heels for a few more days, with a formal demerit added to his file for sexual harassment against one of his shipmates?" Jenkins asked.

"Sexual harassment?" Li rolled his eyes.

"Everyone's got a façade to protect," Jenkins said with a light, hollow chuckle as he wore his best poker face.

For a moment, Jenkins thought the other man would call his bluff and that he would not only be down a valuable member of the battalion, but that the inquiry into him would reveal that it was Styles, not Podsy, who had fashioned the anti-Jemmin program.

It had been a minor miracle for General Akinouye to keep Styles out of Fleet's hands following Durgan's Folly, given the talented technician's stunning success in overcoming the Arh'Kel mind-link system. But if word broke of a second, equally stunning maneuver under his belt in as many deployments, Jenkins knew there was no chance Styles would remain under his command.

And frankly, without Styles, the battalion would have already died twice over. The battalion needed Styles *at least* as much as it needed Jenkins. And Styles wouldn't survive the regular army.

"Fine," Li reluctantly agreed, "but that man will never again receive authorization to so much as flip a light switch aboard my ship. Is that clear, Colonel?" the century-old officer snapped.

"As a Solarian's conscience." Jenkins nodded in agreement.

Li gave him a withering look before cutting the line, and when the feed died, Jenkins exhaled a sharp sigh of relief. So long as Podsy played his cards right, the battalion would remain intact long enough for Jenkins to face down what he expected would be yet another "informal" inquiry.

19

THE JEMMIN CONSPIRACY?

Lee Jenkins sat outside the TRF *Red Cliff*'s main conference room, where he had waited for nearly two hours in total silence while the board of inquiry within reviewed after-action reports and other materials authorized for release by General Akinouye. The *Red Cliff* was 6th Fleet's flagship and was one of the most decorated dreadnoughts in the entire fleet. It had been at the head of the flotilla that turned back the Arh'Kel before they could reach Durgan's Folly, which said that Fleet wanted to keep Armor Corps' performance under Colonel Jenkins compartmentalized while they reviewed the after-action reports.

The general had redacted significant portions of the official report, which was his duly-recognized prerogative as Armor Corps' ranking officer. Those redactions would remain in effect until the Joint Chiefs had fully examined the events of Shiva's Wrath. Such reviews generally took a few months, but in this case, the general had expected it to take a small fraction of that time given the gravity of the situation.

As a consequence of the general's information fog, this particular review board was unaware of the battalion's success in meeting with the Zeen. To their knowledge, which was informed by the carefully-manipulated facts General Akinouye let slip through his wall of redactions, the insect-like species had been Armor Corps' enemy on the frozen worldlet.

But one didn't become an admiral by being a fool. Jenkins knew he was about to come under fire from one of the most clear-minded, incisive, and aggressive officers in the Terran Fleet. He had no illusions about "winning" the certain-to-be-contentious interview; Lee Jenkins merely needed to survive so that General Akinouye could come in and sweep up the debris after he exited stage left.

The door to the conference room suddenly slid open, revealing a sharply-dressed ensign in her black uniform. "The admiral will see you now," she reported.

"Thank you," he replied, standing from the bench and making his way into the conference room.

"Lieutenant Colonel Jenkins," greeted the granite-hard voice of Vice Admiral Zhao, who gestured to the lone chair situated before the five-person board of inquiry's bench, "be seated."

"Thank you, Admiral," Jenkins replied, tucking his dress beret beneath the crook of his arm as he approached the unprotected position at the center of the chamber. The curved bench, which featured two empty chairs, wrapped around Jenkins' isolated chair, giving that spot the undeniable impression of being surrounded. He made for the chair and sat down, meeting the eyes of the review board one-by-one.

"I understand this is not your first time in front of a panel like this, Colonel," Admiral Zhao said, while his flanking officers looked on in silence. One of those figures, a heavyset woman with light brown skin wearing a multi-colored sash over her green uniform, was unknown to Jenkins, but her uniform designated her a commander in the Terran Planetary Defense Coalition or TPDC. With each of the Terran colonies' individual

Planetary Defense Forces under local, wholly sovereign control and funded locally without Republic funds, the TPDC was less a governing body than a regulatory one. Generally regarded as the "fifth wheel" of the Terran Armed Forces, in part due to PDF usage generally centering on major planet-wide infrastructure projects, the Republic's various PDFs nonetheless featured more active-duty servicemen than all other branches combined. The TPDC's representative looked up from her data slate with practiced disdain the very instant Jenkins' gaze fell on her.

The third member of the board was known to him, and frankly, Jenkins was surprised to see him there as Admiral Zhao gestured to the TPDC representative. "This is Major General Kylie Kavanaugh of the Terra Africana PDF, currently assigned to the Terran Planetary Defense Coalition. And this—" He turned to the man wearing dress blues. "—is Colonel Jonathan Villa of the Terran Marine Corps."

"General." Jenkins nodded to the TPDC rep before doing likewise to his longtime friend. "Colonel."

"As you can doubtless deduce," Admiral Zhao continued, "this board is conducting an informal, preliminary inquiry into the events on Shiva's Wrath." Jenkins noted that the admiral had not used the planet's official designation of EO-5293, which seemed to bode well for the rest of the meeting's tone and direction. "You are not required to answer any questions posed at this time," the admiral continued, "nor will the product of this informal inquiry be admissible in any official proceedings from this point forward. Consider this to be a purely fact-finding debriefing, Colonel Jenkins, so that the rest of us can come up to speed on what went on down there."

Major General Kavanaugh's darting eyes flicked back and forth between her data slate, Jenkins, and Admiral Zhao while her expression remained an unreadable mask. Colonel Villa, on the other hand, was neither tense nor relaxed as his eyes barely lingered on Jenkins for more than a second while he studied the reports arrayed before him.

Jenkins nodded, reading his longtime friend's body language: a battle was about to be waged, and everyone in the room was ready for it.

"I understand, Admiral," Jenkins acknowledged.

Admiral Zhao leaned forward, and his fierce grey eyebrows gave him a decidedly predatory appearance as he intently met Jenkins' gaze. "Under General Akinouye's orders, you and your battalion were deployed to Shiva's Wrath for what purpose?"

Jenkins had expected yes or no questions to begin with, but it was now clear that the admiral had no intention of making this easy for him. He drew a short breath, gathering his wits as he replied, "General Akinouye had received word of a unique opportunity on Shiva's Wrath, which included safeguarding automated mining installations of critical importance to Terran security interests."

"Was that all that the general told you about the mission to Shiva's Wrath?" Zhao asked, his expression unreadable and his tone pleasant.

"No, Admiral." Jenkins shook his head. "The mining installations were merely a cover for the real operation."

At that, Major General Kavanaugh recoiled as she asked, "And what was this 'real' operation's nature, Colonel Jenkins?"

"Using contacts within Durgan Industrial Enterprises," Jenkins explained, "the Vorr reached out to the Terran Republic through unofficial channels in order to facilitate a clandestine meeting."

"Under what security protocols was this meeting to be conducted?" Colonel Villa asked.

Jenkins shook his head. "General Akinouye never went into specifics on that front, Colonel, and given the nature of the assignment, I chose not to pursue the matter. Operational security was deemed paramount even during the planning stages, which meant that code clearance level was irrelevant to my people until after the deployment was completed."

"You claim that operational security was paramount—" Villa leaned forward intently. "—but if that was the case, why was a reporter embedded in your unit?"

"You would have to ask the general about that, Colonel," Jenkins said matter-of-factly. "But I can say that we cooperated with the directives given to us regarding Ms. Samuels' presence and her authorization levels."

Admiral Zhao sliced a brief, but pointed, look at Villa. "The matter of the reporter can be examined at some other time. This meeting is about the mission itself, not civilian observers."

"Of course, Admiral," Villa agreed, giving Jenkins a short-lived look that said, "That's all the help I can give."

Jenkins was not yet certain why his friend had played that particular card, but he was grateful that Villa had done so as Admiral Zhao continued, "You were aware prior to deployment that you were to meet a Vorr contingent, is that correct?"

"Yes, sir," Jenkins agreed.

"What was your objective during that meeting?" Zhao pressed.

This was where the rubber met the road, and Jenkins knew that how he played the rest of this meeting would determine the fate of his unit and, potentially, his entire branch of the Terran Armed Forces.

Without hesitation, he replied, "Our objective was to rendezvous with the Vorr so that they could arrange a meeting between ourselves and a third, previously unknown alien species for the purpose of establishing a potential diplomatic dialogue. Before we touched down on Shiva's Wrath, the Vorr were driven off by Jemmin forces, and we were unable to establish contact with any Vorr representatives. As a result, we were unable to make contact with the third species, and in fact exchanged fire with them on several occasions. I am prepared to describe those engagements in detail at this time since I assume some of those details were redacted in the preliminary report."

Jonny Villa's eyes went as round as saucers, and Major General Kavanaugh's brow creased in surprise. But the admiral's brow lowered thunderously, and his eyes narrowed into serpentine slits at hearing this unexpected turn.

Unexpected to everyone except Colonel Jenkins, that was.

Jenkins had spent every hour of every day since receiving General Akinouye's initial briefing on the Shiva's Wrath operation planning for this very moment. He knew it was a risk, but he also knew there was no other way through this particular firestorm. He was as ready as he would ever be, and it was time to see if he was equal to the task before him.

Admiral Zhao could sense a flanking maneuver when he saw one, and the fierce-looking officer leaned forward with his eyes pinning Jenkins to the chair. "All right, Colonel Jenkins," he said, his pleasant demeanor replaced by one that was openly hostile and predatory, "let's get right to it."

"As I said, Admiral," Jenkins reiterated six and a half hours later, "we detected an orbital exchange between the *Dietrich Bonhoeffer* and the lone Jemmin warship in orbit of Shiva's Wrath. Using the last of our orbit-capable platforms, we engaged the enemy from the surface."

"Did Colonel Li, the *Bonhoeffer*'s CO, authorize you to deploy danger-close nuclear strikes against that Jemmin warship?" Zhao asked, re-phrasing the question for the third time.

"Negative, Admiral." Jenkins shook his head firmly. "I had no direct contact with Colonel Li during the orbital engagement."

"And yet," Zhao pressed, "you authorized the fire of a ground-based, low-orbit-capable railgun platform called..." he trailed off, flipping through pages on his slate as he failed to summon the mech's name.

"The mech in question is the *Sam Kolt*, Admiral," Jenkins interjected, knowing that by doing so, he was antagonizing the nearly-unflappable officer. "It features the only low-orbit-capable direct-fire system in the battalion, and I did indeed authorize it to engage the Jemmin target in orbit at the same time I authorized the deployment of tactical nuclear devices against said target. As you can see—" He gestured to the data slates before the inquiry panel. "—my crew have provided sworn statements which corroborate this timeline."

"The internal integrity of your report is not in dispute, Colonel," Admiral Zhao said, slicing a hard look in Jenkins' direction.

Jenkins feigned surprise, which quickly morphed into a veneer of equally false indignity. "If the admiral is suggesting—"

"I am not *suggesting* anything, Colonel," Zhao interrupted tersely. "I am saying, unequivocally and without reservation, that this story of yours stinks worse than an Arh'Kel's guts. Never in my..." he trailed off, his jugular veins bulging in tandem with a particularly gnarled-looking vein in his forehead. The admiral looked ready to explode with anger and forcibly sat back in his chair as he tried to relax.

Seven hours earlier, Jenkins would have never believed what he was seeing were possible. Admiral Zhao, one of the most fearsome living human warriors, was flustered and cracks were beginning to form in his impeccable veneer. But Jenkins didn't put it past the man to be laying some sort of trap designed to lower his guard, and a quick look at the white-faced Villa at Zhao's side seemed to support Jenkins' assessment.

The admiral leaned forward, his glare furious but his voice once again controlled. "Never in my career have I seen such a painstakingly crafted and patently absurd narrative, Lieutenant Colonel Jenkins. You expect this board—" He gestured to the officers flanking him. "—to believe that you went to this planet to conduct a secret diplomatic mission, using an intermediary alien species to introduce your contingent to representatives from yet another, hitherto unknown alien species, only to run into a string of such historically bad luck that not only were you unable to *contact* said species, but you ended up fighting them to the death instead?" Zhao snorted scornfully. "Frankly, Colonel Jenkins, *no one* is that unlucky—and this board is not that stupid. No one in Terran Armed Forces history who has attained the rank of field officer, as you have *somehow* managed," he sneered with unveiled contempt, his veneer of control peeling further back with each passing word, "and been entrusted with such an important mission has been so utterly incompetent that he misplayed a diplomatic situation to the unfathomable degree that he ended up killing the very envoy he was sent to meet. It *stinks*, Colonel!" he roared, standing from his chair and driving his knuckles into the bench-top. "And I intend to get to the bottom of it!"

"Admiral?" Major General Kavanaugh scowled, tearing Zhao's gaze from Jenkins. "A word?"

"Of course," Zhao replied, and Jonny Villa moved to crouch beside them as the trio conferred in private for several long, agonizing minutes.

Every few seconds, Admiral Zhao would send a sharp look Jenkins' way, but the Armor Corps Lieutenant Colonel Jenkins remained stoic throughout the sub-conference. He was so close to getting through this meeting that he could taste it, and once the conference room doors closed, he knew his turn on the grill would be over.

For now.

Eventually, the review board's private conversation ended, and the trio returned to their respective places on the bench.

"Why don't we cut through this façade, Colonel?" Zhao urged, the intensity of his gaze belying the gravity of his tone. "Tell us, right here and right now, what really happened down there. You've got one chance, so don't just make it good..." He raised a finger pointedly before placing it, tip-down, on the bench before him. "Make it the truth."

"The truth, Admiral Zhao?" Jenkins repeated, legitimately surprised by the admiral's sudden shift in direction.

"So help you God," Zhao replied grimly.

Jenkins drew a long breath, which he exhaled audibly while lowering his eyes to the floor in front of the bench. He silently kept his gaze fixed there for a full minute, before finally saying, "The truth, as far as I can tell, is that the Jemmin didn't want us to contact the Vorr or the third species. They did everything in their power to prevent us from making contact and achieving our objective, and it worked. We killed the very creatures we were sent to meet with, and we did it because the Jemmin manipulated events and information with such expert ability that we didn't even realize we were being manipulated. The truth, Admiral Zhao—" He lifted his gaze to meet the admiral's, meaning every single word he next spoke. "—is that the Jemmin don't want the Terran Republic to survive out here, and the events of Shiva's Wrath prove that beyond the shadow of a doubt." He leaned back in his chair, shaking his head in bitter resentment as he wrapped that truth in perhaps the most important half-truth of his entire report. "We only made it off Shiva's Wrath due to Colonel Li's resourcefulness in neutralizing the Jemmin computer virus at a key moment of the engagement.

Without his efforts, I wouldn't be here today and neither would my people."

Admiral Zhao was unconvinced, but something in his expression suggested that Jenkins might have bought himself enough time with what he hoped were his closing remarks. The admiral looked down from the bench, looming imperiously as he studied Jenkins from head to toe in silence while Major General Kavanaugh and Colonel Villa looked on.

"Thank you, Colonel Jenkins," Zhao finally said. "You are dismissed."

"Thank you, Admiral." Jenkins stood from his chair, turning to the other members of the board in turn. "Major General. Colonel."

He turned on his heel and made for the door, half-surprised that the admiral failed to call after him before he exited the room.

"Nuts flush," Xi declared triumphantly, laying down her king-high flush. "All right, pubes, pay up."

"Aww, man," Lieutenant Winters groaned, throwing his hand in while snickers echoed around one of the sickbay's bedside-tray-turned-card-table. "How the hell can you be so lucky?" he muttered as Xi raked in the pile of makeshift currency, most of which consisted of coffee cream packets and other condiment sachets.

"She's not lucky, Winters," Lieutenant Ford chuckled. "She's plain good. And *mean*," he added, dramatically cradling his crotch.

"What's the matter, Ford?" Xi quipped. "Can't handle a little game of footsy with a chick?"

"You're not a chick, Captain." Ford shook his head. "You're a Goddamned buzz-saw."

"Aww..." She pursed her lips in her best, sickly-sweet pout. "That's the sweetest thing anyone's ever said to me."

"Jesus..." Ford backed away, his hands held up in mock surrender. "When she starts talking like that, it's time for me to run fast and far. I can't handle another ruptured testicle." Styles and Winters' laughter was joined by Private Staubach, who to this point had been an onlooker in the four-hand game.

"Men these days." Xi sighed as Ford collected his things, patted the sleeping Lu on the leg, and made for the sickbay's door. "You guys really don't know how to deal with women, do you?"

"I have to side with Ford on that front, Captain." Styles grinned after *Forktail*'s Jock had gone. "You're not a woman. You're the angel of death. A guy'd have to be suicidal to make a move in your direction."

She cackled with glee before gesturing to the empty seat. "You're up, Blinky."

"Really?" he asked, his eyes lighting up as he rummaged through his pockets for two handfuls of currency. "Thanks," Staubach gushed as he set up his stack and checked his cards.

Before Xi was set to start the bidding, Lu stirred in his hospital bed. The *Bonhoeffer*'s doctors had kept him sedated for two full weeks longer than Fellows had thought, but Xi was convinced it had been the right call. Just a few hours earlier, they had removed the sedation drugs, and the card-players had gathered to welcome him back to the world.

"Heads up," Xi said, moving to Lu's bedside while everyone else did the same. Even Blinky, whose prior excitement at entering the game vanished in the blink of an eye, made his way to the foot of the bed.

Lu looked up, his puffy, pink face no longer bandaged as the replacement skin had finally gotten strong enough to be exposed to light and air. "What..." he croaked, and Xi offered him a sip of water that he gladly accepted. "Where are we?" he asked, his voice barely above a whisper.

"Back on the *Bonhoeffer*," Xi replied, looking around at the other mech crewmen present. "We made it off Shiva's Wrath."

"Mission accomplished?" he asked, wincing in pain as he shifted in the bed.

She nodded. "Mission accomplished. All thanks to you."

Lu gave her a muted look of disapproval, but Winters jumped in. "It's true, Chief. When that thing dropped the thermite on *Elvira*'s topside, it would have poured straight into the ammo cans without you closing the emergency slides."

"We'd be dead if you hadn't stuck your nose in there and closed that breach, Lu," Blinky said solemnly, patting Lu on the foot.

Xi gripped Lu's one good hand and made firm eye contact with him as she said something she had felt since the very moment she saw Lu's burned body in *Elvira*'s rear compartment. "I failed you, Lu. I'm sorry."

Lu's brow creased in confusion, along with everyone else's, as he said, "What?"

"I failed you," she repeated firmly, remembering all the times she had longed for Podsy's presence during her deployment on Shiva's Wrath. "As commander, it was my job to deploy my people to the best of their abilities. I didn't do that...I tried to hold you up to some kind of arbitrary standard. I acted like there was only one way to be my Wrench, but that's not right," she continued with feeling. A pair of tears ran down her cheeks as she continued to hold his good hand tightly in both of her own. "You deserved better than what I gave you. I know that now. And when you're well enough to ride, I hope you'll give me a second chance. I'd be proud to have you as my Wrench."

Lu returned her grip with a weak squeeze of his own before surprising everyone with his reply. "You were right, Captain. I needed a boot up the ass."

The quartet at Lu's bedside erupted in laughter, and Xi wiped the tears from her cheeks as she patted his hand. "Maybe you did," she agreed as Winters clasped her approvingly on the shoulder.

"I'll ride with you any day," Lu assured her, "but right now... could you people please clear a path for the busty nurse brigade?"

Laughter filled the room before Xi gestured to the door. "You heard the man. Roll out!"

———

"General, you asked to see me?" Jenkins greeted after rejoining the *Dietrich Bonhoeffer* in orbit of Terra Americana, his homeworld.

General Akinouye was standing beside a viewing portal on the observation deck, his hands clasped behind his back. "Colonel," he greeted without turning, "take in the view with me."

Jenkins approached, unable to avoid looking down on the rocky, frozen world below. In the midst of a thirty-thousand-year ice age, New America was still in the relatively early stages of terraforming. The coastlines were lush and green, and just this year, a thin band of green stretched across the equator for the first time since humans had arrived in the system.

That band would grow at a painfully slow rate over the coming decades before the planet's climate was Gaian-class like Earth, but the heavy lifting of that project had already been done as orbiting reflectors redirected the system primary's radiation back down to the world's surface, slowly but surely melting the ice until the planet's natural climate systems began to augment the jumpstarted process a full ten thousand years before it would have naturally occurred.

Looking down on the rocky, water-rich world, Jenkins could not help but feel pride at his forebears' accomplishments in transforming the previously uninhabitable planet into the second-most prosperous in the Terran Republic. Home to nearly a hundred million hard-working, ruggedly independent colonists, the surface of New America was home to the second-most-populous human society in the Republic, behind only the world of Terra Han.

The coastlines below the *Dietrich Bonhoeffer* were dotted with tidal settlements, half-submerged and half-exposed as fusion reactor waste heat cleared the shoreline of ice. Those settlements cultivated tremendous amounts of food from New America's five major oceans, and nearly a third of the planet's population lived in underwater habitat modules that oversaw the expansion of the bio-rich coastal shelves.

Standing there at General Akinouye's side, Jenkins saw his birthplace, New Boston, nestled on the northern edge of a massive tributary unimaginatively named Three Rivers Delta.

"Beautiful, isn't it?" Akinouye asked reverently.

"It is, indeed, General," Jenkins agreed.

"You did good with Admiral Zhao," the general congratulated, though his tone was far from jubilant.

"I hope I didn't cause you any undue duress, sir," Jenkins said, knowing that several of his maneuvers had been purposefully kept from the general so that they would have the maximum desired effect.

"You played your hand perfectly, Colonel," Akinouye chuckled. "The look on that bastard Zhao's face was the most satisfying thing I've seen in a long time. Except, of course," he added pointedly, "the fast-approaching surface of Shiva's Wrath as the *Zero* dropped to the deck." He sighed. "I hadn't thought I'd ride the old girl into battle again."

"Havoc made his presence known on the field, sir," Jenkins said with feeling, knowing that everyone in the battalion felt likewise.

"Enough pleasantries," Akinouye said, pointedly turning his back on the viewing portal. "Fleet's not going to let this thing go, and it sounds like they've got enough support to spur a full-on Senate investigation."

Jenkins winced. "I'm sorry to have let you down, sir."

"I said you played your cards perfectly," Akinouye grunted, "and I meant it. But it seems clear to me, now more than ever, that the Zeen were right. There *is* a rot in the Republic, and I'd bet my fast-fleeting ability to take a satisfying morning crap that the Jemmin are behind it."

"Yes, General," Jenkins agreed.

"Unfortunately," Akinouye sighed, "we might be outgunned here. I've stonewalled as long as I can, but the next Senate session kicks off in three days, right here in orbit of New America. If something doesn't break our way before then, we can expect the Legion to be buried so far under paperwork and reviews that we'll never drop another can before Armor Corps is officially reorganized under Fleet."

Jenkins recoiled in surprise. "I'm sorry, sir?"

"Everyone knows Armor Corps has been on the ropes for decades," General Akinouye explained. "What no one outside of the Joint Chiefs and their staffs know is that gears have been in motion for a long time which would fold the Metal Legion into the Fleet. Not only would that remove Armor Corps' seat at the big table, but it would consolidate even more power into the Terran Fleet. Once the Legion folds, it's only a matter of time before the Marines follow suit."

Jenkins nodded slowly, finally taking the general's meaning

after contemplating the situation from a tactical perspective. "You think the Jemmin are behind the consolidation of the various Terran military branches."

"I do," Akinouye agreed. "And their efforts have intensified in the last few months, ever since word of your victory on Durgan's Folly reached the Senate's intelligence committee. The political machine is picking up speed, Colonel," the general said, fixing Jenkins with a hard look, "and if something doesn't break our way in these next three days, I'm afraid that nothing will be able to stop it. And if that happens..." He turned and cast a haunted look over the icy sphere of Terra Americana. "God help us all."

20

THE EXCLUSIVE REPORT

"It can't be that bad..." Styles said in disbelief after Jenkins had brought him and Xi up to speed on the political situation. He looked back and forth between Jenkins and Xi before finishing with less than his usual confidence. "Can it?"

"The general's convinced it is," Jenkins replied flatly. "He's been doing this for nearly a century, and has served with the Joint Chiefs for four decades."

"How?" Xi demanded. "How can we be so successful, do so much good, and still end up on the chopping block?"

"The problem is a lot larger than that, Captain," Jenkins said heavily. "Our careers, and even Armor Corps' future, are less important than safeguarding the Terran Republic. The politicians have a different idea how to do that than we do."

"Hear, hear," Styles agreed with conviction, and Xi frustratedly nodded in agreement.

"But we're out of moves," Jenkins continued. "We've been cut off, our supply lines frozen, and even our communications restricted following our extraction from Shiva's Wrath. The *Bonhoeffer* is under strict orders not to break orbit, so we're stuck here until the higher-ups decide our fate."

"The next Senate session convenes in two days," Styles said, rhythmically rubbing his temples with his palms. "Are we really going to sit here and do nothing?"

"What *can* we do?" Xi asked in bitter resignation.

"Hack New America's data net," Styles said fiercely. "We dump whatever information we think might help our cause straight into the feeds. Let the people decide if this Jemmin conspiracy is an actionable threat or not."

Xi nodded approvingly, her enthusiasm growing with each word to pass Styles' lips. "We can use the *Bonhoeffer* to go and physically upload files to one of the main comm satellites. From there, it would only take a few minutes to spread the files across the whole planetary network…"

"We're not doing that," Jenkins interrupted with finality. "Not only would it breach protocol at near-treasonous levels and land everyone aboard this ship in the brig, but frankly?" He let out a long, frustrated sigh. "I'm not sure it's what the Terran Republic needs right now.'

"The Jemmin are undermining our entire society!" Styles cried. "How can we stand by and do nothing while an enemy who had zero compunction about opening fire on us actively manipulates the Republic for its own benefit?"

"We still don't have all the answers, Chief," Jenkins said emphatically. "We think we know that humanity was uplifted by some other species, and we have reason to suspect that if we're right about that—" He held up a hand, forestalling Styles' protest. "—it was the Jemmin who uplifted us. But if that's true, why would they attack us?"

"They didn't uplift *us*, Colonel," Xi said pointedly. "They uplifted *Sol*. When the wormholes closed, cutting the colonies off from Sol for the better part of a century, humanity's role in whatever plan the Jemmin are playing out was thrown out of alignment. The Terran Republic is clearly an obstacle to that plan, whatever its end goal might be, and they're trying to neutralize us."

"That's our best current theory," Jenkins allowed. "But we don't have enough proof to justify throwing the entire Republic into chaos, and possibly outright war, with the entire Illumination League. We *barely* managed to fight off that last major Arh'Kel offensive, people," he said, snapping his eyes back and forth between Xi and Styles. "How do you think we'd fare against the League? For that matter, how do you think the Terran Republic would handle being cut off from the Nexus and, by extension, from itself? We only think the wormhole gates are two-way and two-way only. What if the Jemmin have a back door? What if, within five minutes of declaring war against us, our wormholes go offline—*again*," he said pointedly, "and the Jemmin move a fleet of two or three hundred warships into the colonies, sweeping through them one by one until there's nothing left of the Terran Armed Forces but a few tattered flags waving beneath flaming skies? Is that what any of us wants?"

The duo was silent for several seconds before Xi leaned forward intently. "We can't just sit here and do nothing, sir."

"I don't like it any more than you do," Jenkins admitted. "But we're backed into a corner here, and the last thing we should do is lash out in desperation. We still have time, and we still have allies," he added with a knowing look that suggested confidence he in no way felt. "This isn't over. Not yet. Right now, we need to keep our heads down and our foxholes in order so that when something breaks our way, we're ready to take maximum advantage of it."

Styles' wrist-link chimed, and after checking the inbound message, a look of confusion filled his features. "What the..." he muttered before his eyes went wide and he quickly forwarded the feed to the office's main display. "Colonel, you have to see this."

Jenkins couldn't tell if it was hope or fear he heard in Styles' voice, but after the image appeared on the screen, he realized it was probably a bit of both.

Standing there, against a backdrop of frozen tundra, was the image of Sarah Samuels with *Elvira* at her back.

"Too often," the reporter said, apparently in the middle of an introduction, "we, the people of the Terran Republic, take our security for granted. Out here, far from the site of humanity's deepest roots, the people who call the seven Terran colonies home are the bravest and most self-reliant in the history of our species. That's not false bravado or self-important jingoism, but a simple matter of fact. Never before have humans had so little, yet done so much, as what we of the Terran Republic have achieved since our forebearers reached out for the stars and grasped them with both hands, refusing to let go even when the opportunity to do so seemed like the only sane thing to do. And maybe we're not sane. Maybe our reach has in fact exceeded our grasp. But maybe, just maybe, it's the resolve demonstrated by men and women like those in the Terran Armor Corps that keeps us moving forward against all odds. My name is Sarah Samuels, and I'd like to introduce you to a group known to itself as the Metal Legion."

Images of human colony ships, flanked by relatively meager escorts, flitted across the screen as music swelled and screen-shots of every original colony in what eventually became the Terran Republic flitted by one after another. Eventually, armor units of every shape and size appeared, most of which were presently represented in Jenkins' battalion. Heroic figures from the TAC's past were shown, along with its current brass and, eventually, even members of Jenkins' battalion appeared in the stream of images.

"This isn't what I expected," Xi said in surprise.

"She never said anything about this being a patriotic puff

piece." Styles nodded in agreement. "All she talked about was winning journalism prizes by hitting as hard and as fast as possible."

"Something changed..." Styles mused.

"Or she was lying all along," Xi suggested.

"Let's see how this goes," Jenkins urged, and the trio sat in silence while the program unfolded over the next forty-two minutes.

"We're being tested, Ms. Samuels," the image of Colonel Jenkins said on the special report, which Xi was shocked to find was unflinchingly supportive of the Armor Corps. She swelled with pride at hearing his words as he continued. "The universe is asking if we're ready to stand on our own two feet and deal with whatever it can throw at us. Some might be tempted to retreat to the safety of their homes and hope that someone, somewhere, can keep them safe. But the Terran Armed Forces doesn't run *from* fights. We run *to* them. You don't point a gun at someone unless you're prepared to pull the trigger. And you don't deploy armor unless you're ready to use it. This isn't about minerals, Ms. Samuels. This is about standing up for what's right, and that's exactly what the Terran Armor Corps does damn single day."

"Even if it gets you all killed?" Samuels challenged, though the pickup never switched from the image of Lieutenant Colonel Jenkins as his lips curled in a confident smirk.

"*Especially* if it gets us all killed," he replied confidently.

Jenkins' face was replaced with that of Sarah Samuels, this time from within the *Dietrich Bonhoeffer* in orbit around Shiva's Wrath. As she spoke, she slowly walked along the drop-deck where mechs were being unloaded from drop-cans during the last stages of their withdrawal from the world. "As I spent these last few weeks with the men and women of the Terran Armor Corps, I came to understand them, not only as servicemen and women, but as Terrans. These people carry a proud tradition on their shoulders which stretches back to the first mounted cavalry charges on Old Earth, and I think it's clear to anyone watching this program that theirs is a tradition worth preserving," she said with such conviction and gusto that it sent chills down Xi's spine. "The culture of camaraderie I found in the Metal Legion is stronger, and more intensely *human*, than anything I could have imagined. And I'm proud to say that I learned more about myself, and about them, than I ever thought possible during my time inside this very mech." She gestured to the battered *Elvira* as it was unloaded from a nearby drop-can. "And as I close this program, I would like to convey just a slice of the wisdom expressed by its pilot, Xi Bao, a former criminal convicted of data theft for which she was sentenced to thirty years in prison. She's also the youngest woman ever to attain the rank of captain in Armor Corps history, and quite probably the wisest person of her age that any of us will ever meet."

Xi felt herself squirm uncomfortably as an image of her shaking her head with overt disapproval filled the screen. "Do you know what Thomas Jefferson said about an informed populace?" she heard herself ask with more than a hint of contempt.

"Tell me what he said," Samuels asked with clear professionalism.

"He said 'a well-informed populace can be trusted with its own government,'" Xi heard herself reply, and she found herself mouthing the words as her recorded-self spoke them. "But those words weren't what he was *really* saying. They were a negative image of his true message, which was this: an *uninformed* populace absolutely *cannot* be trusted with its own government. I was informing the public with my data release, whether they were going to like what I showed them or not. I'm not the enemy here. The real enemies in my criminal case are the institutions which think they get to decide what information is or isn't fit for public consumption. I broke the law, and I knew I'd be punished for it, but I did it anyway because I thought that the information I was putting out there was important and needed to be understood."

Xi felt her CO's eyes swivel over to her, which only made her feel like she was about to turn to sludge and fall through the chair onto the deck beneath her in a puddle of self-conscious goo. But the recording continued on, heedless of how uncomfortable its author felt at hearing her words repeated on air.

"Not because I agreed with what it suggested or represented," the recording continued with a surprising degree of passion that she didn't remember feeling in that moment, "or because I thought it would lead to a particular outcome, but because I always, *always*, think that more information is better than less. My government threw me in jail because they disagreed, and I can't blame them for dropping the hammer on me since I disrupted their plans." Her image shrugged indifferently. "The real problem in my case, Ms. Samuels, is the media that failed—and *continues* to fail—the people who depend upon it to present all of the facts so that we, the people, can make up our minds."

The image of Samuels returned, and this time, she stood atop the highest building on Terra Han, the Bronze Phoenix Tower. The commanding view behind her was truly breathtaking, and it was impossible to ignore the new watermark on the lower righthand corner of the screen that read "DIN."

"Strong words. And they were spoken by a particularly strong, dedicated woman who I'm not ashamed to admit makes me proud to call myself a Terran," Samuels continued. "And the more I thought about what she said, the more convinced I became that Captain Xi Bao is right. We, the people, *cannot* be trusted with our own government if we do not have all the facts at our disposal. As a lifelong journalist, it gives me no pleasure to say that we can do better to bring you the truth than we have done. No..." Her eyes hardened into icy pools that seemed to pierce Xi's soul. "We *must* do better. Which is why I'm proud to announce—" She splayed her hands wide, gesturing to the interior of the Bronze Phoenix Tower, where dozens of technicians sat at data-feed workstations. "—that this report is the first of many we'll be featuring here on the newly-founded Durgan Investigative Network. Our goal isn't to tell you what to think. It's to investigate where others won't, to dig up stories that others ignore, and to present you as many facts as we can gather. And then we'll move on to the next story, leaving the conjecture and opinion to you, because that's what we're *supposed* to do. It's what you deserve, it's what humanity needs, and it's what DIN will provide. This is Sarah Samuels, signing off."

The screen went blank, leaving the trio in a stunned silence that lasted three full minutes before Styles snickered. "You'd better dust off your makeup kit, Captain."

Xi shot him a bewildered look, but Colonel Jenkins nodded in total agreement. "He's right," Jenkins explained. "You're about to be swamped with interview requests."

"I'll set up the feeds." Styles stood and quickly made his way to the door.

"But...we're on information quarantine!" Xi objected, more than a little dismayed at the thought of sitting in front of a camera to provide satellite interviews. "The *Bonhoeffer*'s transceivers are under complete blackout! You just said so!"

Jenkins grinned, showing greater determination and resolve than she'd seen in him for two full weeks. "I think our friend Mr. Durgan just lifted the blackout...the hard way."

Xi groaned in despair, sinking as deep into her chair as it would let her go while her CO laughed.

"Look on the bright side," he said, enjoying her discomfort as he schooled his features into a reasonably neutral expression. "You'll probably have a few thousand marriage proposals by this time tomorrow."

She glared at him in irritation before finally flashing a lopsided grin. "I guess there might be an interesting gift or two..."

"That's the spirit," Jenkins declared as she stood from the chair and sighed.

"I hate cameras," she muttered, "but I hate makeup even more."

Less than an hour after the DIN's inaugural program was broadcast across the New American data net, the *Bonhoeffer's* information quarantine was provisionally lifted. They were not permitted to discuss any details of their deployment, but they were able to receive a lengthy stream of communiques while Captain Xi was given the ability to conduct "character inter-views" with the nearly two hundred media outlets that had lined up to speak to her as soon as Samuels' report had ended.

A dozen or so requests had come in for Jenkins himself, but he had declined since he had more important business items to address.

Foremost among those items was a sit-down with Chief Podsednik, who soon appeared at Jenkins' door sporting a poorly-coordinated but fully-functional pair of prosthetic legs.

"Enter," the lieutenant colonel commanded, and the wily chief known to the Legion as "Podsy" entered the room.

He was thin and sported a nearly-healed bruise covering the left side of his face, but his posture was upright and worthy of an Armor Corps officer in spite of having just spent three solid weeks in the spaceship's brig. To say nothing of this being the first time Jenkins had seen him with his new, prosthetic legs beneath him.

"Chief." Jenkins gestured to the seat opposite his own, and Podsy assumed the chair. "First off, how's the eye?" he asked, gesturing to Podsy's still-red eye. Likely a gift from Li's people from when they initially delivered Podsy to the brig.

"Doc says it'll be good as new in another couple of weeks, Colonel," Podsy replied confidently.

Jenkins knew he needed to deal with this carefully. It was possible, even likely, that Colonel Li had him under constant surveillance while aboard the *Bonhoeffer*. That made every word he was about to say to Podsy of significant importance.

After all, the Armor Corps had just the one combat-ready assault carrier, and Li wasn't the type to give up his command willingly.

"All right, I'll cut straight to it," Jenkin said. "You violated the *Bonhoeffer*'s data system integrity without prior authorization, and in doing so, you broke two dozen regs. Do you dispute this?"

Podsy shook his head firmly. "No, sir, I do not."

Jenkins nodded approvingly. "When you're a Wrench on one of my mechs, you're your Jock's problem, which means there's someone between you and me to save me the frustration of dealing with a hotheaded, loose cannon like you every minute of every day. I don't enjoy taking blowback for things I didn't do. Do you understand me, mister?" he demanded with steadily-increasing volume.

"Yes, Colonel, I do, sir." Podsy nodded stiffly. Jenkins only hoped the other man could read the situation without external cues, and respond as he hoped he would.

"You've jammed me up here, Chief." Jenkins grimaced. "Because on the one hand, I'd like to bust your ass back down to a deckhand and watch you spend the next six months scrubbing the deck with your tongue. But on the other—" His face twisted sourly. "—everyone under Colonel Li's command during our latest deployment has been recommended for commendation for scrapping the first Jemmin ship in Terran history. I can't in good conscience allow you to be commended for breaking regs, Chief, but Colonel Li has insisted it would be unfair to you not to receive some sort of recognition for the part you played in neutralizing the Jemmin at Shiva's Wrath."

Podsy's eyes flickered with confusion before finally, he seemed to understand where Jenkins was going with this.

"On top of all that," Jenkins continued blithely, producing a stack of requisition forms as thick as his forearm, "it seems that you've managed to call in more ordnance, perishables, and even derelict vehicles," he said with legitimate surprise that Podsy had somehow succeeded in horse-trading for three mechs previously held in private collections, "in the last few weeks before we shipped out than I managed to put aboard the *Bonhoeffer* prior to deploying to Shiva's Wrath."

Jenkins took out a pair of silver lieutenant's pips still in their decorative case and tossed them onto Podsy's lap.

"I'm not putting those on you, Chief, because I don't think you've earned them," Jenkins snapped. "But there's someone aboard this ship who might. My advice to you? Go to him right now, this instant, and demonstrate not only that you're remorseful but that you can be an indispensable member of the team going forward. Make him *believe*," he said with perhaps a bit more theatricality than he was going for, "that you're a changed man, and I might be inclined to believe it myself." Jenkins stood from the desk, looking down with as much measured disdain as he could summon. "I've got an inspection to make of the drop-deck, where the rest of the battalion is doing their duty." He shook his head and hoped he conveyed ample disappointment. "You're dismissed."

"Thank you, Colonel," Podsy said, bracing to attention and saluting before awkwardly turning on his prosthetic heels and leaving Jenkins' berth aboard the *Bonhoeffer*.

A few minutes later, Jenkins arrived at a specially-prepared drop-can where Styles and Xi were putting the finishing touches on their latest project. Everyone was in place, and everything was prepared. Now the only thing left to them was to wait.

Minutes steadily ticked by until the faint footfalls of boots on the deck approached the drop-can. Andrew Podsednik soon emerged at the open mouth of the can, which erupted in cheers and a relatively meager but well-deserved shower of confetti as the newly-minted lieutenant was greeted by every member of the battalion that had been deployed on Shiva's Wrath.

"Congratulations, Podsy." Xi was the first to embrace him, and she was soon followed by every other member of the battalion. They knew he had been the key part of their lifeline during deployment, and they knew the risk he had taken by uploading the antivirus.

"Thank you, everyone," Podsy said after a few minutes of celebration. "I'm just glad you're all okay."

"Lieutenant Podsednik." Jenkins lifted a glass of what had to be the worst hooch ever distilled by servicemen in human history. "Well done."

"Thank you, sir," Podsednik said with feeling as his eyes began to mist over.

"Enjoy yourselves," Jenkins urged before disembarking the drop-can and leaving his people to enjoy the moment.

God knew they'd earned it.

21

CHAIRMAN OF THE BOARD

High above New America was the DSV *Kirin*, the most powerful non-government warship to fly the Terran Republic's banner. The flagship of the Durgan Security Fleet, its armaments rivaled the *Dietrich Bonhoeffer*'s, and it served as the mobile headquarters for none other than Chairman Durgan himself.

Jenkins followed the private security officer through the ship's snake-like corridors before arriving at a gilded wooden door carved with religious iconography from essentially every human society throughout history.

He took a moment to appreciate the carvings and their quality before passing through the door and seeing a breathtaking compartment beyond.

Fully thirty meters across, the semi-circular room's curved, far wall was a transparent viewing portal beyond which the icy sphere of New America loomed.

"Colonel Jenkins," Durgan greeted, standing beside the viewing portal and uncannily reminding Jenkins of General Akinouye's similar stance near one of the *Bonhoeffer*'s viewing portals a few days earlier. "Come in."

Surprisingly, this particular image was undeniably more impressive than even that struck by the Armor Corps' top officer aboard his flagship.

Jenkins made his way to stand beside Director Durgan, who said, "I never tire of this view. When I look down there, I don't see a planet in the middle stages of terraforming. I see the future of humanity, carried on the backs of a hundred million hard-working people who want nothing more than to sink their roots as deep as possible so they might secure our species' future."

Jenkins nodded silently, surmising the director hadn't asked him here to interrupt his speeches.

"You did well on Shiva's Wrath," Durgan congratulated after a brief but pointed pause. "Well enough, in fact, that I was able to recruit Ms. Samuels after nearly a year of failed attempts to do so. Her former employer was...displeased with her departure—" The magnate's mouth quirked in satisfaction. "—which came at a most inopportune time, from their perspective."

"What changed her mind?" Jenkins asked with genuine curiosity.

"You did, of course," Durgan chuckled. "I've prepared a little presentation I hope you'll indulge me in watching?"

"Of course," Jenkins agreed, and the lights dimmed before Sarah Samuels' image sprang to life via holo-emitter in the center of the room.

"This is Sarah Samuels, embedded reporter with the Terran Armor Corps on the frozen world known as Shiva's Wrath," the reporter began, standing on the same ice-field from which she had opened her DIN report. "Some say the Armor Corps is outdated, that modern warfare requires flexibility and versatility which is simply impossible to achieve with vehicles whose designs often date back two centuries. Critics say the battlefield for the Republic's future is changing faster than we are, and if we're not careful, we'll find ourselves on the losing end of a race for the future of our Terran way of life."

Durgan accelerated the recording, skipping past several minutes of her continued monologue while he casually remarked, "I trust you get the idea."

"I do," Jenkins said, setting his jaw as he realized just how dangerous Sarah Samuels had been to the Armor Corps' future. She had prepared two separate, conflicting narratives during her time with the Legion. One had been intended to bury Jenkins and his branch, the other intended to canonize them.

He shuddered to think of the difference in his peoples' lives if she had opted to air the former and not the latter.

"I can assure you, Colonel Jenkins," he said, pausing the recording on the image of a Zeen vehicle-bug's wreckage, "that she was not cheaply bought. Suppressing this portion of her report cost me very, *very* dearly." He turned to Jenkins with an expectant look. "Are we on the same page?"

Jenkins nodded resolutely. "We are."

"Good," the director said, his gaze lingering on Jenkins before he deactivated the projector and caused the lights to resume their previous luminosity. "Because what I'm about to show you could cost me even more dearly than Ms. Samuels' silence," Durgan said, beckoning for Jenkins to follow him to a door on the far wall.

Jenkins followed the director to the door, and Durgan keyed in a series of codes, then did a biometric scan. The door slid open, revealing what looked like an airlock beyond. Durgan stepped into the airlock, and Jenkins followed. The door slid shut behind them, locking with a hiss before a decontamination cycle initiated.

When the cycle completed, the second door slid open to reveal a dimly-lit, circular chamber.

Durgan moved into the room, followed by Jenkins, and

when the airlock door secured behind them, it plunged the room into darkness.

"This room contains my two most precious secrets, Colonel," the director said from a few meters to Jenkins' left. "The first of which I do not expect you to recognize," he explained as a soft, blue light illuminated a six-foot-tall, two-foot-wide transparent cylinder three meters in front of Jenkins.

The cylinder was filled with a pale blue liquid, and floating motionless at the cylinder's center was the shriveled form of something bipedal, but beyond that, Jenkins had no reasonable guess as to what it was.

He stepped closer to the cylinder, examining it from top to bottom for several seconds before determining its head was in fact above, and its caudal section was below in what was only barely-suggestive of a bipedal form. Its bony, emaciated arms were covered in what looked like sores, and its face was a twisted mockery of anything deserving to be called such.

But there was something strange about that face which caught his attention. Something unnatural. Something...

"Not symmetrical," Jenkins realized aloud, recoiling as he understood what he was looking at. "This is a Jemmin?"

"Impressive, Colonel," the director said with mixed surprise and approval. "Yes, this is a Jemmin. But to refer to it in the singular might not be linguistically consistent with our concept of individuality."

"It doesn't look anything like the images we saw transmitted by the *Azure Spire*." Jenkins peered closer at the thing's sunken, misshapen head.

"This particular Jemmin was a rogue," Durgan explained, "but in order to gain its freedom and become an individual, it had to undergo a painful, self-destructive, and ultimately fatal series of operations."

"How do you know this?" Jenkins asked warily.

"Because it told us so," Durgan replied matter-of-factly. "More precisely, it told my grandfather so shortly before it died over a hundred years ago."

Jenkins felt the hairs on his neck stand on end. *Durgan's family has interacted with the Jemmin for over a century?* His mind began to race through the possible repercussions.

"You're probably wondering whether you can trust any of this, now that you know my family has been directly exposed to the Jemmin and their potential lines of misinformation," Durgan continued, correctly identifying Jenkins' present misgivings. "Which is why I've arranged for you to meet someone who, I hope, will put your mind at ease on that front."

A second faint light filled the room, but this light was a verdant green and grew steadily in brightness until it dwarfed the pale blue of the Jemmin's specimen container. Jenkins turned toward the source of the green light and was strangely unsurprised at what he saw.

Floating in a second transparent container, this one egg-shaped and supported on a rolling chassis about two meters long, was an octopus-looking creature. Its tentacles waved hypnotically, and its skin flashed with a bizarre, far-too-fast sequence of colors and patterns that were nothing short of dazzling.

"Colonel Jenkins," Durgan introduced, "meet Deep Currents of Radiant Warmth, my personal contact with the Vorr Cooperative."

"Colonel Jenkins," a distinctly feminine voice emanated from the Vorr's fluid-filled pod, "we are pleased to formally meet. Director Durgan speaks highly of you. On behalf of my people, I extend an offer of friendship and clarity," the Vorr said, and Jenkins watched as it seemed to "pop" a third of one of its tentacles off, which it carefully gripped in two others and gently lowered to the floor of the egg pod.

Jenkins watched with mixed alarm and fascination as the dismembered segment of the Vorr's body was sucked off the pod's floor and quickly presented on a small, tray-like apparatus built into the pod's drive system.

He hesitated, and Director Durgan made no attempt to hide his amusement at Jenkins' apparent squeamishness. But Jenkins had prepared for this since before arriving on Shiva's Wrath, and he took the gently-squirming tentacle reverently in his hands before making the appropriate reply. "I accept your offer of friendship and clarity in the hope of promoting future harmony between us."

With that, he schooled his face into a mask and tried to swallow the ten-centimeter-long tentacle in a single go. Unfortunately, it stuck in his throat partway down, and he was forced to chew the surprisingly tender and tasty bit of flesh a few times before it would go down. He looked around for a blade of some kind, with which to cut himself and offer a small portion of blood as they had come to learn was appropriate when reciprocating the infamous Vorr gesture.

The Vorr's skin flashed with a rainbow-like array of colors. "We do not expect you to reciprocate the traditional exchange of our people. It is sufficient that you recognize the significance of this gesture."

"I do." Jenkins nodded agreeably, forcing himself to avoid thinking about what he had just done so he could focus on the exchange. "Thank you." He turned to the dead Jemmin in the tube. "What is your issue with the Jemmin?"

"Jemmin do not respect sovereignty," Deep Currents of Radiant Warmth replied serenely. "We Vorr are mistrustful of outsiders and resisted Jemmin efforts to influence our culture and technology. This angered Jemmin. This Jemmin—" The Vorr turned pointedly toward the dead, misshapen corpse in the cylinder. "—was not like the rest of Jemmin and tried to help Vorr."

"It gave the Vorr," Durgan explained, "information which painted a clear picture of how the Jemmin have uplifted several different species throughout the last few thousand years. These uplifts were raised using the same package of technological 'gifts,' which the uplifts weren't even aware they had been given. The proof, which the Vorr and the Zeen recovered together as part of a joint operation on Shiva's Wrath, was deposited there by this Jemmin shortly before it arrived in Terran space and made contact with my grandfather. This particular Jemmin was appalled by its species' mistreatment of lesser races."

"Races like humanity." Jenkins nodded grimly.

"And the Arh'Kel," Vorr agreed.

"And at *least* three others," Durgan said somberly.

Jenkins narrowed his eyes in contemplation. "I'm guessing the Vorr weren't among them."

"No," the Vorr agreed, "we reached the stars on our own merits, and as a result proved less susceptible to Jemmin inter-ference than less-developed species. We nonetheless attempted to integrate to the Illumination League, as it contained a diverse array of lifeforms with which we might cooperate for mutual gain. But it soon became clear the Illumination League is not a cooperative, but a hostile system used by the Jemmin against species which might threaten its supremacy."

"There are currently only four member nations in the Illu-mination League," Durgan explained. "The Jemmin, the Solar humans, the Finjou, and the Brek. The Finjou and Brek rarely come out of their home star systems, much like the Solarians..." he said leadingly.

"Which means," Jenkins concluded, "that even if the Finjou and Brek are two of the other species the Jemmin uplifted, which judging by their behavior being similar to the Solarians seems likely, then..." He felt a shiver run down his spine at the implications of his thought's natural conclusion.

"The third uplifted species is no longer accounted for," the Vorr finished for him, her voice filled with sorrow and regret. "We have searched for this species, but the Jemmin control the only vessel capable of transporting the wormhole gates at speeds exceeding the light barrier. We must conclude that this species no longer exists."

Jenkins closed his eyes as he processed her meaning. "You're saying they might have killed off this third species and then removed the gate leading to its star system, essentially erasing all traces of their existence?"

"That's our best theory, yes," Durgan agreed. "Eventually, every advanced civilization's activity leaves evidence that's easily detectable, even at distances of tens of thousands of lightyears. But during the time it takes that evidence to reach us at the speed of light, there won't be a single clue outside the Jemmin databanks that they ever existed."

This was a lot to process, but Jenkins did his best to keep his feet firmly beneath himself while he considered the information being presented to him. Eventually, he formulated what was probably the most important question on his mind, which he put to the Vorr as candidly as he could.

"The Terran Republic is tiny," he said emphatically. "We have a few dozen dreadnoughts, yes, but the Illumination League has *thousands* of warships. What use can we be to any Vorr plan that hopes to deal with the Jemmin?"

"We do not require Terran help to address the Jemmin problem," the Vorr said confidently, and Jenkins wasn't sure whether he should be more relieved or concerned to hear those words.

"This isn't about the Vorr, Colonel," Durgan said tightly.

"It's about humanity's survival...and it's about preventing a holocaust from wiping our species from the cosmos."

"I don't follow," Jenkins said warily.

"We cannot, in good conscience," Deep Currents of Radiant Warmth explained, "initiate action against the Jemmin while they hold your entire species hostage, as we believe it currently does. The Terran Republic is small, yes, but you hold the future of your species in your hands."

"There is a planet," Durgan explained, "which the Vorr think contains direct evidence of the Jemmin conspiracy. Even more important than the evidence, they are convinced there is a piece of technology there which will help us to save humanity from extinction at the hands of the Jemmin. The Vorr can't risk being detected at this world for fear that the Jemmin will intercept and destroy the prize. I've already prepared the excavation equipment you'll need for the dig. Bring back that tech, Colonel Jenkins, along with the evidence," he said, his eyes blazing passionately, "and together, we can preserve the future of the human race and ensure Terran independence."

"And what do you get out of this, Director Durgan?" Jenkins asked. "You're obviously a patriot, but you're putting your entire legacy and empire on the line. The contentious report launched by your new news network, the overt support of Armor Corps when the rest of the Terran government wants to sweep us under the rug, and now exposing me to enough information to sink you and your company indefinitely if I decide to go public? What's your aim, Director?"

Durgan met Jenkins' gaze steadily, and when he spoke, Jenkins was surprised to find that he believed what the other man said. "The Terran Republic has been exceptionally good to my family, Colonel. We have prospered unlike any other in human history, and it was made possible because of the most fundamental principles upon which our Republic was founded:

justice, liberty, self-determination, and the freedom to chase the horizon no matter how dangerous that chase might be." He shrugged, for the first time looking very much like just another human instead of the wealthiest person in all history. "I want to safeguard the opportunity for others to do as I have done— nothing more, nothing less—and if that means personally taking hold of the reins of government...well, that's something I'm prepared to do."

"Every tyrant in history has said something similar," Jenkins said grimly.

"True," Durgan agreed, "and I expect my coming weeks and months to be fraught with danger. In fact," he added pointedly, "I wouldn't be the least bit surprised if this was the last time you and I ever spoke, Colonel."

Jenkins eyed the other man skeptically. "You think someone might try to assassinate you?"

"Might?" Durgan scoffed. "No, Colonel Jenkins. I receive credible attempts on my life at least once a week. But I expect those attempts to increase in both frequency and severity as I begin the work of peeling back the carefully-woven layers of corruption which conceal the rot in our Republic's government. Which is why—" He produced a data slate. "—I've arranged a series of meetings for you with some of my friends, associates, and even rivals who might be persuaded to provide material support for your cause."

Jenkins looked down at the slate, knowing that by accepting it, he was crossing a line from which there no return. Director Durgan had committed nothing short of treason by secretly conspiring with the Vorr, and if evidence leaked about that conspiracy, it would taint everyone and everything which had ever touched Durgan Industrial Enterprises. As a military officer, Jenkins had sworn an oath to abide by the Terran Armed Forces Code, which included reporting potential threats to

Terran sovereignty such as the one he had just discovered in the form of the Durgan-Vorr alliance.

But he had also sworn an oath to uphold the Terran Constitution and everything it stood for, and as he looked down at the data slate, he made the only decision he knew with every fiber of his being that he could live with.

Taking the slate in his hands, Jenkins said, "I'm going to need to include both Styles and Xi on this."

"Styles, yes," Durgan agreed. "But Xi...she's too high-profile and, to be blunt, too unpredictable. She's young, reckless, and has a history of flouting authority."

"She's also the finest young officer I've had the privilege to serve with in my entire career," Jenkins countered, "and is the future of the Metal Legion. If you're right about this evidence and technology holding the key to saving humanity from the Jemmin," he said, waving the data slate, "and if I'm going to need to go fundraising while my people begin to dig for it, then she needs to know what her mission really is when I deploy her at the head of my battalion."

"Battalion?" Durgan scoffed. "Colonel Jenkins, you didn't really think I'd send you on a mission to save the species with a mere *battalion*, did you?"

Jenkins eyed the other man for a moment before scanning the first screen of the data slate's contents. His eyebrows rose in surprise at what he saw. Over a hundred mechs were listed there, and while it was clear many of them would need significant work to bring them to combat-readiness, at least two full companies were already at that level. Most of those vehicles were currently under lock and key at facilities whose owners he guessed were on the list of names Durgan had assembled for the "fundraiser" drive.

"I still need to inform Xi," Jenkins said firmly after reviewing the itemized list.

Durgan seemed to consider the matter before extending his hand. "You're the field commander, and I think it's clear from the product of this meeting that I'm officially all-in, so if you think Xi can be trusted, then I'll support that decision. I'm content to let my fate, and the fate of our Republic, rise and fall on your efforts. Are you?"

Put that way, Jenkins was unable to keep a knot from forming in his throat before he clasped the other man's hand. "Yes, I am, Mr. Durgan."

"Then let's do this," the magnate declared.

EPILOGUE: A HEART-TO-HEART

Xi sat outside Colonel Jenkins' office awaiting her CO's return to the *Dietrich Bonhoeffer* following a short, previously unscheduled trip off-ship. No one knew where he had gone when he left four hours earlier, save General Akinouye who had personally authorized his sojourn.

Twenty minutes ago, Xi had received a priority summons to Colonel Jenkins' office, only to arrive and discover he was not yet back aboard the assault carrier. Whatever he wanted to discuss with her was important, but the lack of company awaiting his arrival filled her with more than a little trepidation.

The outer door slid open, and Xi reflexively stood as Chief Styles entered the office's cramped waiting room, holding a stack of data slates. "Captain."

"Chief," she replied, and together, they sat on the short bench outside Jenkins' inner office door.

"What's this about?" she asked.

"I don't have a clue," Styles replied. "But I do know he wanted our full personnel roster, vehicle status report, list of incoming transferees, and just about everything else he'd need for a full review of the battalion's status."

Xi felt her guts tighten at hearing the suggestion they might be undergoing a formal review. Such a review could take months to complete, and it would effectively ground the entire unit. They had fought so hard to navigate the perils of Shiva's Wrath, but despite their efforts and the bit of unexpected good fortune with Ms. Samuels' report, the early indications were that they had failed.

Fleet had won the political war, and now the Metal Legion would know what it was like to be defeated without firing a single shot.

Her mood darkened with each passing second while she and Styles sat in silence for several long, frustrating minutes.

Then the door suddenly swished open, and through it passed Lieutenant Colonel Lee Jenkins, whose purposeful strides never faltered as he made for the office's inner door. "Captain, Chief," he acknowledged without making eye contact. The door automatically opened before he reached it. "In my office."

Xi and Styles shared a worried look before following their CO. When the door slid shut behind them, she couldn't help but vent her frustration. "I can't believe Fleet would do this to us, Colonel. A week ago, nobody even knew Armor Corps existed, but now? It's got a popularity rating nearly as high as the Marines! We've received thirty thousand unsolicited enlistment submissions since the report went public, and it's only a matter of time before the Senate has to authorize a budget that expands the Legion..."

"I hate to cut short a good tirade, Captain," Jenkins interrupted with a bemused grin she only noticed after he had spoken. "But I'm on the clock here. My shuttle departs in eighty minutes, and we need to use that time as effectively as possible."

"Shuttle, sir?" Styles pressed, proffering the data slates.

Unexpectedly, Colonel Jenkins not only declined to accept them, but he gestured for Styles to hand them to Xi.

Xi recoiled in alarm. "They took your command?"

In spite of his serious expression, the colonel let out a short laugh. "No, Captain. But time isn't on our side, and the quicker we get off the blocks, the better our chances will be." He gestured again for Styles to hand Xi the stack of slates. "Captain Xi, I'm temporarily placing you in command of the newly-formed Dragon Brigade."

"Brigade, sir?" Xi asked in confusion as Styles thrust the stack of slates against her chest. "We barely have enough combat-ready mechs to redeploy the battalion."

"And a battalion is all you'll be breaking orbit with in twenty-six hours," Jenkins replied heavily. "But General Akinouye personally approved this restructuring of the Armor Corps to buy us the maneuvering room we need to make our next move."

"Which is, Colonel?" Styles asked while Xi looked down at the stack of data slates in a mixture of confusion, pride, and despair. Xi Bao didn't mind fighting and bleeding on the battle-field, and she didn't even mind dealing with insubordinates and rival officers...

But she absolutely *hated* paperwork.

"Our next objective—" Jenkins produced a slate of his own. "—is an inhospitable, desert world in Finjou space. We are to convey, deploy, and protect excavation equipment on that world until the excavation effort produces evidence of the Jemmin conspiracy," he said, causing Xi to unexpectedly flush with excitement, "along with some sort of artifact which might prove useful in exposing the Jemmin."

"Terran interests aren't permitted to enter Finjou space," Styles said warily.

"That's correct." Jenkins nodded. "Which is why Armor

Corps is sending a full brigade there to bring a band of dissident Terran colonists into compliance."

"That's our cover op?" Xi asked, silently thinking it was awfully thin as cover stories went.

"The colonists are real, Captain," Jenkins assured her, "and they won't pack up without a fight. But we can expect to encounter a presumably hostile Finjou contingent, and we also need to prepare for Jemmin interference should they discover what we're doing there."

"Firing on our own colonists, sir?" Styles said, sounding every bit as squeamish at the idea as Xi felt.

"They broke the law, Chief, and their rebellion against Terran and League authority might kick off an interstellar war," Jenkins said heavily. "But let me be clear. I don't like this any more than you do. Unfortunately..." He gestured for them to sit across from him, which they did as he continued. "We've got a much bigger problem to solve than a few errant colonists. The fate of humanity is at stake, and right now, the Legion is the only outfit that can make a difference." He looked back and forth between Xi and Styles with stony determination. "Are we up to the task?"

"Yes, sir," Xi and Styles replied in perfect unison.

"Good." Jenkins nodded. "Because what I'm about to tell you next will make your head spin."

Right on schedule, Colonel Jenkins' shuttle departed the *Dietrich Bonhoeffer* en route to a rendezvous with the corporate luxury liner, *Endless Oceans*. Owned by a Terra Han-based virtual appliance manufacturer, it held offices for a dozen of the Republic's wealthiest individuals with whom Colonel Jenkins was about to negotiate for material support of the Metal Legion's efforts.

Xi didn't know if she should envy or pity her CO for undertaking his latest assignment. Being surrounded by the rich and shameless, who were only ever exposed to the finer things in life, seemed like a dream job in comparison to running a battalion— no, make that a brigade—of the Terran Armor Corps in preparation for a fast-turnaround redeployment.

"I'll give you a couple hours to go over the reports," Styles explained. "Meanwhile, I'll go sift through those thirty thousand enlistment applications. There might be a few gems worthy of plucking fresh off the vine."

"Agreed." Xi nodded, gesturing to the stack of slates. "But I'm going to need Podsy's help with at least the material requisitions and inventories."

"He's the right man for the job," Styles agreed before snapping a salute. "Captain."

"Chief." She returned the salute before making her way to the drop-deck, where Podsy and the rest of the battalion were working on a seemingly endless list of work orders.

"Captain Xi," Podsy greeted, walking over on his shiny new pair of prosthetic legs. The proportions were picture-perfect for his physique, and beneath his jumpsuit, it was almost impossible to recognize they weren't his original legs. His gait was still jerky and slow, but he was well ahead of the standard rehab schedule, which filled Xi with pride at her former Wrench working to overcome his physical trials.

"Lieutenant Podsednik," Xi acknowledged, causing him to cock his head in surprise.

"Awfully formal, Captain," he chided.

She gave a wan smile by way of apology before proffering a pair of data slates. "Which means you know that a total bone job is coming. Here's the deal. I've been placed in temporary command of the battalion, and I need a dedicated quartermaster. Do you want the job?"

Heads turned in alarm at hearing Xi was now in command, and she felt extraordinarily self-conscious at that moment as all eyes quickly fixed on her.

"I heard the word 'deal,' but there was a distinct lack of anything deal-like." He shook his head at her smirk. "Of course, Captain." Podsy nodded, accepting the data slates and scanning their contents. He was doing the best of anyone present at hiding his surprise at her revealing the temporary change in command structure, but even he was unable to keep it entirely from his voice and visage as he asked, "When are we shipping back out?"

"Twenty-four hours and change," she replied, turning to the nearby teams working at the deck's various machining stations and workbenches. "Which means we need to re-prioritize this repair schedule to get as many vehicles back in the green as quickly as possible."

"Understood, Captain." Podsy nodded with professional conviction, and for some reason, Xi felt as though a wall had just sprung up between herself and the man she considered her closest friend in the entire Legion...and probably the entire universe. "We'll shuffle the board and get mechs back in their cans ASAP."

Chief Rimmer came over from one of the benches, wiping grease from his hands and nodding in agreement. "We'll get the deck stowed and ready for departure on schedule, Captain."

"Good." Xi nodded. "Chief—" She caught herself too late before setting her jaw and starting over. "Lieutenant Podsednik, I'll need a full report on those requisitions and inventories in three hours. Chief Rimmer." She turned to the *Bonhoeffer*'s deck chief. "How close is the other drop-deck to getting back in rotation?"

Rimmer cocked his head dubiously. "If I pulled everyone currently off-shift, along with a few of the mech crews, and worked round-the-clock...we can get the hull patched up and the deck re-pressurized in time for departure. But I can't do anything about the armor damage without a week in a proper shipyard," he added with finality.

"Understood. Forget the armor and make your top priority getting both decks functional," Xi commanded. "We can catch up on lost sleep after we break orbit."

"Yes, Captain," Rimmer said, displeased but equal to the task.

"Good. As you were," she said with a nod, causing both men to spring into action and begin barking orders.

She allowed herself a moment to linger, savoring the energy of the deck as nearly two hundred men and women went about the task of preparing for battle. Colonel Jenkins had done an outstanding job assembling this team of passionate, dedicated warriors. Some of them fought as Xi did, aiming ordnance and holding positions inside the most fearsome armored vehicles humanity had ever developed. Others fought with rifles, grenades, unbreakable spirit, and unshakable ferocity like the Trappers and their infantry. Still others fought like Podsy and Rimmer, with wrenches and welders to keep the war machine relentless pressing into the heart of the enemy.

Only a fool could look at the lot of them and see anything but a united band of hard-edged fighters. And as Xi basked in their unity of purpose and intensity of spirit, she knew then more than ever that it was her duty—no, her *honor*—to lead them into battle. They would follow her orders, and those orders would lead some of them to victory and others to their deaths. It was a sobering thought, and one which made her doubt her worthiness to lead.

Podsy turned, catching her eye as he gave her an approving

nod. And at that moment, her doubt melted away and two words crystallized in the fore of her mind. She pointed to him and nodded back.

"We're ready," she said with satisfaction, turning and leaving the men and women of Dragon Brigade to prepare for their next battle. Their enemies were numerous and would stop at nothing once they learned of the Legion's latest mission. Speed and surprise were of the essence, and Xi knew she would need to maximize both if she hoped to achieve victory in Colonel Jenkins' absence.

"Ready or not..." She allowed herself to smile as she entered the lift and punched in the bridge code, where she and the ship's CO would prepare for the most important game in the Metal Legion's history. "Here we come."

The End

If you like this book, please leave a review. This is a new series, so the only way I can decide whether to commit more time to it is by getting feedback from you, the readers. Your opinion matters to me. Continue or not? I have only so much time to craft new stories. Help me invest that time wisely. Plus, reviews buoy my spirits and stoke the fires of creativity.

Don't stop now! Keep turning the pages as Craig talks about his thoughts on this book and the overall project called Metal Legion.

AUTHOR NOTES - CRAIG MARTELLE

WRITTEN NOVEMBER 20, 2018

You are still reading! Thank you so much. It doesn't get much better than that.

I love this series! I can't thank Caleb Wachter enough for doing the heavy lifting. I met him through Matthew Thrush and ours was a writing match made in heaven! Caleb brings the characters and the flow, an innate understanding of the characters, and how to keep the reader riveted. I bring the military experience and lingo to punch up the realism. I am blessed to have found someone with Caleb's talent to bring these stories to life.

I just returned from Las Vegas, where I ran the 20Books Vegas 2018 convention with my good friend, Michael Anderle. He came up with the 20Booksto50k® premise and it is this.

"I've talked in the past about how I wanted to create an

income of $50k a year by having a backlist of 20 books. I came up with this number because I noticed after the first few days of selling my first book, I was averaging about $7.50 a day in income. At that number ($7.50 a day for each of the 20 books) I'd make $54k. You only need $36k to enjoy a very nice retirement in Cabo San Lucas. That was my goal." Michael Anderle

A little group called 20Booksto50k® was born on Facebook and it now boasts over 26,000 members. We decided that it would be great for the authors to meet face to face, so we took the show to Vegas, where they are professionals at running conferences. I planned for 150 for the first show in 2017. We had 420 sign up. In 2018, we had 720 sign up. Because of space, we have to limit 2019 to 850. It is the single largest gathering of self-published authors in the world. It takes a bit of my time over the course of the year, especially since I also have self-published author conferences in London, Edinburgh, and Bali, too. We travel a fair bit, but the stories still get written.

And Michael Anderle is a total party. He doesn't eat vegetables, which is okay and if you order family style, then be prepared to eat the entirety of the green bean casserole yourself. We went to what is touted as the best Chinese restaurant in Vegas. Hidden in Gold Coast is Ping, Pang, Pong. Don't judge it by that. It was incredible. I had no heartburn from the orange chicken which had the lightest breading and sauce that wasn't overly sweet. The chicken was tender inside. I wish I had a monster order of it sitting in front of me right now, but alas, I'm back in Fairbanks and Winter has arrived. Only five months left until Spring!

It's dark eighteen hours out of the day, soon to be twenty. That means more writing time.

Because first and foremost, I write science fiction. I'm branching out into cozy mysteries and some fantasy, but that keeps the science fiction juices flowing. I hope it does anyway. Maybe it's that I love telling stories, regardless of the genre.

I hope everyone enjoyed Metal Legion. It was fun to write in a way that I found most relaxing. James Caplan, Micky Cocker, and Kelly O'Donnell keep me on the straight and narrow with in-process reads and ideas, language smoothing, continuity, and overall readability. They are an amazing bunch who help make me and my stories better.

No one goes on this journey alone. If it weren't for being surrounded by great people and the incredible readers who keep picking up my books, none of these stories would be possible.

Peace, fellow humans.

Please join my Newsletter (www.craigmartelle.com – please, please, please sign up!), or you can follow me on Facebook since you'll get the same opportunity to pick up the books for only 99 cents on the first Saturday after they get published.

If you liked this story, you might like some of my other books. You can join my mailing list by dropping by my website **www.craigmartelle.com** or if you have any comments, shoot me a note at craig@craigmartelle.com. I am always happy to hear from people who've read my work. I try to answer every email I receive.

If you liked the story, please write a short review for me on Amazon. I greatly appreciate any kind words, even one or two sentences go a long way. The number of reviews an ebook receives greatly improves how well an ebook does on Amazon.

Amazon – www.amazon.com/author/craigmartelle

BookBub – https://www.bookbub.com/authors/craig-martelle

Facebook – www.facebook.com/authorcraigmartelle
My web page – www.craigmartelle.com

That's it—break's over, back to writing the next book.

CONNECT WITH THE AUTHOR

Craig Martelle Social

BookBub:
https://www.bookbub.com/authors/craig-martelle

Facebook:
https://www.facebook.com/AuthorCraigMartelle/

BOOKS BY CRAIG MARTELLE

Craig Martelle's other books (listed by series)

For a complete list of books from Craig, please see www. craigmartelle.com

Terry Henry Walton Chronicles (co-written with Michael Anderle) – a post-apocalyptic paranormal adventure

Gateway to the Universe (co-written with Justin Sloan & Michael Anderle) – this book transitions the characters from the Terry Henry Walton Chronicles to The Bad Company

The Bad Company (co-written with Michael Anderle) – a military science fiction space opera

End Times Alaska (also available in audio) – a Permuted Press publication – a post-apocalyptic survivalist adventure

The Free Trader – a Young Adult Science Fiction Action Adventure

Cygnus Space Opera – A Young Adult Space Opera (set in the Free Trader universe)

Darklanding (co-written with Scott Moon) – a Space Western

Rick Banik – Spy & Terrorism Action Adventure

Become a Successful Indie Author – a non-fiction work

Enemy of my Enemy (co-written with Tim Marquitz) – a galactic alien military space opera

Superdreadnought (co-written with Tim Marquitz) – a military space opera

OTHER BOOKS FROM LMBPN PUBLISHING

For a complete list of books by LMBPN Publishing, please visit:

https://lmbpn.com/books-by-lmbpn-publishing/

All LMBPN Audiobooks are Available at Audible.com and iTunes

To see all LMBPN audiobooks, including those written by Michael Anderle please visit:

www.lmbpn.com/audible